WARRIORS OF THE APOCALYPSE

Book 2

DARK HOLOCAUST

ANTHONY GIANGREGORIO

Copyright © 2014 Anthony Giangregorio
ISBN Softcover ISBN 13: 978-1-61199-080-5 ISBN 10: 1-611990-80-7
All rights reserved. Open Casket Press is an imprint of Living Dead Press.
www.livingdeadpress.com

Prelude

The day of World War 3 began as any other day. That is until bombs began falling from the sky.

In the blink of an eye, the world we knew was gone, replaced by vast sections of radiation and nuclear fire. EMP pulses knocked out all radio and television frequencies in seconds, thus preventing further communications. The population of the world found itself blind, deaf and burning.

Major cities in the United States had been decimated, leaving behind massive craters of twisted metal, smoldering steel, and charred corpses. Even places that served no purpose in destroying were hit, thanks to faulty weapon's guidance.

But despite this, the entire planet was not laid waste to become nothing but barren landscape as scientists once assumed.

Pockets of refugees still existed, and due to the shifting winds, the radioactive fallout wasn't as bad as predicted.

But the civilized world was gone, in that there was no doubt.

After the initial confusion of that fateful first day, survivors who had escaped the worst of the bombs began to crawl out of their holes, to face a new world. In shock and overwhelmed, many simply fell to their knees and cried. But others saw opportunity, and began to prey on their fellow survivors.

There were no longer local authorities to keep the peace, and though some tried to maintain order, it was soon clear this would be impossible.

In too short a time, the things every human being relied on began to run out: food, water, electrical power, medicines to treat the sick and dying, all gone—all exhausted.

Slowly and inexorably, the survivors came to the realization these items were gone, and that there would be no more for the foreseeable future, well, not for their future anyway. There would be no international relief, for other countries were suffering just as bad, or worse.

As each man and woman came to grips with their new reality, some went mad while others simply killed themselves…and then there were the ones that turned opportunistic. They became the worst of all, capturing men and women and making them slaves to help them rebuild their small but growing empires, or to use the survivors as cattle to practice cannibalism, which became popular thanks to a lack of food.

The thin veneer of civilization had finally been peeled away, to show the true face of humanity: that of a greedy, selfish, and uncaring animal that was both malicious and cruel. America had gone insane, where the law of the land was ruled with a gun and kill or be killed was the mantra sung over campfires. Out of the ashes of this decimated country, came a man who refused to accept this reality, who still believed in honor and kindness. Though not afraid to kill, he would show mercy when necessary, and still believed in the America of old.

Together, Hank Summers, with his three companions, Laurie, Carl and Stewart, traveled the blighted nukescape in search of a home, for a place where the acid rains didn't fall or the radiation lepers didn't exist, where slavery and cannibalism was abhorred.

In a world gone to hell, only a special breed of human could survive—a new warrior for a new age.

The age of the apocalypse.

Prologue

Hank Summers, along with his three companions, Laurie, Carl and Stewart, came across the information that could lead them to a secret government redoubt in the heartland of Nebraska.

Having no particular destination in mind, they decided to give it a try and see if the information would pan out.

After a difficult search, they finally found the underground bunker, but before they could enter, they were besieged by marauders. A desperate battle was fought, with the backs of the companions pressed against the impenetrable steel door of the facility.

But when all seemed lost, a desperate gamble paid off, and they gained access to the bunker, the few surviving marauders from the battle locked out.

Exploring the underground redoubt, they found it filled with treasures that would make any man a king: an armory filled to the brim with newly-oiled weapons, a motor pool fully stocked with vehicles, tools, and condensed fuel; hot and cold running water, a fully-stocked laundry room, shelves of BDU's and footwear still sealed in plastic, and living quarters perfect for them all to relax in.

The redoubt had everything they could ever want except for one thing.

Food.

There wasn't so much as a crumb of food anywhere in the facility.

The one thing that hadn't been delivered to the state-of-the-art cafeteria before the bombs fell was food. Nor was there a single soul—living or dead—found anywhere. No one had reached the subterranean shelter before Armageddon claimed the world.

With only the sparse amount of food they had brought inside the redoubt with them, the four companions still relaxed and enjoyed the security of the bunker, and when food was too low to stay any longer, they packed up in one of the brand-new Humvees, loaded it with weapons and fuel, and prepared to exit the installation and brave the world once more—only now fully stocked to the teeth with firepower and ammunition.

But upon reaching the exit, the door wouldn't open, and it was soon discovered that a countdown had been tripped accidentally upon entering the facility. The countdown was for a hundred years, the time the original developers of the bunker believed that the earth would need to heal itself from nuclear war. There was no other way to exit the facility, nor was there a chance in hell of hotwiring the circuitry or blasting their way free.

They were trapped.

Exploring the bunker some more in a desperate attempt to gain their freedom, Stewart discovered hibernation chambers on one of the levels, where row after row of units were lined up so that all the missing personnel could have slept in stasis until the chosen time arrived to wake them up ten decades later. Stewart quickly deduced how they functioned and was confident he could get the chambers to work for each of the companions.

With no other option than to die of starvation, the four trepidatious friends did the only thing available to them. They entered the hibernation chambers, hoping they would come out the other side alive and well, and as each of them began their century-long sleep, the facility also powered down, to wait for life to once more fill its cold, dark corridors.

Chapter 1

Hank Summers opened his eyes.

At first he didn't know where he was and his mind struggled to focus, his vision doing the same. Figments of dreams long forgotten drifted through his mind like will-o-wisps.

Slowly, he raised his right hand to bring it up to his face, but when it was halfway there, and above him, the hand struck something, halting it. Not understanding what it was, he touched the object, feeling that it was smooth.

His vision cleared slightly and he saw that he was encased in a glass chamber. The feeling of being in a coffin overcame him and he began to feel nervous, agitation filling him from head to toe. Taking his other hand, he used both of them and pressed on the glass but it wouldn't budge.

As adrenalin suffused his system, Hank's mind grew clearer and he instantly knew where he was and why he was in a glass coffin.

It wasn't a coffin, it was a hibernation chamber. The room he was in was dark except for the glowing lights. The illumination made a dull gloom that suffused the room.

Suddenly everything that had had happened only minutes ago came crashing back in his mind like a thousand video tapes being played at once. He remembered finding the bunker and how the main blast doors had closed after he and the others had entered, sealing tight for a hundred years. With no food and little options, Stewart had suggested they use the chambers to survive the hundred years, and when it was over, the door would be unlocked and they would be free. A risky venture but when there were no other options, the decision was easy. So it had worked, he guessed.

He didn't know what day or time it was so for all he knew he had only been asleep for a few days, maybe even hours.

With his head clearer, he now knew where he was and why. Glancing to the left and right, he saw his three companions in similar chambers. There was Stewart Matheson, Carl Rivers and Laurie Collins.

Like the others, Laurie's eyes were closed, sleeping softly. Her lips were pursed slightly, as if she was waiting to receive a kiss.

"Laurie," he called out to her with no response. He pressed on the glass of his chamber once more but it wouldn't budge. Why was he awake when the others were still asleep? Straining his head upwards and to the side, he was able to see the glowing numbers on Laurie's chamber in the gloom, slowly counting down to zero. According to what he saw, she still had another three weeks before she would wake. Turning to the opposite side, he was able to see Carl's chamber and the glowing numbers, and it was the same with his. Stewart's wasn't able to be seen but Hank had a feeling if it was, just what those numbers would say.

Deep down in his gut the first flutterings of panic began to set in. Had his chamber malfunctioned, and though he was awake, the chamber would remain sealed for another three weeks? Was he trapped inside his chamber with no way to escape? Thinking that it was possible he'd been sleeping for a hundred years didn't come to mind, only the here and now mattered.

Would his friends wake up to find nothing but a mummified corpse in his chamber, after he slowly died of starvation and dehydration?

Slapping both palms against the glass of the chamber, Hank pushed with all his might, but unfortunately, that wasn't much. He was as weak as a baby, no doubt a side-effect of the hibernation process.

Dropping his hands onto his stomach, he sucked in air as he stared out through the chamber at the room with rows of computers, all with glowing lights and dials. He felt so tired, which to him didn't make sense. If he'd been sleeping, then why was he tired?

It was as he mused about this that he drifted off into a dreamless slumber.

Time held no meaning when Hank awoke, but when he looked at Laurie's hibernation chamber, he saw that almost an entire day had passed. Had he really slept for that long?

His stomach rumbled, feeling as empty as a bottomless pit. Thinking back, he recalled that he had gone into the chamber hungry and now, after sleeping for how long he didn't know, he was so hungry that he would eat the leather on his shoe if given the chance.

He raised his right hand to his chin and rubbed it, feeling a scruff of beard there. So though in hibernation, his hair grew still, even if it was so little that it was like a week had passed.

He felt a twinge of pain in his gut and knew instantly his bladder was telling him it needed to be emptied.

Great, he thought. *I have to take a piss.*

Once more, in the dull gloom he began trying to figure out how to escape his glass coffin. At least he felt stronger now that he'd slept for a day.

Once more he pushed on the glass but it didn't so much as budge. He did this three times, and after the third try, he let out a yell and punched the glass, but only managed to damage his knuckles. Feeling stupid, he willed himself to calm down. Losing his cool would get him nowhere.

Damn it, he had to pee. It was like his eyeballs were floating within his head. He tried to ignore it and focus on getting out of his tomb once more, but as he lay there, the pressure on his bladder increased until there was no choice. Either he urinated or he would piss his pants. Hating what he had to do, he unzipped his fly and turned to the side, then began to pee. The hibernation chamber was perfectly level, and in a matter of a minute he found himself lying in a quarter of an inch of his own urine. At first it was warm but it quickly became cold.

Doing his best to ignore the sensation and odor, he once more focused on escaping. His eyes roved over the chamber, the dull gloom making it difficult to see. If he didn't get out he would die, there was no question about it. An errant thought crossed his mind. Was the thing air tight?

He sure as hell hoped not. No, it couldn't be air tight; it somehow must allow air into the chamber when it turned off and he woke up, otherwise he wouldn't have slept for a day to wake up alive.

But that didn't change the fact he was trapped.

His eyes shifted to Laurie in her chamber, sleeping softly. He wanted to reach out and touch her, caress her cheek. Wanted to hold her in his arms, kiss her. She was the love of his life. When the world had exploded in nuclear fire, she had been the one thing that had kept him going, made him want to survive. Life without her was unthinkable.

Shifting a little to the side, his urine sloshed across the bottom of the chamber.

"Well," he said, his voice echoing inside the chamber. "At least it can't get any worse."

That was when his bowels churned inside him and he realized he had to take a very large shit.

Chapter 2

Doing a mental search of his body, Hank knew he had maybe an hour before he shit his pants. Shifting to the side, the now cold urine sloshed back and forth around him. He needed to get out of his coffin and fast or it was going to become even more unbearable.

What was worse, if he didn't find a way out, he would end up dying with a load in his pants, his body then marinated in his urine. Not a way he would want his friends to find him when they woke up.

He began studying every nook and crannie of the hibernation chamber, his mind trying to figure a way out. He pounded on the glass some more but of course that did nothing, or so he thought. When he had just about given up for the third time, he spotted a screw above and behind his head that connected the glass to the frame of the chamber. Apparently, all his banging had caused enough vibration to actually loosen the screw a little so it wasn't flush with the glass anymore.

It wasn't much to work with but he wasn't in a position to complain. Any edge was worth its weight in gold, as far as he was concerned.

But he needed something to use as a screwdriver.

It only took him a second to pull off his military-issue belt from his pants, part of the BDU's he was wearing. Though there had been no food in the bunker, there had been plenty of clothes, plus the armory and motor pool had been fully stocked.

Using the edge of the belt buckle, he began worrying at the screw, but it wasn't working well at all. He thought about the motor pool, where there were tables full of tools, and dozens of screwdrivers. But they were on Level 4, one floor above him. He remembered he was on Level 3, where the armory was also located.

Sweat coated his face and dripped into his eyes, but Hank shook his head to free his vision and continued working at the screw. Time passed without notice and even his bowels quieted down as he concentrated on that one screw over his head.

Nothing else mattered, only that one, single screw, for Hank knew deep down that if he didn't loosen it, he would die in the chamber, a long, slow death, too.

Once, when he gave up, he began beating the glass with the belt buckle, but it did nothing, not even so much as scratching the surface. He screamed and yelled his anger but eventually he would calm down and go back to work, for though excruciatingly slow, the screw was all there was in a hope of escape.

Hours later he had managed to turn the screw one full revolution. That was it. Well, what did he expect? He was trying to unscrew a Phillips screw with a goddamn belt buckle? He laughed out loud, his voice echoing inside the chamber, and he wondered if he would go mad before he either got the screw free or he died.

He laughed so hard that he shit himself, and immediately the inside of the chamber was filled with his own filth. As his ass cheeks stuck together, he curled his nose and got back to work, feeling shame at what he'd done. He was ashamed yes, but if he could get out of the chamber then he could wash up and no one would ever know of his embarrassing situation. He knew if he got out, it would be a secret he would take to his grave.

More time passed and he felt tired, so tired he could barely keep his eyes open. This surprised him. He would have thought that lying in a puddle of urine with his ass coated in shit, that the last thing he would want to do is sleep. But he was weak from hunger, and without nourishment his body needed to rest, no matter the condition it found itself in.

Finally, he managed to turn the screw one more revolution. But the damn thing wouldn't move easier and in fact seemed to go even slower. But he kept on, fighting off sleep until he could do so no longer, then he closed his eyes and rested. He told himself he would rest for a few seconds, but when he opened his eyes again, he saw that three hours had passed, thanks to the glowing red numbers on Laurie's hibernation chamber.

Cursing his weakness, he got to work again, forcing the edge of the belt buckle into the X of the top of the screw. A full hour later he had managed to turn it one more revolution and he felt elated. That was three or so revolutions, at least he thought it was. Truth be told, he wasn't thinking too clearly anymore. He'd been weak from hunger before going into the chamber and now it had been more than a day since he'd awoken. He was running on fumes and he knew he didn't have much longer to go.

So with narrow-minded determination, he got to work for what he knew might be the last time, and pressed and twisted at the screw. When he had it another half revolution, he dropped the belt buckle and squeezed the tip of the screw between his thumb and forefinger. Squeezing as hard as he could, the stainless steel metal tip digging into his flesh, he began turning the screw. It was painfully slow work, and after a full five minutes he had to switch hands, as the first hand was covered in blood from where the metal had dig into his fingertips. But it was working. Slow, ever so slowly, the damn screw was moving smoother now, until finally, to Hank's amazement, it popped free and fell onto his face before bouncing off to land somewhere around him.

Cheering, he clapped his hands and whooped up a storm. If anyone had been watching him it would have seemed bizarre to see a man lying in a chamber, cheering and clapping happily.

When he was done celebrating, Hank pushed on the glass and saw it separate minutely from the frame it was mounted to, at the top over his head. There was a gasket between the frame and the glass. Hank pushed up on the glass to separate it as much as possible and then shoved the belt buckle inside the slim line of space, pushing it as far as he could. When it was in as much as he thought possible, he began pulling down on the buckle, using it like a lever. At first nothing happened, the glass more than strong enough to withstand the force being put on it. The glass wasn't really glass, but was a mix of plastic and plexiglass so that it wouldn't shatter like normal glass, nor would it melt like plexiglass.

Screaming with the exertion he was putting on the glass, Hank used every ounce of his remaining strength. He was yelling so loudly that he didn't hear the soft crack of the glass. It started up by his head and then began to spiderweb across the surface. He had his eyes closed as he forced the buckle downward, the edge jammed into the glass being force upward.

In fact, he was so focused on what he was doing that at first he didn't know what was raining down on him, but were small bits of something that peppered his face before falling off to splash in the urine around him. It was only when he opened his eyes and saw that a one foot section of glass directly over his head was gone, and that the air smelled slightly sweeter now that he wasn't trapped inside the chamber.

Using the belt buckle, he made the hole large enough for his shoulders, and then without a second's hesitation, he crawled out of the hibernation chamber and fell onto the floor, sucking in air that tasted sweet, despite being a little stale and recycled. All around him, the motion of his escaping the chamber triggered the overhead lights, and the room was bathed in illumination, almost blinding him with its intensity.

He passed out, but not for long, and when he came to, he sat up, and on shaky legs stood up. He touched Laurie's hibernation chamber once, staring down at her beautiful, sleeping face. His fingertips left a bloody smudge on the glass but in his present condition he wasn't able to wipe the glass clean.

He was covered in shit and urine, the latter dripping all over the floor. He stripped right there, leaving the foul-smelling clothes where they lay, then he turned and left the room, his destination Level 2, where the showers were along with the sleeping quarters. That was also where his weapons were, too.

When the four companions had gone into hibernation, Hank had told Stewart that he'd felt naked without his weapons, but Stewart had made a point of explaining that while they were sleeping, the guns would do them no good if someone breached the bunker so leaving them in the sleeping berths was fine. Of course, if Hank had been armed with his SIG-Sauer, even his panga, escaping from the hibernation chamber would have been a lot easier. He planned on having a long talk with Stewart when the man had woken about going anywhere at anytime unarmed ever again.

But for now a shower was in Hank's future, and then he would figure out what to do next. His friends were still sleeping and would be that way for the next three weeks. That left Hank waiting for them to awaken inside an underground government redoubt with no food, the same situation they had all been in before going into the hibernation chambers.

As he entered the elevator, the fluorescent lights in the hallway he'd just been in flicked off now that he was gone, and as he rode the lift down to Level 2, his stomach reminded him of exactly what he'd been thinking with a loud grumble.

Chapter 3

The hot water in the shower cascaded over Hank's body and he thought back to the last time he'd been here. He'd been with Laurie then, the two making love under the warm spray. As he washed and shaved, he discovered that the bullet wound on his shoulder was healed, nothing but a white scar to ever show it had happened. This made him think. If the wound had healed, then it was all true, and he had slept for a hundred years.

Opening his mouth, he let the water fill his throat and he greedily sucked it down into his stomach, quieting the hunger pains for at least a little while. He drank enough water to float an elephant, and by the time he left the shower, his skin was wrinkled and he was pretty sure the hot water was running out. He also felt like he sloshed each time he took a step, his stomach so full of liquid.

After dressing in new BDU's taken from storage, he did a few things in quick succession. One was that he went back to the chamber room and retrieved his soiled clothes, then brought them to the laundry room, tossed them into a washer, and let them wash, thereby erasing his humiliation and the situation he'd been in. The next was a quick cleaning of the floor where he'd gotten out of the chamber, then with a few t-shirts taken from storage, he sopped up most of the urine in his hibernation chamber. Now that he was on the outside, he had easily opened the glass door to allow access to the interior of the chamber.

When that was done, all the clothes were taken to the laundry, and once more thrown into a washer. He didn't need the clothes as the storage shelves were lined with walls of uniforms, but he did need to erase what had happened. In fact, when the washing machine cycled off after being on 'spin,' Hank was nowhere to be found to take the clothes out and toss them into the dryer.

The last chores he did was to gather all the weapons left in the sleeping berths and bring them to the chamber room, so that when the others awoke, they would have their weapons close at hand.

When he was truly done, he drank even more water to silence his grumbling stomach and then sat down with Laurie and the others, staring at their sleeping faces as they waited to wake up. He smiled as he stared at Laurie's face, wishing he could kiss her, even once. But he couldn't tamper with the chambers. He knew nothing about them and if he pressed a wrong button or did something wrong, for all he knew he would kill them. If only Stewart had woken up first, he thought. The older man had learned a lot about the hibernation chambers and no doubt all there was to do to shorten the stasis cycle was press a button, but Hank knew nothing of it.

He had no choice but to wait for the chambers to count down to zero on their own. He only sat with the others for an hour though, then his hunger reminded him that he had a serious issue on his hands.

Standing up, he did a quick check of his weapons out of instinct. On his right hip was his SIG-Sauer P-226 9mm pistol. On his left was a sixteen inch panga with a razor-sharp edge, the worn leather sheath it was in stained a dark black. Over his shoulder, hanging by a sling was a Heckler and Koch G-12 automatic rifle. The rifle used 4.7mm rounds, which were in a small backpack, along with ammunition for the SIG. Also included in the bag of death were a few hand grenades and a block of C-4 with detonators. He didn't know what he was going to do with the weapons at the moment but it felt good to be armed, even if he was the only person moving around inside the redoubt.

There was no reason to explore the bunker—that had been done thoroughly before he and his friends had gone into hibernation, so he went directly to the motor pool, jumped into the black armored Humvee that he, Carl, Laurie and Stewart had prepared before, but had been halted when they found that the bunker had been sealed for a hundred years, and he drove it out of the garage and up the ramp that led to the outside world.

As he left the motor pool, he noticed the countdown timer on the wall. It had said that one hour remained before it struck zero. He didn't bother to give it much thought about how he had woken up early and then though the timer on the bunker was done, that the three hibernation chambers containing his friends had three weeks left on them. The technical science that made any of it happen was far beyond him, and he just figured that none of the electronics had ever been tested in reality, and the fact that any of it had worked for what Hank believed was a hundred years was simply amazing.

Though he told himself that he'd been asleep for a century, deep down he had to wonder if that was really true. It didn't feel that way. Hell, he sure didn't feel a hundred years old. He felt like he'd just gone into the chamber yesterday and had simply taken a regular night's sleep.

No doubt Stewart would have been able to explain it better to Hank, but in the end it really didn't matter. He was alive, and his friends were alive, and in a few weeks they would be joining him.

But for now he needed to leave the bunker and find food, or else he would be nothing but a dead skeleton when the others woke up. He'd left a brief note in the hibernation chamber room, the piece of paper attached to Stewart's chamber. When the man awoke, it would be staring right at him. The note detailed what Hank was about to do, and why, and that if he didn't return when they had woken up, it was probably because he was dead. Not only did he need food for himself but when the others woke up, they too, would need sustenance, so he had a double reason why he needed to strike out on his own.

As he drove up the ramp to the one-foot thick bunker door, the lights in the ceiling flickered on, then went out as he passed. A few of the lights stayed off and Hank assumed a hundred years without maintenance was the reason. He slowed to a stop at the blast door, letting the Humvee idle. Vents in the wall near the ceiling began sucking out the exhaust fumes almost immediately, and the heating and/or air conditioning adjusted for the idling vehicle. Hank pulled a wrinkled map from his back pocket. The map stank of urine as he'd had it in his pocket when he'd been in the chamber, and though it had been dried, it still had that ammonia smell—it couldn't be helped. On the bottom of the map were seven numbers. Reading the numbers, Hank went over to a keypad mounted to the wall next to the blast door. He took out his panga and used it to carve the seven numbers into the wall directly over the keypad. By doing this he knew that Stewart and the others would be able to leave the bunker, even if he didn't return. Then he punched in the numbers into the keypad, but when nothing happened, he realized he had to wait for a few more minutes, as the digital display over the door counted down to zero. He watched it slowly ticking down to zero, and when it finally reached zero, the display flashed once and went dark.

It was time.

He went to the driver's side door of the Humvee to the passenger seat, where he grabbed the gas mask he'd placed there earlier. There was no way to test the air before he opened the door, and for all he knew the door would open and a toxic cloud of radioactive dust would roll in. Better to be safe than sorry he figured. So he quickly slid on the mask and adjusted the straps. With his breath hissing through the mask like a villain from an old movie, he input the seven digit number sequence and pressed the 'enter' button. Immediately, an alarm began to sound and red lights in the ceiling began to flash, both warnings that the blast door was about to open and to stand clear.

At first nothing happened, and when almost thirty seconds had passed and the door still remained immobile, Hank began to get nervous. Then suddenly the entire door began to shake as massive hydraulics started to slowly begin working.

Dust from the ceiling rained down on his head as the door fought to open. Hank could see something was preventing it from opening, and as the sound of metal rubbing against metal grew louder—so loud Hank had to press his palms to his ears to stifle it—the door finally let out one massive squelch and began to slowly rumble downward into the ground.

Sunlight began to spill into the tunnel and Hank backed away until he was standing behind the open driver's door of the Humvee, his SIG-Sauer in his hand in case there was trouble waiting for him outside the door. The last time the door had closed raiders had been attacking, and the door had closed only seconds before the bunker had been breached. The air purifiers may have scrubbed the tunnel free of the odor of burning gasoline, but Hank remembered it well from his memory.

When the door was halfway down, Hank peered over it to the outside world. From what he could see it looked deserted, only high grass and trees in all directions. That was odd as Hank didn't remember trees at all, only a field of rolling grass and hills. The sky was clear and so was the air so carefully, so as not to risk choking in case the air was still tainted, he cracked the seal and sucked in a lungful of what he hoped was clean air.

When he didn't start choking or gagging, he took off the mask until he was breathing the air fully. It was fine. He tossed the mask back into the Humvee, glad he didn't have to wear the damn thing.

When the door was more than halfway down, he darted over to the keypad so that if there was trouble he could close it quickly. He should have done this before and cursed himself for being a fool. Taken in by everything that was happening, he'd dropped his guard for a moment. In the world he lived in he knew to drop your guard for even a second could get him killed.

But as the door rumbled into the ground with a screeching of metal, he saw that his concerns were unfounded. The area he could see through the opening was indeed devoid of human life, and as he looked, he didn't see much of the animal kingdom either. He could hear it though. As the door rumbled to a stop and the alarm went quiet, the sound of bird calls came to Hank, as well as a coyote from somewhere in the distance, more than a mile if he guessed right.

He took in the terrain in an instant, but he quickly realized that none of that mattered at the moment. Even if there had been an army waiting outside as the door rumbled open, Hank saw that he would have been safe.

For before the door was a giant crater more than twenty feet wide as well as deep. Leaning out of the doorway, Hank could see the scorch marks around the frame where the attacking SUV had plowed into the door at the exact moment the door had sealed itself shut. Past the crater and through the tall grass and trees, he could also see the rusted-out wrecks of the other vehicles of raiders that had been trying to gain access to the bunker. Now, the vehicles were nothing but red piles of rust that were slowly seeping back into the earth. Anything of value that had been on them, such as tires or remaining glass and metal, had been long taken and only the shells remained to fade back into the dry dirt.

The trees were large, looking as if they'd been there for a hundred years. That made Hank think about his situation, and though he wanted to, he couldn't deny what his eyes were seeing. He chuckled to himself. Son of a bitch, it was true, he'd actually slept for a hundred years. He wished his friends had been by his side to share this moment, but alas, he was alone.

Movement caught his eye and he spotted a fox come out of the brush across from the crater. The fox studied Hank for a few seconds, its nose rising in the air as it took in the smell that the bunker was leaking out of it. Hank sighted on the fox, wanting to shoot it, for the meat would be life-saving, but the fox was too fast. Before he could get a bead on it, the animal turned and dashed back into the tall grass. Hank nodded happily, despite losing his lunch. At least he would be able to find food, even if it would have to be cleaned and cooked. The bunker had a cafeteria, and though the kitchen was empty, it was ready to go to prepare food once it arrived.

Looking down into the crater, Hank frowned. There was no way he was going to be getting the Humvee across that. Perhaps, with Stewart, Carl and Laurie's help, together they could somehow manage to make a bridge out of supplies found in the redoubt, but alone, this simply wasn't an option.

There was a pool of water at the bottom of the hole. He kicked a pebble at his feet off the ledge and into the pit. The pebble plummeted and plopped as it hit the water, but it gave no sign as to how deep the crater might be. For all he knew, the water could be a foot deep or ten feet deep. The side closest to the bunker was solid granite and it was clear to Hank that the raiders, upon not getting inside, had begun excavating to find a way in. Deep scars and blast marks were on the wall of the crater, but other than a few gouges in the facade, the reinforced concrete had held up to all attacks. On the edges of the crater there was what looked like fresh-turned dirt, as if people were still trying to dig deeper into the crater, but Hank may have been imagining it. From where he stood, the dirt may have only looked fresh. Until he got across it, there would be no way to tell for sure.

He went to the outer keypad, assuming it would be nothing but mangled electronics, but was surprised to find that the metal box with the keypad was intact. It looked like someone had tried to hotwire it but the keypad still glowed. Wanting to try something, as it mattered greatly, for if he couldn't regain access to the bunker once he left it, then his plan would have to be changed, he pressed the seven digit code and then 'enter' and waited. At first nothing happened and the keypad began to flicker on and off, but then the alarm sounded, red lights flashing, and the door began to rumble closed. Hank stepped back into the tunnel as the door crawled upwards at a snail's pace. The keypad still worked, if a little faulty, but that would mean he could regain access after he left. Whoever had tried to get inside years before had been smart enough not to mess with the keypad too much. No doubt someone with computer experience had been assigned the task of hacking the keypad. Lucky for Hank. If the idiots that had been the raiders' main force had been responsible, no doubt the keypad would now be nothing but bits of frayed wire and burned-out parts.

By the time the door rumbled closed, Hank was already inside the Humvee and turning it around so he could return to the motor pool. The Humvee wouldn't be of much use at the moment to escape the bunker, but as he drove back down the ramp to Level 4, an idea was already forming in his head on how he was going to get past the crater.

Chapter 4

Upon returning to the motor pool, Hank turned off the engine to the Humvee, left the keys in the ignition, and went to the far north corner, where there was a blue tarp covering something.

Pulling off the tarp, he exposed a 1960 Triumph TR6A. The Roadster looked fully restored, and with the exception of the tires having no air and having some cracks from dry rot, looked pristine. He spotted something on the floor near the front tire. Picking it up, he saw it was a yellow, disposable Bic lighter. Shaking it, he was surprised when it still had some fluid in it. Testing it once and satisfied when the small fire erupted, he slid the lighter into his pants, for you never knew when a lighter would come in handy.

Ignoring his growling stomach, Hank pushed the bike over to one of the work tables and got to work, checking the sparkplugs, putting air in the tires, and filling the gas tank with gas from a container of condensed fuel. The tank took three Imperial gallons. An Imperial gallon equaled about one and a quarter gallons in the states, so he put in about four gallons total before the fuel reached the top of the tank. After filling the tires, he checked the pressure with an air gauge he found on a work bench.

The Triumph had a set of saddlebags draped over the back, and Hank quickly began transferring ammunition, grenades, and as much water as he could carry into the bags, and once done, he got on the machine, turned the ignition key—which thankfully was in the ignition—and kicked the bike over a few times. It took him more than ten times before the motor finally sputtered to life, and with a belch of exhaust smoke, he played with the choke until the engine smoothed out.

Satisfied the engine was in good working order, he turned it off and went back to the Humvee. After gathering supplies that he needed to make his escape from the bunker, he loaded it all into the rear of the Humvee and drove it back to the main door, and after dropping off the items, he rode back to the motor pool. Once there, he left the Humvee and drove the Triumph to the main door for what he hoped would be the last time.

The Roadster was fifty feet back from the blast door, sitting on its center stand in the middle of the ramp, idling softly. The ramp was slightly on an incline here as it trailed away to a sharp corner, where it then disappeared into the redoubt.

The main door was down again, and Hank stood where the door had slid into the ground. He placed a large piece of plywood that was reinforced with two-by-fours at the edge of the door, so that when the door began to rise out of the ground, the wood would go up with it, thus making what Hank hoped would be a useable ramp. On the top edge of the plywood, on the side facing the ground, Hank had nailed in two, three-inch nails, so that the wood wouldn't slip off immediately as the door rose—or so he hoped. His plan was beyond crazy, and if Stewart or Carl or even Laurie had been there beside him, Hank knew they would have given him a ration of shit, telling him he was insane for what he was about to do. When the blast door was open on the inside, all he had to do was press a button that simply said 'close,' so at least he didn't have to type in the code again. The Triumph's saddlebags were overflowing with gear. Hank adjusted his rifle on his shoulder, wanting it out of his way. He took one last glance at the crater and the land beyond before going to the keypad and standing before it. He would only get one chance at this, and with no practicing, it was a hell of a gamble.

He took a deep breath, readying himself for the mad dash to the Roadster. When he felt he was ready as he would ever be, he pressed the 'close' button on the panel, and as the alarm began to sound and the hydraulics began to operate within the ground, he was already running to the Triumph.

By the time he reached the bike, the door had risen two feet, but Hank didn't see this; there was no time. He pushed the Roadster forward so it rocked off its center stand, squeezed the clutch, kicked the transmission into first gear, and gunned the motor as the rear tire spun so fast it began to smoke on the ramp.

The British motorcycle shot forward like a rocket, and before Hank had gone six feet, he had already kicked the bike into second gear, then third and finally, when he was no more than ten feet away, fourth gear; each time redlining the engine before shifting into a higher gear. He didn't even know how fast he was going, there was no time to glance down at the speedometer. By the time the front tire of the bike touched the plywood ramp, the door was over four feet high, which was about where Hank wanted it.

He let out a yell as the bike rolled onto the ramp and soared through the opening in the doorway. Then he was airborne, the crater below him, but Hank barely saw any of it. Everything was all a blur to him, the adrenaline suffusing his system and making him feel like he was on some new-age drug.

Before he realized it, he was over the crater and was hitting the ground—hard. He didn't land properly though, and he went head over heels over the handlebars, the bike flipping over and past him as he found himself tumbling across the ground like a doll tossed out of the window of a truck going sixty.

He knew enough to go limp and then prayed when it was all over that he wouldn't end up a cripple.

The tall grass helped a lot, cushioning his body, and when he finally stopped moving, he was lying on his back, staring up at the sky. That was when he realized that the sky was blue, not the reddish color it had been the last time he'd been outside.

Not moving an inch, he did a mental inventory of his body. Though he had a few aches and pains here and there, nothing felt broken. Carefully, he moved his left arm, then his right, then his legs. All were working just fine. His rifle was lying under him, and he shifted so that it wasn't pressing on his back any more. He was beyond lucky. If he'd fallen differently, he could have easily become impaled on the end. Not something he wanted to think about.

The Roadster was lying a few feet away, idling softly, the rear wheel spinning as the bike was still in gear. Getting up, Hank ignored the rush of dizziness and walked over to the bike.

"Any landing you can walk away from…" he said to himself.

Upon reaching the Triumph, he turned it off and raised it so it was upright. The saddlebags were still closed, the belt buckles secured firmly. As he scanned the bike, all he saw were a few scrapes and a small dent in the gas tank. A signal light had snapped off; he chuckled at that. It was doubtful he would need them anyway.

The handlebars looked a little bent too, but when he sat on it and tested how it felt, it didn't seem like there would be a problem. Hell, after a few miles, he wouldn't even notice the difference probably. There was grass stuck in the front wheel and he leaned over and pulled it out, then kicked the bike to start it, relieved when it turned over and began to idle on the first kick.

Those Brits knew how to make a motorcycle, he thought as he drove the bike back to the edge of the crater. The blast door was closed once more, and just like he'd hoped, the plywood ramp had fallen away as the door had risen. He gazed across the chasm to the door and the keypad inside the metal box. When he returned and had to get back inside it was going to be a challenge. He would have to get some fallen trees and build a walkway to get across the crater or something similar. But that would be later; for now he needed to find food for himself and his three sleeping companions.

He studied the outside of the bunker now that he could see it from his vantage point. The once brown and green paint on the door was almost completely gone. There were a lot more scorch marks on the outside of the door than the last time he'd seen it, and to Hank it looked like hundreds of explosions had been set off before the opening. But none had so much as dented the thick blast door. With the trees all around it, the redoubt truly was hidden from sight, and as he scanned the area, he still saw nothing stirring. His hand reached down to his SIG-Sauer out of instinct, but when nothing moved he took his hand away.

His stomach growling pulled him back to his mission and he spun the Triumph around. Spraying dirt behind the bike, he drove off. He didn't have a particular direction to go, and even if he'd remembered how he'd arrived upon first finding the bunker, well, nothing looked the same. The terrain had been transformed to something totally new. The handlebars bucked under his hands as he drove over the tall grass, and he hoped he didn't end up falling into a deep ravine or some such thing hidden under the grass.

With the whine of the engine fading away, Hank disappeared amongst the trees.

As Hank drove away, a man stepped out from behind the tree he was hiding behind. The hunter had been out looking for game, and to say he was shocked when he heard the alarm sounding and the bunker door opening would have been an understatement.

His village knew about the underground bunker, but the door had never opened, not in his lifetime nor his father's anyway. There had been excavations over the years to try and get inside but no one had ever managed to gain access and eventually, everyone had given up. The crater had been dug years ago, the baron wanting to see if digging underground would work, believing it was a way to get inside. He thought he could burrow underground, but no matter how far his men went, the wall of stone was always there. In the small village of Sunset the hunter called home, there were countless stories about the riches beyond imagining that were inside the facility. Everything from tons of canned food to enough fuel and guns to last a lifetime, or better yet, to make any man who found it a king. And now, unbelievably, a man had come out, and what a way to make an exit, the hunter thought. The hunter had been in such awe that he hadn't had time to shoot the man off the motorcycle until the rider was already too far away to hit.

As he watched the motorcycle disappear into the forest, the hunter knew he needed to get back to his village. Their leader — Baron Sharpe — would want to know what he'd found and hopefully there would be a reward for the information provided. He planned on leaving the part about how he could have shot the man and captured him right then and there, deciding some things could be left out of the story. Baron Sharpe wasn't a forgiving man, as those that spent time in his prison could attest to.

To become a baron in the first place, a man had to be cold-blooded, and ready to do anything it took to get ahead. Baron Sharpe was just such a man. Around sixty with graying hair and an avuncular appearance, beneath that inviting exterior was a man made of ice, who'd kill in a heartbeat if it would further his agenda. But then, almost all the barons that had enclaves in the area were of the same breed, and compared to most, Baron Sharpe was positively an angel.

Already thinking about how he was going to spend his reward, the hunter began running back home to report his news.

Chapter 5

A mile from the redoubt, amidst a small glade of trees, Hank slowed the Triumph and then stopped it. Before him was a half dozen apple trees, the ground littered with fallen fruit. The trees still had half their crop, however, and Hank put the Roadster on its center stand and went to one particularly large tree. Reaching up, he plucked an apple from the closest branch, feeling like Adam in the Garden of Eden.

He took the first bite rather hesitantly, as if he expected the apple to be riddled with worms, but when nothing was inside it but sweetness, he quickly devoured it and ate six more. By the time he finished the last one, his stomach felt like it would burst.

Well, that took care of the food problem, he thought, and with the trees so close to the bunker, he could easily grab as many as he wanted so that the others would have something to eat upon waking. A little voice in his head said he should gather what he could carry and go back now but he pushed it down.

Now that he was outside, he didn't want to go back just yet. He wanted to explore his new world. Though it was hard to believe it had been a hundred years since he'd last been outside, Hank had to admit that trees around the bunker hadn't sprouted up overnight. That took years, decades, to become the sizes they were.

Besides, his friends were sleeping and there was nothing to do but wait for them to wake up. He had transportation; so why not explore a little, that way when the others awoke, he could tell them the lay of the land?

After all, what was the worst that could happen?

Dividing up about a dozen apples in his saddlebags, he drove off once more. He hadn't traveled far before coming upon a road. It had been paved once, but that clearly had been a long time ago.

In many places the pavement was missing or had been raised five or six inches off the ground, thanks to weeds working their way beneath. Vegetation grew tall on both sides of the road, giving it the look of an unused roadway.

But the Triumph was more than a match for the rough path and Hank drove onto it, weaving his way down it. He drove for a half hour and then began to see signs of habitation, though sporadic.

Off in the distance were scattered farmhouses, but if they were occupied was unknown. No smoke wafted from cracked and worn chimneys nor did the land look like it was being worked.

Hank glanced down to the radiation badge on his shirt. It was something he always wore, as did the other companions. The small, circular badge had proven invaluable for living in a world where the bombs had been dropped, scattering radiation across the land. He was pleased to see the little arrow was in the green, meaning there was no radiation present. If it had been in the yellow it would mean he was in a place that he wouldn't want to stick around in long, and red would mean get the fuck out of there before your ass begins to rot off.

Rounding a corner in the road, he had to hit the brakes hard or risk driving into a man who was walking in the center of the road. The man was naked and his skin was covered in red welts, the flesh bubbling in places. Hank had seen enough men with radiation burns to know it when he saw them.

But the man seemed harmless so Hank drove up until he was right behind the slowly-plodding figure. When the man didn't so much as turn his head upon hearing the idling motorcycle behind him, Hank drove around him and slowed until the bike was alongside him.

The man resembled one of the living dead, his eyes blank, the nose looking as if it was about to fall off at any moment. The skin on his face resembled Silly Putty more than flesh, and the hair was all but gone, a few wisps at the very top all that remained of a once full mane. The man seemed lost in thought, placing one foot in front of the other, while he mumbled something that only he understood.

Though he looked harmless and on death's door, Hank still knew not to take any chances, and with his left hand on his panga while his right hand kept the Roadster moving slowly, he said, "Hey, buddy, where you going? You okay?"

The man said nothing, not so much as blinking at the sound of Hank's voice.

"Fine," Hank shrugged. "Just thought I'd be friendly."

He drove off, leaving the naked, slowly-dying man to himself, but he didn't go more than a hundred feet, when he rounded a corner in the road and found even more people walking single file on the left shoulder, their left arms brushing the tall weeds as they walked. There were a dozen of them, both men and women, and they all walked with heads held low, eyes staring at their feet, each mumbling something.

With the Triumph moving at no more than a walking pace, Hank drove up until he was even with the last walker, then slowly passed him, until he was even with the second to last one.

They all looked the same, red welts and sores, skin sloughing off the bones and eyes filled with blank stares. Hank glanced down at the radiation badge and was surprised to see that it had moved slightly from the green into the yellow. So these people were radioactive, red hot, which explained the burns and sores.

The word 'zombies' came to mind as he stared at the line of what was basically the walking dead. A few had foam coming from their mouths and Hank knew it was from exposure to radiation. It was a sickness similar to rabies but at the moment these people seemed to be harmless, but still, he stayed wary, in case one decided to try and jump him.

Hank drove until he was at the front of the line, then pulled the Roadster to a stop, and with the engine idling, he placed his hand on his SIG-Sauer, as he watched the line of walking dead folks reach him and begin passing him, not one of them gazing his way.

As they passed by, their mutterings grew louder, and Hank heard words like, "God will save us. He is everywhere, we are his vessels. We will die and rise to be by his side."

There were other passages but it was hard to understand, as they had to speak using mouths with cracked and dry lips, teeth that fell out even as they talked, and tongues swollen and bloated.

Some looked like nothing more than walking skeletons, their skin already gone to expose the red meat beneath. The odor was overwhelming and Hank had to cover his nose or risk vomiting right there on the spot. Flies buzzed from head to head, each scalp raw and bloody, boils weeping and puss flowing. They were a truly disgusting bunch and Hank couldn't remember seeing something so gross as the line of men and women passing him by.

"Jesus Christ," he muttered under his breath when he could take it no longer.

Whether it was coincidence or because he had mentioned the savior Jesus Christ, one of the men in line looked up and straight ahead, then stopped walking, the watery eyes never blinking. A few pieces of red meat slid off the man and slapped the ground wetly. The others simply walked past him, ignoring one of their brethren that had stopped.

"You speak of the Son of God, are you one of us too then?" the man asked, spittle flying from his lips in a fine mist. One of the boils on the right side of his face popped, and pus started to dribble down until droplets slid off his chin. Flies played in the mucous, having a pool party right on the man's face.

"Uh, no, sorry, I'm not. I was just passing by and I saw you guys walking. Ah, you all don't look too good."

The man's head began to swivel so he could look squarely at Hank. Until now, Hank had only seen the man's right profile, but as he turned slightly, Hank saw that the left side of his face was all but gone. Bone could be seen past bits of muscle, that side of the nose having rotted off to leave a jagged hole that dribbled mucous continually. Veins pulsed slowly as blood still pumped through them, and to Hank the whole mess seemed to glow with an eerie light. It may have been the way the sun hit the man's face or his imagination, but either way Hank almost fell off the Roadster when the man turned to face him, such was the shock of rot and decomposition.

The eyes were almost totally white, two hardboiled eggs floating in a see of red.

Swallowing the knot in his throat, Hank put on his best face and said, "So uh, why are you all walking like this?"

"We are in search of the one true God," the man said, his voice a hoarse whisper. "He is found in those places where no one remains, where the bombs destroyed everything, the fires cleansing the earth of all evil." The man sneezed, and the rest of his nose flew off to strike the road three feet ahead of him. It rolled once and lay still. Wiping his imaginary nose with the back of his arm, he then slid two fingers into his mouth and pulled out a loose tooth that was bothering him. He flicked it away absently. That only left a few remaining teeth, and soon they would be gone, too.

"You mean the rad zones? But why?" Hank asked as he winced at the sight of the man taking out his teeth with his fingers. He was amazed that this guy and others like him had willingly walked into rad zones and cooked their bodies to a crisp in search of God.

"Man is a sinner which is why the fires of Hell rained down on him a century ago. Man needed to be punished. But now we hope to find Him and ask Him to take us back into His loving embrace, and by suffering we hope to have Him see that we are pure. That by bathing in the atomic zones we are worthy to be by His side."

"Ah, okay, I guess." Hank blinked at the man's ravings. They were all alone now, the last walker about to turn the corner up ahead. The man, seeing he had fallen behind, began walking again. Red splotches were left behind from each slap of his bloody feet.

But then the man did something that Hank wished to never see. As he walked, the man reached into a hole in his side and pulled out a chunk of something bloody, a pancreas or perhaps a liver. Then he raised the bloody organ to his cracked lips and took a bite, chewing at it slowly, the few teeth left in his mouth barely up to the task.

To Hank it was the most disgusting thing he had ever witnessed and his stomach roiled inside him, threatening to disgorge all the apples he ate. He had to close his eyes and think of something pleasant or risk losing it all right there on the road.

The naked, bloody dead-man-walking continued onward, chewing on himself as he plodded down the road, oblivious to Hank or anything else around him.

Hank pointed the Triumph the way he had been going, and with bile tickling the back of his throat, he gunned the engine and flew up the road, passing each of the walking dead until he was past them and the road ahead was clear, nothing but sunshine and tall weeds before him.

He let out the breath he was holding, not even aware of it, and he sucked in the air around him. For some reason it tasted a hundred times better now that he was clear of the dying men and women.

Taking a look at his radiation badge, he saw that it had gone back to green. For the needle to move even a little as he stood near those people meant they were positively radiated. He wouldn't have been surprised that they glowed in the dark when night fell.

With the wind in his hair and the road ahead clear of rotting things, he felt infinitely better.

He did make a mental note to take an alternate route back to the bunker, not wanting to come across the pus-covered group again.

Chapter 6

Hank had only traveled about five miles, when over the sound of the Triumph's engine, he heard gunshots coming from just over the rise before him.

Screams sounded as well, but they didn't last long. Driving the Roadster over to the side of the road, he rolled it into some brush so that it was roughly hidden from view, then he got off the bike, made sure to take two grenades with him from the saddlebags, and headed off on foot. The rise was only a hundred feet before him, and with him running, it only took a minute to reach the top. He had a good view from where he was, and staying to the side of the road so that he was hidden in the tall weeds, he looked out onto a wide open field to see his first tableaux of humanity of a hundred years later.

Though it didn't surprise him, it looked like man was just as much of an asshole as he had been a hundred years ago, and if possible, maybe even a little meaner.

To the left of the road, in the open field, were three vehicles, each of them on fire. What the vehicles had been when they had rolled off the showroom floor ten decades ago was unknown, and would be forever. They were such a patchwork of different cars and pickup trucks to be virtually unrecognizable as any kind of model that Hank recalled.

Not that it mattered, as all three were burning funeral pyres, right down to the human bodies within each one, trapped behind the steering wheels. The only good thing about the terrible scene was that the burning humans were long dead, riddled with bullets from the raiders turned scavengers that were even now running around the field, digging through the clothes and bags of the ten corpses strewn about the area. The wind shifted, blowing in

Hank's direction, and the unmistakable odor of burning human flesh came to him. He wrinkled his nose, knowing the scent well and hating it as much as ever.

More than a dozen corpse-strippers flitted from body to body, calling out at what they'd found to the others. Many were laughing, having a grand old time at slaughtering the innocent travelers.

Filthy fingers rifled through bloody clothes, searching for anything of value. A few of the coldhearts had pliers in their hands, and they used them on the open mouths of the corpses, pulling out silver fillings to get a payday.

Boots, belts, jewelry or any weapons, such as knives or guns, were quickly stripped from the corpses, leaving some naked, ass up to the sun, to meet their maker without a stitch of clothing.

Hank's jaw set in a grimace as he watched the scavengers picking the corpses dry, but other than not wanting to be seen by them and having to either run or fight, he quickly decided he would simply stay hidden. Soon the scavengers would have all that they had killed for and would leave, and then Hank would make sure to go the other way. Twelve to one were bad odds and he didn't feel like gambling today.

"I found a juicy one here," one of the scavengers called out.

Hank saw the buck-toothed man sawing at the corpse, and a second later he stood up with an ear in his hand. When he turned so that Hank could see him better, Hank saw that the man wore a necklace of human ears, at least fifty from the looks of it, each one wrinkled and shriveled so that they resembled dried prunes.

"Got me a couple of nice ones over here, too," another man said. This man had a large boil on his left cheek, so red and swollen it looked as if it would pop at any second. He wore a necklace of ears, too, though not as many. The piece of human shit was holding up his ears with a proud look, examining them in the sunlight.

Another scavenger, a man with a misshapen face that looked like it had been squeezed into a vice and left there to bake in the sun, came running towards the other men, holding a handful of ears in his hands, blood from said ears dripping through his fingers to be lost in the tall grass. He had a necklace that must have had a hundred ears, and as he ran, the necklace swayed back and forth, the ears rubbing together, the sound like dry leaves rustling in the wind. "I got me a shitload here," he laughed as he joined the other men. Part of his nose was eaten away by some kind of fungus, and his entire face was pockmarked with scars from old sores that hadn't healed well.

It took everything Hank had not to unsling his Heckler and Koch rifle and take out a few of the bastards from where he was hidden. No doubt if he took down three or four, the rest would run away, the cowards they probably were. But he knew it would be pointless. The people were all dead and he wasn't in the revenge game for total strangers. It was terrible what had happened to the people, but even now, a hundred years later, the rules of the jungle were still active. Only the strong survived, and though all coldhearts and cutthroats, in this situation, the scavengers were the stronger.

Still, a lot of people had died to make the corpse-stripper's necklaces. Hank's hand went to his SIG, making sure it was safely on his hip.

"Hot damn!" the ugly one yelled out happily. "I'm gonna need to start makin' a new necklace after this haul."

Hank gazed off to the left, where two men were lying on top of the corpses of two women. Both men had their pants off and the dresses the women had been wearing were pulled up so that their faces were almost covered. The men were fucking like wild animals, yelling and whooping up a storm. Apparently, the women being dead wasn't a turn-off. Hell, for all Hank knew, it was a turn-on for the sick fucks. To the scavengers, a warm piece of meat was all they needed and the corpses were still warm, having only become dead minutes ago.

Once more Hank's moral code fought with him. He wanted to kill the scum below, but knew it would be for nothing. Even if he killed them all, there were a hundred more in the area, probably more like a thousand, just like them waiting to do the same deeds to other helpless people.

No doubt Hank would have been able to remain exactly where he was, and would have stayed as only an observer, if not for what happened next.

As he watched the scavengers cutting more ears from prone bodies, suddenly from behind one of the burning vehicles, a young woman around seventeen or eighteen appeared, running for her life as two laughing scavengers followed right on her heels. Her white shirt was torn, exposing the pair of firm breasts beneath, and the curves hidden within.

She was beautiful, with long blonde hair that reminded Hank of Laurie, who was sleeping gently back at the bunker. Whether he would have done something to save the girl if she hadn't reminded him of Laurie was unknown, but the fact that Hank at first glance thought he *was* seeing Laurie, certainly was a factor in what came next.

In a well-practiced motion, Hank unslung the rifle off his back and lined up the first man to enter his gun sight. The man managed to take another three steps before a 4.7 mm bullet ripped through his neck, blowing out tendons and muscle and leaving the man with nothing to support his skull. The head lolled to the side, devoid of support, and though already dead thanks to a severed spinal cord, the body still ran a few more feet, as if unwilling to accept that it was dead. Then the body tumbled forward into the grass, the legs rising up slightly from the momentum before the corpse lay still.

Hank saw none of this, as he was already shifting his aim to the other man chasing the woman. Firing again, the round took the man in the side of the chest, blowing out his heart before continuing into his lungs, then exiting out the far side, leaving a fist-sized hole in its wake. The man's eyes popped from his head, in shock as to what was going on below his neck, and he thrust out his arms, as if wanting to reach the girl even as his nerve endings shut down for the final time.

He actually sped up, a surge of adrenaline forcing him to go faster, and he struck the girl on the back, pushing her forward and to the ground. He landed on top of her, dead before both bodies had settled. He was twice her size and she found herself trapped, unable to extricate herself from the heaving bulk of the scavenger, who was bleeding all over her back.

By now the other ten men had figured out they were under attack and began firing back at Hank's general direction. Bullets whined around Hank's head and he had to drop low and retreat or risk being hit by a stray round. The enemy had been engaged, there would be no stopping now.

He searched for the girl, trying to pick her out amidst the carnage, but he couldn't see her trapped under the body of the scavenger. Assuming she was dead, all Hank could do now was finish the job, and leave this part of the world just a little bit cleaner than when he'd found it.

But simply sitting on the rise and taking potshots at the now hiding scavengers while they did the same to him was futile, especially when they might be smart enough to figure out they could flank him. Hank needed to take the fight to the enemy, and as he crawled back to his motorcycle, an idea was already forming in his mind.

Chapter 7

"**W**ho the fuck is shooting at us?" the man with the boil called out to his men, who were taking cover behind anything of use, which were bodies, battered suitcases taken from the burning cars, and a few big rocks the size of large dogs. All served well as decent cover.

"I don't know," Buck-tooth replied, "but the fucker's gonna get what's comin' to him when I get through with him." On the tail end of his words, two things happened back to back, so close they almost occurred simultaneously.

The first thing was a small object came soaring from the same direction of the shooter, and an instant behind it a motorcycle erupted from the brush, flying through the air like something out of an action movie.

To the surprise of five of the scavengers, they found out to their unhappiness that the small object was a grenade. It landed between them, rolling right up to where one of the men lay behind a dead body. The man had time to open his eyes wide, and was about to yell a warning, when the grenade exploded, spraying all five men with shrapnel and gore from the body, but also because it was so close, destroying the man who had seen it first, leaving behind nothing but a bloody paste.

As a pink and red mist floated around ground zero of the blast, the motorcycle landed a few yards away, the rider already spraying the remaining scavengers with bullets.

As Hank landed with the Triumph between his legs, he almost wiped out and only sheer luck kept him upright this time. He landed with the back wheel first, and when he felt himself falling to the right, he kicked out with his foot and pushed off the ground, leveling the bike. The telescopic front forks absorbed the impact when the front tire came down, and Hank spun the Roadster in a wide circle, avoiding the debris and flying body parts from the grenade. He then pulled his SIG-Sauer from its holster by way of a cross draw, his left hand having to do the shooting so his right hand could keep the throttle of the bike engaged. He changed gears by banging on the clutch with his foot, which was never a good thing for the tranny, but he wasn't in a position to worry about it at the moment.

Gunning the throttle, the chain drive spun the back tire, spraying dirt behind the bike, the Roadster surging forward as if it had been shot from a cannon.

His plan had worked well. The scavengers were shook up from the grenade and not even one of them fired at Hank as he landed and went on the attack, the SIG-Sauer leading the way as he leaned over the handlebars, using the bar to brace his hand. Of course, he quickly found out this was a terrible idea as the Roadster bounced all over the field, causing his arm to shake as well.

He made a mental note that the next time he was fighting a dozen scavengers with human ears for necklaces in the middle of a field with corpses everywhere, he would make sure to keep his gun arm higher.

The grenade had taken down five men, and he had shot two with his automatic rifle seconds earlier, which left only five more to go. Five to one were odds he could live with, especially when he was dealing with the kind of human scum he was trying to kill.

A man wearing pieces of radial tires as armor jumped up and began firing at Hank, the bullet missing by inches. Hank swiveled in his seat and shot the man in the face, thus avoiding the tire-armor the scavenger was wearing. Armor only protected what it covered, and face-armor wasn't used too often. As the man went down, Hank bet that the man had wished he'd made some kind of mask or helmet right about now.

A bullet ricocheted off the handlebars and Hank was so startled that he swerved too hard to the right, the bike sliding out from under him. A second later he was flying through the air.

He hit the ground on his right side and made sure to tuck his arms in as he rolled. His rifle strapped to his back whacked the side of his head three times before he had stopped completely. The entire time he was falling and rolling, he never let go of his SIG, and the instant he stopped he jumped up, then searched for a target. He found one immediately and another corpse-stripper went down with a face full of lead, the back of his skull no longer in existence.

That left three enemies: Boil, Buck-tooth and Ugly.

"Kill that son of a bitch!" Boil yelled at his remaining men, who did their best to comply, but Hank wasn't staying still, always a moving target.

The ground was treacherous, filled with depressions from water run-off and also old animal warrens. Add to this all the debris strewn around the area from the burning, ransacked vehicles, and it was just a matter of time before Hank tripped over something hidden in the grass.

He never knew what it was that tripped him, but one second he was running and seeking cover, and the next he was falling face first into the grass. Out of instinct he put his hand before his face, and when he landed, the SIG slipped from his hand to fall into the grass. Getting up as fast as possible, and trying to bring around his rifle, he found that no matter how fast he wanted to be, it was still too slow for the three remaining ear collectors.

Before the rifle was even halfway off his shoulder, the three men had run over to him, their guns leveled at Hank's chest.

Knowing when the odds were against him, Hank put on the friendliest grin he could manage and raised his hands into the air. "Now, now, boys, let's not get too carried away. We're all friends here, aren't we?"

Boil spit into the grass and said, "You aren't no friend of mine, stranger and after what you did to my men, you're gonna die real fucking slow." He gestured to Buck-tooth and Ugly to take Hank into custody, as it were.

The men did as they were told, but when they were only a few feet away, one of the flaming vehicles exploded, the gas tank finally erupting and sending blazing debris off in all directions. Everyone turned towards the explosion for a brief second, well, everyone but Hank, who saw the explosion as an opportunity. As the three men were distracted, he lunged forward, grabbed Boil by the cuff of his filthy shirt, and pulled him close, drawing the panga at the same time and placing the razor-sharp steel edge against the scavenger's throat.

When the other two corpse-strippers looked back, they found that things had changed dramatically from only seconds ago.

Hank swallowed the knot in his throat and pressed the panga even tighter to Boil's neck, ready in case the coldheart moved so much as an inch. But the man remained still, too afraid to move. Like most scum, Boil was only brave when he had the upper hand. Hank kept the man directly in front of him so that the other two men couldn't get a shot off without risking a bullet hitting Boil.

As the four of them stood immobile in the field, Hank felt slight relief when the other two men didn't try anything. Apparently, Boil was high up in the chain of command.

"Shit, what the fuck do we do now?" Ugly asked Buck-tooth as the two scavengers stood stock-still, not sure how to approach the present situation.

"You stay right there or you're pal gets a new mouth," Hank hissed as he pressed the edge of the panga so close to Boil's neck that a small bead of blood seeped from around the blade.

"Now, now, stranger, let's all take it easy here. There's no need for violence." Boil's voice trembled slightly; the man knew he was a half ounce away from death if Hank decided to kill him. "Just let me go and I promise me and the boys will let you walk away from here. Free and clear, hell, take anything you want from our booty, too. We won't stop you or nothin', I promise."

"Fuck this, kill the bastard!" Ugly yelled, taking a step forward, getting some courage back now that he had a moment to think about it. After all, if Boil was killed, maybe he could be in charge. Buck-tooth was thinking the same thing too.

"Don't you assholes move a muscle!" Boil yelled. "If you do, this guy'll kill me and so help me if he does, I'll come back from the dead and get both your asses. I'll cut you ear to ear and add yours to my necklace! So help me God!"

Both coldhearts stopped in their tracks; evidently their fear of Boil was enough for the moment to prevent them from doing anything rash. Hank began to back up, wanting to reach his motorcycle, where he hoped to use it to escape.

As he watched the two scavengers, seeing that they weren't moving a muscle, Hank actually began to believe he might actually make it, when suddenly, Boil sank his teeth into Hank's arm just above the wrist.

Before the teeth could do much damage, Hank let out a curse and pulled the panga across Boil's throat. The blade sliced into the man's neck like a warm knife through butter, severing the carotid artery and jugular smoothly, then continuing deeper and severing the voice box. Boil was a dead man before he knew what was happening, and with blood geysering from the large gash in his throat, Hank pushed the twitching corpse away from him.

Boil fell straight to the ground, his hands at his throat as he tried to keep his blood inside him, though it didn't seem to want to cooperate, and it squirted out between his fingertips with each beat of his heart. His mouth opened and closed, spewing out red bubbles as a waterfall of crimson spilled down his chest.

So much for making a hasty escape, Hank thought. As if an alarm had sounded at the killing of Boil, the other two scavengers rushed Hank with knives in their hands, wanting to take him alive and make him suffer, murder filling their eyes. Hank thought for a quick second that he was lucky they wanted him alive to torture, for two against one, and with guns in their hands, the fight would have been over before it started. But he wasn't going to look a gift horse in the mouth when it was presented to him. If the two men were overconfident, that was fine with Hank. He knew when in a situation like this, to turn and run would be the worst possible move, so instead, much to the surprise of the two coldhearts, he ran at them with the bloody panga held before him, screaming at the top of his lungs like a warrior going into battle.

For a split second the two scavengers were shocked to see their prey charging them, and Hank was ready to use that surprise to his advantage. Buck-tooth raised his knife to slash at Hank, but the blow never came, for Hank got in under the man's guard and plunged the tip of the panga all the way up the hilt into his guts. The man stopped like he'd run into a cement wall, the blade pushing up and then out of his back an inch, almost like it was a snake peeking out of its warren to see if it was safe to come out. Then the blade tip receded as Hank withdrew the weapon, stepping to the side so he didn't get splashed with guts. He made sure to twist the blade to the left and then right as he pulled it out, thus making the wound tract even larger. The instant the panga came out, Buck-tooth's intestines spilled forth, hot and slimy as the coils landed wetly in the grass to stain the blades red.

Buck-tooth looked down at his escaping insides, not under-standing why they were doing that. His stuff was supposed to stay in him, wasn't it? What the hell was it doing on the ground? "I…can't die, not like this. I've killed everyone, no one gets away. I can't die…not like this."

"Sorry to disappoint you, pal, but you're already dead," Hank said and then sliced the panga across the coldheart's throat, spar-ing the man a slow death with his guts spilled onto the grass. Buck-tooth tumbled over to twitch his last in the dry grass.

Hank turned to see where his last enemy was, and saw that Ugly was making a fast track away from the area. Not wanting to let the man go, he unslung the G-12 automatic rifle from his shoulder, went to one knee, and sighted the coldheart's back in the scope. A second later the gun barked and the scavenger threw his hands up wide, like he was gesturing to God that he was coming home to the Promised Land, then he tumbled face first into the grass. He didn't rise.

Reslinging the rifle, Hank wiped the panga on the back of Buck-tooth's shirt, then prepared to gather his gear and get going. It was as he turned and set one foot before another that he saw a rat-faced looking scavenger step out from behind one of the burning vehicles, the one next to the vehicle that had exploded. The distance was no more than thirty feet, and the man's thin face and beady eyes put on what was definitely a smile, as the man knew he had Hank dead-to-rights. The rat-faced coldheart had a hunting rifle aimed right at Hank's chest, and from the distance between shooter and target, there was no question that Hank was a dead man when the scavenger squeezed the trigger.

Even from the distance he was standing from the man, Hank saw the gleam in the coldheart's eyes, the man's finger already pulling the trigger to send a bullet straight into Hank's heart.

Chapter 8

The report of the gunshot echoed across the field, making Hank jump slightly where he was standing. He even closed his eyes, expecting to feel the rat-faced man's bullet hit him square in the chest. He imagined that in a split-second he would feel a sharp impact, and then pain and numbness as the bullet shredded his heart, and he dropped to the ground, dying on the way down. But he didn't feel anything other than the wind on his face, and when he opened his eyes, he was surprised to see that the scavenger was lying face down in the grass and there was a young woman standing behind him, holding Hank's SIG-Sauer, which he'd thought was still lost in the grass somewhere. The second he saw her Hank recognized the woman as the one he'd seen running, the one he'd tried to save, but when she'd gone down he'd assumed she was dead.

The young woman stood with the gun still level, her eyes wide with shock. Tears ran down her cheeks. Hank walked closer to her, his hands out and away from his body, not wanting to take any chances that she thought he was just another scavenger.

He made it all the way up to her and he carefully took the SIG back, then touched her shoulder. "Hey, you all right? I owe you my thanks for taking that asshole out. I thought he had me there for a minute."

At first she didn't move, then she slowly turned her head to face Hank. A full minute passed before she said, "They killed my family, my friends."

"I know, and I'm truly sorry for it all," Hank said. "What were you all doing out here?"

She blinked more tears and sniffed heavily. "We left the village we lived in. The baron was a horrible man, killing and torturing anyone he wanted. If you didn't pay him enough in taxes he'd send his men to take you to either be a slave if you were a man or if a woman he'd put you in his whore house. My father lost his job, and we ran out of money. He was taking care of the whole family on his salary. So we had no choice, we had to run for it. When we left a few others came with us, people in the same situation as us. But we were followed by the men you killed. They were mercenaries the baron sent after us." She stared down at the bodies scattered around. The flames of two of the vehicles were still burning brightly, though the one that had exploded had died down with nothing else to burn. Small fires burned here and there, and if the wind went the wrong way, the entire area for miles could end up being engulfed.

A low moan came from a few feet away and Hank glanced over to see that the rat-faced man wasn't entirely dead, though he had a spreading blood spot on the back of his shirt. "Looks like he's not quite dead yet," Hank said.

The young woman seemed to stand taller at Hank's words, then going to another body and taking an eight inch Bowie knife from it, she walked over to the rat-faced man, climbed onto his back so that the man's face was in the grass, then grabbed his hair with her left hand, pulling his face up and exposing his neck.

"No, please don't kill me, please, I..." the man begged but his words fell on deaf ears. In a hand shaking from nervousness, the girl pressed the blade to the man's throat and drew it slowly across, slicing as she slid it. Hot blood gushed out of the gash in the man's throat, spraying the grass and painting it crimson. The man began to buck and jerk, but the girl stayed on his back, keeping him from moving. Such was the wound that he bled out in less than a minute. When his twitches grew still and the body went slack, she climbed off the corpse, and after wiping the blade clean on the man's shirt, she walked back to Hank, who had silently watched the killing, his face devoid of emotion.

"He's dead now," she said flatly; for the moment the tears had dried up. It was as if the killing had fueled her with inner strength.

"Yeah, he sure is," Hank said. "I thought you were dead, too. You know, back when I took down the man chasing you."

"I almost was. When you shot him, he fell on top of me. He was twice my size and his dead weight was on me so that I couldn't get out from under him. But finally I managed to do it."

He nodded, understanding. Looking her up and down, he saw she couldn't have weighed more than a hundred and ten pounds soaking wet. She had small, pert breasts, the nipples poking up from the cotton of the shirt she wore. The shirt was stained with blood but it wasn't hers, it was from the man that had fallen on her. She wore a pair of patched jeans and sandals, and despite the disheveled appearance, Hank had to admit she was even more beautiful up close than when he'd first seen her from up on the rise.

"Well, I'm glad to see you're all right." He gazed out over the death field and then looked back to the girl. "I'm sorry about your family. Anyway, I gotta be going. Best of luck." He turned and walked back to the Triumph. Once he'd reached the bike, he picked it up, pulled out the few errant grass blades that had become wedged here and there and got on the bike. He kicked it over once but nothing happened. "Shit, I hope it's not flooded," he muttered and kicked it over again.

Once more nothing happened. He played with the choke a little and then kicked it again, and this time the engine surged to life with a belch of black smoke. He revved the throttle a little, getting whatever gunk was inside out of the carburetor, satisfied when the smoke subsided and it burned cleaner.

He was about to drive away when the girl called out to him, running up as fast as she could. "Wait, you're not just going to leave me out here alone, are you?"

Hank shrugged. "Why not? I saved you. I did my civic duty and all that. Hell, I should have minded my own business, but you reminded me of..." He stopped talking and looked down at the handlebars.

"Reminded you of who?" she asked.

"No one that matters at the moment."

"Please take me with you. If you leave me out here alone, my chances aren't good."

Hank stared at her, needing more. He wasn't in the business of adopting wayward women. He'd done his part by saving her, after that she was on her own.

"I can cook," she said and when Hank's face didn't so much as twitch, she began to get desperate, so she put on her sexiest look and added, "I can make you happy if you let me. I'll make it worth your while to take me with you." She moved up close to him, brushing her body against his.

He took her by the shoulders and separated her from him. "That won't be necessary," he said. "I don't need that."

"Really? Well, you'd be the first man I ever met that didn't. Maybe if I was a man instead you'd..."

"No, it's not like that. I already have someone, and I wouldn't want to be unfaithful to her."

"Oh? Where is she then? She's not here."

"She's close by and I'll be with her in a few weeks. Besides, I never needed to take sex from a woman as a form of payment and just 'cause the world has turned to shit, I wouldn't start now."

"Then you're the most honorable man I've ever met other than my father," she said. At the mention of her father her eyes began to tear up and she gazed off to where the man's body lay, cold and still in the grass. "I need to bury him, and my mother and the rest of my family, too." But then she looked back at Hank. "Would you please take me with you? I can be of help to you. I can watch your back when you need a second set of eyes. I can shoot too, you saw me."

"Yeah, I did see that, all right." Whether it was her uncanny resemblance to Laurie or just because though he hated to admit it, in the end Hank was a big softy, he finally said, "Okay, fine, you can come with me for a while. But I don't have a destination, I'm just driving around to see how it is around here, then I have to go somewhere you can't come."

Her face lit up and she clapped happily, looking more like a young child than a woman of twenty. "Oh thank you, you won't regret it, I promise. But wait, what about my parents? They need to be buried."

Hank looked over at the bodies lying everywhere. Soon, the four legged kind of scavenger would come out, as well as the flying kind, ready to feed on the fresh meat of the recent kills. His eyes looked over the land and at the two still burning vehicles. "I have an idea how to deal with that faster than burying them," he said.

Chapter 9

The fire on one of the vehicles was burning even brighter, thanks to the fresh corpses that had been tossed into it. The funeral pyre burned strong, eagerly devouring flesh and bone.

Around the pyre, the bodies of the raiders lay where they fell. They didn't deserve any form of burial or cremation. They could stay there and rot, or become food for the animal scavengers already preparing to come in and begin feeding. Only Hank and the girl kept them at bay, though insects had already begun to harvest what they could from the corpses.

Hank and Harmony—the name she had given Hank—had worked fast, picking up all of her loved ones and friends and tossing the bodies into the fire. Hank had really done most of the work, and Harmony had merely prepared the bodies for cremation by clasping hands together and closing eyes that had stayed open in death. Tears fell freely from her eyes the entire time, and only now, as she stood a few feet from the raging fire, did her tears finally subside, mostly because they evaporated as soon as they left her eyes thanks to the oven-like heat coming off the pyre.

Hank waited for what he thought was enough time, then he touched her on the arm to get her attention. When she looked at him, he gestured to the Triumph with his chin, telling her it was time to go. She nodded, knowing he was right. She had managed to salvage a few items from everything that had been strewn about the area, and she had shoved it all into an old and worn backpack, with more patches to keep it whole than the actual material that it was made with. She also kept the Bowie knife, and took a .45 pistol from the body of one of the scavengers along with five full clips for it. Hank thought the gun was a little much for her, but when he'd commented on it she'd merely mentioned how she'd saved him with the SIG. He couldn't argue too much after that. Hank had gathered a couple of revolvers from some of the corpses, along with some rounds for the weapons.

"Thank you for doing this," she said to Hank as they walked over to the Triumph, which was waiting on its center stand. Almost an hour had passed since Hank had agreed to help her with the bodies, and once he'd begun doing the morbid task, he'd decided time wasn't an issue and just wanted to do it right.

"You're welcome. At least now your parents and friends can rest in peace." He climbed onto the Roadster and she hopped on behind him. She weighed so little he barely felt her get on. Kicking over the engine, it started with the one kick, and after driving around the blaze, he drove back to the road. At least now he had a guide in this strange new world, he figured, and hopefully she would be of help to him.

The wind blew Harmony's hair behind her head, and ten minutes after they'd left the glade of death, Hank glanced in his right handlebar mirror to see her in the reflection. She was smiling, her eyes creased a little from the wind, but she looked content.

While they rode, Harmony began telling Hank about the area, about the village of Sunset ten miles away and the baron there, who ruled with an iron fist. She explained more about the whore houses and the men who had been enslaved to pay what they owed.

Hank said nothing, listening intently. It appeared that over the past hundred years nothing much had changed, with the exception that now items that he had taken for granted, such as canned food, were now all but gone, or worth their weight in gold if a stash was found and the food was still edible. Harmony told of the baron's wealth of canned foods, and how he was obsessed with finding all he could get. He almost never opened the cans though, and ones that still had faded labels were the most valuable to him, his 'pride and joy' as he called them.

Hank thought it amusing that a man would think of a can of beets as his most valuable possession, but then this was a new time, where the things he had admired and thought as valuable were long gone, now only stories of the past.

He knew better than to tell Harmony about who he really was and how he came to be with her. First, she probably wouldn't believe him, but he quickly found out that if she or anyone else knew that he'd come from the redoubt, he would find himself a very popular individual.

She told Hank stories about the bunker and what was told to be hidden within its giant metal door. He smiled as she talked, knowing a lot of what she said was pure fiction, still, it was amusing to hear. The baron believed the bunker was filled to the ceiling with canned food, gold and weapons, which was why he had tried over and over again to break inside, each time failing miserably. He was the one that had commanded that the crater at the bunker be created.

Though no gold or food had been found, the bunker did have an impressive armory, and the motor pool with its condensed fuel would be a valuable commodity in the post-apocalyptic world Hank now found himself in. Maybe when the others awoke, they could take as much as they wanted and set themselves up somewhere as barons themselves.

Harmony asked Hank a few times where he had come from and where he was going, but each time Hank had diverted her questions, changing the subject to something she knew about. So far it had worked, and each time she began her questions, she had quickly been derailed and was soon off and talking about her family, the baron, or the town of Sunset that she used to call home.

An hour or so later, when Hank rounded a bend in the road he was on, a cracked and twisted stretch of pavement with weeds growing out of the myriad cracks that lined the faded pavement like spiderwebs, he spotted movement off to the left, across an open field of dead earth. He pulled over to the weed-infested shoulder and put the Triumph in neutral.

"Why are you stopping?" Harmony asked, stopping her story about how her father used to take her out hunting when she was a child.

Hank had let her ramble all she wanted, hoping it was a way for her to deal with the loss of her family. He merely pointed to the movement across the open area of bare ground. Harmony squinted but couldn't make out what she was seeing. Hank reached around past her leg and opened a saddlebag, taking out a small pair of field glasses. Holding them up to his face, he zeroed in on the movement until it was crystal clear.

At the far end of the denuded ground was a large oak tree, though by the looks of it the oak was almost dead, too. Still, a few green leaves struggled to fight through all the brown and yellow ones.

But that wasn't what had caught his attention. At the foot of the tree, chained to it by a thick metal chain with links more than an inch thick, stood one of the largest men Hank had ever seen.

The man stood a little over seven feet tall, and his shoulders were as broad as the tree he was chained to. He wore pants that were a size too small for him, and a shirt that had more tears than not. Sandals made from old radial tires were on his feet, but they were also too small and his thick toes protruded from the tips, as if he'd grown in size while wearing them.

The top of his head was covered with shaggy black hair, as were his legs and arms, the dark color matching his beard. He was like a giant grizzly bear that looked human. Thick muscles snaked under the tan skin, the wide chest strong and powerful. There was no fat on the giant, only more muscle.

Hank saw all this in a matter of seconds, for there was a lot going on over by the dying oak tree he needed to take in. The giant wasn't alone, chained to the tree. He was surrounded by more than a dozen wild dogs, the pack liking the idea that their prey couldn't run from them. Though the man was huge, the dog pack outnumbered him greatly, and their hunger spurned them to attack, despite the size of their prey.

The dog pack was a wild collection of breeds, from pit bulls and German shepherds to a couple of collies and Dobermans. All were mangy specimens; none had ever seen the inside of a home. 'Man's best friend' were words the canines had never heard of, nor would they have cared if they did. The dogs were as wild as a mountain wolf pack, and generations past their mothers and fathers, who had first found themselves alone in the cold world after the bombs fell, their owners dead or not returning to free them from their locked homes.

Hank watched as the giant fought the dogs with a matched ferocity, using a large branch taken from the oak tree to fend them off. One dog made a leap for the man's throat and was stopped cold by the swinging club, which connected on the side of the dog, cracking its spine and nearly ripping the animal in half. With entrails hanging from the split hide, the dog went spinning away to land in a heap of internal organs in the dust.

But the other wild dogs barely hesitated at seeing one of their number go down and in fact, they actually renewed their attack.

"Let me see," Harmony said and he handed her the government-issue binoculars.

"Oh my God, that poor man," she said while watching the battle. "Hank, you can't just leave him like that. You have to help him."

"It's not my problem, Harmony. I can't save everyone I come across."

"But you saved me," she said.

"Yeah, and don't make me regret it."

"But what if that was you down there? Wouldn't you want someone to come and help you?"

"I wouldn't get into a position like that," he said flatly.

"That's bullshit and you know it. Hank, if you don't help that man than you're no better than the men who tried to kill me and did so to my family. To do nothing when evil is going on is as bad as doing the evil itself by your own two hands. My father used to tell me that."

"Nice speech but it isn't gonna work," he said, crossing his arms over his broad chest.

She scowled at him. "I thought you better than that, Hank, I truly did. But I guess in the end you're right. Fuck the guy, let him die. Serves him right for not having any friends to save his ass."

That hit home. Hank thought about Carl, Stewart and Laurie. How many times had they saved his butt and he theirs? Maybe that was why he had Harmony with him. He knew to travel the land either now or a hundred years ago, alone, was close to suicide. A man needed someone to watch his back; no one could stay alert forever.

With a heavy sigh he said, "Get off the bike." Harmony did as she was told, such was the tone of Hank's voice. "Stay here, I'll be back. You're right. That poor bastard needs help. I can't let a man die like that." He handed her his automatic rifle so it wouldn't be a burden to him. "Take care of that for me."

"I knew you'd come around," Harmony said, holding the stolen .45 in her right hand and the rifle in her left.

Hank nodded curtly and tossed her the field glasses so she could watch, then he was off, the Triumph's rear tire sending out a spray of dirt as the Roadster surged forward. Harmony winced and waved her hand before her face to clear away the dust, then raised the field glasses to her eyes so she could watch Hank approach the battle.

Hank pulled out a shrapnel grenade and a tear gas canister from the left saddlebag as he drove, then let the top flap on the bag fall back down. There was Velcro as well as buckles to hold the top flap closed, and with him driving, the Velcro would have to suffice. The shrapnel grenade he shoved into a pocket for later use, the tear gas staying in his hand.

When he was close to the fray, he slowed the bike and pulled the pin with his teeth, then threw the tear gas canister into the center of the raucous, the smoke immediately enveloping both man and dogs alike.

He felt bad for the man, who now had to breathe in the tear gas as well as fight the dogs, but the ultrasensitive noses and eyes of the animals would have an even tougher time dealing with it.

Suddenly, from his left a dog darted away from the pack and came at Hank. Before Hank knew what was happening, the dog had grabbed his ankle in its mouth. The Triumph kept going, but Hank found himself stopped in his tracks, then was being pulled from the seat of the bike to fall onto the ground. The Roadster kept going for a few yards before hitting a dip in the road, wobbling for a second and then falling over. The rear tire spun slowly, the transmission still in gear.

No sooner did he hit the ground than Hank found something large and hairy on top of him. He barely had time to pull the SIG-Sauer.

Though an ideal weapon for close quarters fighting, it was almost useless to use as a club or muzzle-thrusting into an opponent. But it worked damn good to stop the slavering fangs from sinking into his throat. The SIG went into the slavering mouth sideways, halting the attack of teeth only inches from his face. Hank fought to push the animal off him but the dog was almost as big as him, and was nothing but solid muscle. Living in the wild, there was no time to lie around and put fat on its limbs. It was a killing machine, pure and simple, and at the moment Hank was its prey.

As he fought to get the dog off him, another dog broke from the pack, seeing an easy kill in Hank. Before Hank realized it, he felt a tug on his right boot, as the second dog began to chew on the top of his foot. Only the tough, government-issue leather protected Hank from losing a few toes. But that wouldn't last for long, and though the teeth hadn't penetrated the boot, the pressure from the jaws was enough to make Hank wince.

Fighting with one dog on top of him, the beast doing its best to rip out his throat, while the second made a meal out of his foot, Hank fought for his life, already regretting coming to the chained man's aid.

If he'd minded his own business, both he and Harmony would have already been miles down the road, and Hank's flesh would have remained intact.

Chapter 10

His free foot sweeping around in a wide arc, Hank kicked the dog gnawing on his boot away from him. The dog went rolling, letting out a loud yelp for its trouble.

The SIG was still locked in the powerful jaws of the dog snarling on top of Hank; he tried to buck the dog off him, but no matter how much he tried the animal remained on his chest. He couldn't dislodge the mutt, and the feral beast felt like it weighed as much as a grown man. Though when Hank glanced to his side, he figured that might be a good thing, for there were more dogs waiting to get in on the action, but they didn't want to intrude on the one on top of Hank. It was a big bastard, no doubt about it, and Hank wondered if it was the alpha male of the pack.

His arms were weakening as the dog pressed closer to his face. The SIG was covered in saliva, and it was so set into the dog's mouth that Hank couldn't get it out. Like a vise, the teeth had clamped so tight that Hank swore there would be teeth marks in the metal if he ever removed it.

But then a shadow blocked out the sun and there was a loud yelp of pain from the dog on top of him. Then the dog was suddenly airborne, flying off to the side to land in a heap of limbs. When it had been sent flying, its mouth had opened instinctively, and it had let out a squeal of pain that sounded terrifyingly human. Hank looked up and over to see that the giant of a man had stretched the chain attaching him to the oak tree to the limit, and after stretching as far as he could, the long club had just managed to connect with the dog on Hank's chest, sending it flying with broken ribs and at least two of its legs shattered. It lay on the ground, its head coming up, its tongue hanging out of its mouth as it whined and yelped in pain.

Wounded, the dog lay helpless, and already some of the pack was circling it. Meat was meat, and whether it was human or dog meant nothing to the pack; their stomachs were hungry and they wanted to fill them.

The big man smiled at Hank, but before Hank could do or say anything, a shape lunged from the side, knocking the man back to the tree; he began fighting once more.

Hank had his own troubles. With the alpha dog gone from his chest, more came at him, their fangs dripping saliva, their mouths already tasting his warm flesh.

With the SIG-Sauer now free, he fired at the closest dog, a Brown and black German shepherd. The dog took the bullet in the side and it folded up and dropped to the ground. A Doberman came charging at him, its tongue lolling out of its mouth, and Hank shot it right between the eyes. The animal's head blew apart in a red cloud of blood and brain matter as the body kept running until the legs gave out and it fell forward onto the ground. It slid a few feet and came up only a foot from Hank, the jagged neck opening seeping blood as the heart continued to pump for a few more seconds.

The giant was still holding his own, and with each swing of the club, another dog was sent flying. One was batted against the oak tree so that the club nearly flattened it. The body burst like a rotten tomato, spewing out blood and internal organs, the carcass neatly wrapped around the oak tree like a dirty fur ribbon.

Hank fired at swiftly moving targets, some of his bullets finding a home, some missing entirely. He knew when he hit a dog thanks to the squeals and whines of pain.

Another Doberman, lean and mean, came at him from the side of his gun arm, and before he could turn and shoot it, the dog came at him and locked its teeth on his arm just above the wrist.

Like a trained attack dog, the animal began to shake its head, as if it was trying to make Hank dislodge the SIG.

Not able to get the SIG around to shoot the damn dog, he reached down to his hip, and wrapped his hand around the handle of his sixteen inch panga. Even with all the noise coming from the battle, the long blade sliding from its sheathe seemed to slice clean through the din.

While kicking at a couple of other dogs that came at him, now brave that the alpha dog was gone, Hank swung the panga around and jammed it into the gut of the Doberman, right behind the sharp V of its sternum. Hot blood jetted from the wound, covering Hank's wrist immediately. The dog's teeth didn't let up on his arm though, and it bore down even harder, making Hank scream in pain.

Not ready to lose the fight just yet, Hank twisted the panga as hard as he could, opening the wound in the dog's gut even more. He must have hit something vital, for this time the Doberman's jaws lessoned, and a second later his gun arm was free, as even more blood cascaded out of the animal and onto his arm and chest.

Pulling it up and around, Hank jammed the muzzle of the SIG into the Doberman's mouth and squeezed the trigger twice. There were two muffled pops as the bullets tore into the dog's skull and blew out the back of its cranium, taking a wake of brains and blood with them. The dog twitched once and fell over. Hank pulled the panga free and shoved the twitching animal away from him.

Looking around, he saw that there were only a few dogs left.

The large man was holding a snarling collie in its bare hands, and as Hank watched, the giant picked the dog up and brought it down over one knee. There was a loud *crack* as the animal's spine broke, but still the dog slavered and snapped at the man, trying to bite him. The giant's next punch caved in the collie's ribcage, and as the dog lay on the ground at the man's feet, its bloody tongue lolling out of the side of its mouth, its black lips pulled back in a perpetual growl, the man raised one of his massive feet and brought it down directly over the collie's head. There was a sound like a giant hammer coming down on an anvil, only the anvil was covered in flesh and bone. The head flattened like a pancake and blood and brains squirted out of the sides of the man's foot, needing somewhere to go.

Hank shot two more dogs, leaving only two left that he could see: a German shepherd of formidable size and another collie.

With his eyes on those two, Hank didn't see the biggest damn dog he'd ever seen in his life come at him from the far side of the oak tree. It hit him in the back like a locomotive, knocking him face first into the dirt. With his face buried in the dust, the dog climbed on top of him and tried to bite his neck, only Hank pushed his shoulders up to protect his throat.

The dog was like a thing from Hell, snarling and growling as it tried to tear out Hank's throat. Hank could only curl up into a ball and wait out the attack, and hope he was still alive and in one piece when the attack ended.

But the large man wasn't standing idle, and with his club, he swung at the dog, knocking it off Hank's back. The animal rolled off but came to its feet in a second. Hank jumped up and ran a few feet away, and as he got up, he found that his hands were empty. Both his SIG and panga were lying on the ground between him and the dog, which now that Hank had a better look at it, he recognized as an Irish wolfhound. Behind the large dog were three Chinese Imperials, the small poodles barking and growling like they were tough. The smaller dogs were like baby chicks to the mother hen of the wolfhound, and Hank found it a hell of a thing to see such an odd assortment of breeds living together.

Hank could feel the blood seeping from wounds on his back where the massive dog's claws had sunk into his flesh. Still, when he moved, nothing seemed serious, though a few of the cuts certainly felt deep. His wrist hurt too from where the Doberman had sunk its teeth. He glanced at the wound quickly and was relieved to see it didn't look too bad. For a moment he'd wondered if his damn hand was gone, chewed off by the beast. He had antibiotics in the saddlebags that he would take once he'd cleaned and washed the wounds with Harmony's help. And you better believe she would help. After all, it had been her prodding that had gotten him into this mess in the first place.

The wolfhound lowered its head and its haunches began to twitch as it prepared to attack again. It was an off-white color with spots of fur missing on its back from a previous fight. Half of its right ear was missing as well, but the torn ear was long healed, signifying that it had been torn off over a year ago.

Hank saw the large man chained to the tree out of the corner of his eye. The giant was too far away to help Hank, and he knew he would have to fight the massive dog by himself.

He had seconds to figure out a course of action, but then those were gone as the wolfhound's back paws pushed off the ground, its front paws lunging forward. Like a race horse charging out of the gate, the dog came at Hank, its mouth open wide in preparation of sinking its fangs into him.

Hank once more did what the animal would never expect, and he ran right at it, and it was as he began moving that he felt the shrapnel grenade shift in his pocket. With no other weapon to use other than his bare hands, and those would be useless, he pulled the grenade from his pocket, pulled the pin, and as the wolfhound came at him, he threw it as hard as he could right at the dog's open mouth, then he jumped to the side as it ran past him. But he wasn't fast enough and the dog's head clipped his side, sending

Hank spinning to the ground. But the dog had been running so fast that it couldn't stop to attack Hank, and it had to go past him five yards before its paws could slow it enough to turn around. The grenade was a small object in its mouth, and it tried to swallow it, not knowing what the object was, and with the grenade landing near the back of its throat, it was just easier for the animal to swallow it than try and spit it out.

The grenade was halfway down its esophagus when it exploded.

Hank was on the ground on his side, looking at the dog as it spun around, and he had to turn over and shield his eyes, as the dog's head and upper half seemed to vaporize into thin air, leaving behind a pink mist of evaporating blood.

As the explosion blew off the top of the wolfhound, the last two dogs turned and ran away, seeing that almost their entire pack had been destroyed, and not wanting to join their dead brethren.

The two Chinese Imperials that had been following the wolfhound also ran away upon experiencing the explosion, but one, braver than the other two, began to come at Hank, barking, yipping and growling, too.

Cursing, Hank stood up, and with the Imperial yapping away, he pulled back his right boot and then sent it right at the annoying dog. Kicking the still yapping poodle like a football, he sent it squealing into the air, the small dog twisting and turning in the air as it soared like a wounded bird to land in the dirt fifteen feet away.

It landed heavily and rolled a few times before coming still. It lay immobile for a few seconds and then it got onto its stomach and slowly got up. Shaking its head to clear it, the dog began barking at Hank, though this time it didn't come any closer.

Hank balled his hands into fists and took a step towards it, and the Imperial turned and ran away, its tail between its legs.

Feeling like he'd been run over by a truck, Hank walked over to gather his weapons, then went to the Triumph, picked it off the ground and set the bike on its center stand, and turned off the engine. He waved to Harmony to come on down from the road and join him, then he walked over to the giant who was standing docile, now watching Hank intently. Hank reloaded the SIG with a new clip, pocketing the empty one to refill later. He held the gun in his hand as he went to the giant. The man seemed to shrink back when he saw Hank coming towards him with a drawn firearm.

"Relax, big fella," Hank said, lowering the gun and aiming it away from the man. "This isn't for you. Hell, if I was gonna shoot you, then why the hell would I have fought those bastard dogs to save you?"

It was hard to tell what the large man was thinking, as the beard covered his lower face and his hair was so long it draped over his forehead.

"You should back up a little, in case of shrapnel or a ricochet," Hank said as he stood over the thick chain trapping the man to the oak tree. Lining up one of the links, he fired once, and then again before the link shattered from the force of the rounds. "There, you're free," Hank said to the big lug, who still stood there, staring at Hank silently. Hank frowned at this. "Shit, pal, a thank you would be nice."

Hank was about to say more when the man suddenly went into motion, crossing the few feet separating Hank from him in a split second. One moment Hank was standing there talking to the silent giant, and then the man was sweeping Hank up into his large arms and crushing him. The pressure was unbelievable and Hank could swear he felt his ribs about to start breaking.

The guy was trying to kill him! At least that was what Hank thought at first, but when he looked into the man's eyes, he saw no violence, no malice of any kind. He saw an innocence there, along with a smile as wide as the earth itself, and all at once Hank realized the big lug was 'hugging' him, not 'killing' him.

Barely able to speak with his chest compressed, Hank wheezed, "Okay, okay, you're welcome. Now please put me down, you're gonna kill me."

Hank found himself floating in the air for the briefest of heart beats before his feet hit the ground and so did he, losing his balance and falling on his ass. He got to his knees and knelt over, sucking in air, his chest hurting from the compression. "Christ, he doesn't know his own strength I think."

"I'm Chester," the giant said proudly, patting himself on the chest. His voice was deep but there was something 'off' about it, though Hank couldn't put his finger on it. Maybe if he talked a little more.

"Chester, huh? Well, it's nice to meet you, Chester. I'm Hank and that girl coming towards us is Harmony. She's with me if you didn't know it already."

"She's pretty," Chester said, and after slipping the club under his arm, he began to clap and sing, "Hank is nice and Harmony is swell, and Hank is good and Harmony is pretty."

"What the hell did you just say?" Hank asked. He took a step closer to the big lug and really had a good look at the man's face. That was when he saw the round, soft face and the moonish smile under the thick beard. If a person wasn't up close and personal with the gentle giant, they never would have been able to see these traits. Chester had the distinctive look and slanted eyes of someone afflicted with Down's syndrome.

Chapter 11

After Hank had asked Chester why he was chained to a tree, the big man had shrugged, saying something about bad men from his village didn't like him and had punished him for doing something that Chester hadn't done. Hank had decided after hearing the strange story for the second time that Chester didn't know how to explain what had happened to him.

Hank was under the assumption that Chester had been accused of something he didn't do, and being slow, had no way to defend himself. So he'd been chained to the tree to die, which must have been some kind of sentencing tactic by his people.

Hank got to work on some of the carcasses lying around the oak tree. Meat was meat and beggars couldn't be choosey. Harmony helped, her skills cleaning a carcass far better than Hank's, not that he minded.

"We'll take all we can carry and set up camp down the road a mile or two, away from here. Soon, this place is gonna be filled with every four-legged scavenger in the area. Then we'll cook it all over an open fire. That should allow the meat to keep for a day or two."

While the two worked skinning the dogs and cutting off chunks of meat, Chester stood absolutely still, watching them. He said nothing, only stared in awe. Once he did move but that was only to scratch his butt and pick his nose, then he went back to staring.

"What's wrong with him? He looks like a feeb," Harmony said, pointing to Chester, who smiled wildly when he saw her looking at him.

"No, he's not," Hank said, a little annoyed at her ignorance. "He has something called Down's syndrome. It means he's a little slow but he's far from stupid."

"How do you know what he is has got a name?" she asked. "I've never heard anyone call a feeb that name before."

"Let's just say it's before your time and call it at that, okay?" he said.

She shrugged, not wanting to push the issue because frankly she didn't really care that much.

An hour later, the two had finished and they had a nice pile of meat. Flies buzzed around it happily and Hank wished he had something to cover it with.

He gathered an armful of the stuff and carried it over to Chester, placing it all on a rock near the big man. "This is for, you, Chester, so you have food to eat."

"For me?" Chester asked, his eyes looking at the meat.

"You bet. You should cook it before you eat it though, you don't want to get a parasite."

"A what?"

"Never mind, it doesn't matter. Let's just say that if you eat the meat raw you'll get a tummy ache."

That Chester understood and he nodded. "I can make a fire. My daddy taught me how before he died."

"Good then that's settled. Well, me and Harmony have to go now," Hank said and went to the Triumph, where Harmony was waiting. Hank pulled out a plastic garbage bag from one of the saddlebags, went to the meat, and filled the bag with it, then he carried it back to Harmony, handing her the heavy bag. "Here, you hold this, there's no room in the sidebags; just till we get down the road and make camp."

She took it without saying anything, which surprised Hank. It seemed she liked to protest a lot. But he figured when her stomach was involved she was okay with it.

Chester ran over to Hank as he got on the Triumph. "Can I come with you?"

"Sorry, Chester, but there's only room enough on my bike for me and Harmony. I'm afraid you're on your own again. Just make sure to go that way." He pointed to the west. "You hear me? That way. Don't go that way." He pointed east, where he was pretty sure Chester's village was from. Chester looked both ways and scratched his head like a dullard.

"I don't think he understands you, Hank. After all, he's a feeb."

"He's not a fee.." Hank stopped suddenly and sighed. "Never mind, just stop calling him that, all right?"

She shrugged. "Sure, whatever. If it makes you happy."

"It does."

"Then good, I won't say it any more."

"Good.

"I know it's good," she said.

"Fine."

"Sure, it's that, too."

"Harmony?"

"Yes, Hank?"

"Please shut the hell up or so help me I'm gonna leave you here and drive away."

She crossed her arms and pouted, but Hank was satisfied she was done…for the moment anyway. He was finding she resembled Laurie in ways other than her looks. Her willful spirit for one was a hell of a lot like Laurie's.

"See ya, Chester, good luck," Hank said as he spun the rear tire of the Roadster and drove back to the road. Once there, he aimed the front wheel the way he'd been going before he'd stopped to save the big lug.

Once more the wind whipped at their hair as Hank drove the Triumph a steady twenty-five miles an hour. He wanted to go faster but didn't want to end up coming up on a situation before he could stop.

"Uh, Hank, someone's following us," Harmony said, tapping Hank on the right shoulder as she leaned forward to yell in his ear.

Hank glanced at one of the rearview mirrors mounted on the handlebars of the Roadster and sure enough, Harmony was right. He could see the lumbering form of Chester as the large man ran down the road. His long legs ate up the distance easily.

"Maybe we should stop and let the feeb catch up," Harmony suggested.

He ignored her use of the term 'feeb' and said, "No, he'll get tired eventually. We'll just go another mile or two before we make camp, I'm sure by then he'll have given up." He sped up, leaving the running figure behind.

Three miles and change later, Hank decided it was time to pull over and stop for the day. It was late afternoon, and though there was a few more hours of daylight left, Hank had to admit he was exhausted. It had been a hell of a long day and he desperately wanted to clean his wounds, eat, and lie down and rest.

Harmony gathered wood and kindling for a fire, then got to work by rubbing two pieces of wood together. Hank went off a few yards away to use the bathroom and when he returned, he saw her still working at the two pieces of wood, but with no results.

She leaned back and sighed. "I'll get it, Hank, it just takes time."

"Or we could just use this," he said, and leaned forward with a Bic lighter in his hand, the one he'd found in the motor pool near the Triumph. Instantly, the kindling began to burn and Harmony quickly transferred it to the rest of the wood, then slowly tended it until it was going well. Her eyes were wide with amazement at the sight of the lighter.

"Where in the world did you get that?" she asked, reaching out to take it from Hank, who handed it to her. She began flicking the small wheel like Hank had done, blinking in amazement each time the small fire appeared. "I've only heard about these," she said. "My grandfather used one and he told stories about them. He even had a silver one that had a top that flipped open. It was neat because you could refill it."

"Sure, he had a Zippo," Hank stated. "Here, give that back, stop wasting the fluid. There isn't much left to begin with." She didn't want to give it back but he gave her a look that said not to fuck with him. Finally she handed it back, but that was after flicking it two more times to see the flame.

The campfire was going good, and Hank took a few sticks he'd set aside as skewers and began sliding the dog meat onto them, before placing them over the fire.

Harmony watched him intently. "Who are you really?" she asked.

"I'm the guy that saved you," he said, concentrating on the meat. The odor of the cooking meat began to fill the air and Hank's stomach started to rumble. He was tempted to get an apple from the saddlebags but decided against it. The meat would need to be eaten more than the apples. Better to eat it all first. "I wish I had some salt or pepper for the meat, or better yet, barbeque sauce."

"See, there you go again," she said. "Sometimes you say things that my grandfather used to say. Why is that, Hank? And you have guns and weapons and that shiny new motorcycle over there. No one other than a baron has that kind of wealth."

Hank shrugged. "Call it clean living and karma, I guess," he said and took one of the skewers off the fire. He took a tentative bite, the meat burning his mouth a little. It tasted good, damn good. Who would have known dog would be so tasty? Not him, that was for sure. He took another skewer that had cooked meat and handed it to Harmony. "Here, eat this."

"No," she said, crossing her arms and pouting. "Not until you tell me who you are and how you got to be around here. If you came from far away you wouldn't have so much stuff, you would have used it all up fighting your way across the country. But here you are, loaded up and with a full tank of gas on that bike."

"Okay, fine, I'll tell you who I am and how I got here," he said with a sigh.

"Go on," she said, leaning forward and taking the skewer. She began nibbling on it at first but was soon tearing off large chunks as her hunger got the better of her.

"I'm from the past. A hundred years to be exact. I was in hibernation, which is like a long sleep where I didn't age or grow or anything. It was inside a government bunker, and I have three friends with me, but for some reason I woke up earlier than them. With no food in the place, I had to go out on my own to find some. In a few weeks, I'll return when it's time for them to wake up. I plan on being there with food, waiting for them. But I figured I'd do a little exploring before I return, you know, get the lay of the land. Then I'll go back. Once my friends have recuperated, we'll all set out on our own to see what's changed in a hundred years. There, satisfied?"

She spit out a piece of gristle onto the ground and stood up. "Well, shit, Hank," she said angrily, "if you were gonna lie to me then you might as well have just said nothing." She turned and walked off towards the road, her feet slapping the ground in annoyance.

Hank smiled at her retreating back, then took another skewer and began to eat. He put some more raw meat on the fire with the empty skewers that had just been used.

He smiled to himself. Sometimes, the truth was so far out there that no matter what, a lie would be better.

Chapter 12

After eating, Hank cleaned his wounds, Harmony helping him with any places he couldn't reach, such as his back, where a few claw marks were. The antiseptic had stung when applied, but once his wounds were bandaged, he felt a million times better. The antiseptic had a pain reducer so the areas that had been bandaged were now a little numb. He wasn't looking forward to the analgesic wearing off, though.

Harmony was gone for almost half an hour, and Hank was beginning to get worried, as it was growing dark and all around the campfire the shadows were growing. From where he'd made camp he could see the road, but anyone on the road wouldn't be able to see him, thanks to the angle of the land. The fire had been made in a hole in the ground to shield it from view.

"Hey, Hank, guess who I found?" Harmony asked when she returned.

Hank looked up to see a behemoth of a shadow standing behind Harmony, and he instinctively reached for his SIG-Sauer, bringing it up to shoot the intruder.

Harmony quickly put her hands out to stop him. "Whoa, hold on there, it's Chester. I found Chester out on the road when I went for a walk to find a place to, ah, you know, girl stuff."

"Hi, Hank," Chester said, his bearded face practically beaming. "I thought I lost you and then Harmony came out and I waved to her. She waved back."

"Oh she did, did she?" Hank said, lowering his gun and returning his attention to the fire. "Harmony, could I speak to you alone for a minute?" He pointed to Chester. "Could you go over there for a second, Chester? Just for a minute."

"Could I take some of that meat with me, Hank?" Chester said, rubbing his large belly. "It sure smells good."

"Where's all the dog meant I left you?" Hank asked.

Chester lowered his head, as if he was ashamed. "I ate it already."

Hank blinked in surprised. "You what? There must have been fifteen pounds of meat there."

Chester shrugged. "I was hungry." He smiled again, even wider than before. "It was good, too. Dog taste real good."

"Fine, here, take this," Hank said, shaking his head in exasperation as he gave Chester half a dozen skewers of smoking meat. It was like dealing with a three hundred pound toddler.

"Oh boy, thanks, Hank, thanks a lot." He took the food and skipped away a few yards, until he was only a shadow in the growing darkness. "Meat, meat, it taste like feet, meat, meat it's a real treat," he sang merrily as he began eating.

When Chester was out of earshot, Hank stood up and grabbed Harmony by the arm, pulling her closer. "Just what do you think you're doing bringing him here?"

She shrugged, as if it was no big thing. "What was I supposed to do, Hank? I was near the road and I saw him walking. He was talking to himself. He was saying how scared he was. Shit, Hank, he was acting like a kid, and what can I say, I felt bad for him. Maybe he'll be good to have with us. He sure is big and he can fight like hell. No one'll mess with us once they get a load of that feeb, well, as long as they don't figure out he is one."

"I already told you not to call him that."

"Why? He doesn't know what it means." She turned and called over her shoulder, "Right, feeb?"

"Huh?" Chester asked with a mouthful of meat. "What did you say, Harmony? I like you, you're so pretty."

"See? And what can I say, the guy has good taste. He knows beauty when he sees it." She brushed her hair with a hand with fingers splayed to punctuate her point.

Hank sighed, staring at her with what looked like a father's annoyance with his teenage daughter. "Damn it, Harmony," was all he could think to say.

Harmony knelt down and took a skewer of meat from off the fire. Blowing on it, she began to nibble on the end. "Mmm, not bad, Hank."

"Thanks." He sat down, then called out, "Okay, Chester, come on over here and sit with us."

A minute later Chester lumbered over. He almost walked right into the fire, but at the last second he turned and plopped down on a large rock. Hank could have sworn the rock groaned as it took the giant man's weight.

"So, Chester," Hank said, "Harmony and I have been discussing you and it seems Harmony has already made up her mind for both of us. I guess you can stay with us."

"Really, Hank? Honest and truly? Oh boy, I'd like that. I'd like that a lot."

It was still surreal seeing such an innocent sounding voice coming from such a giant man, with arms so strong they could snap Hank in half.

"Yes, Chester, honest and truly." He pointed a finger at Chester, getting the man's full attention. "But there's nothing for you to ride on, the bike only holds two, so you're gonna have to keep up by running. Is that possible?"

Chester began nodding his head until it looked like it was going to fall clean off his shoulders from the motion. Finally he stopped and said, "Sure, Hank, I like to run. I can run far, too."

"Well, we'll be testing that out tomorrow. I warn you, though, I'm not gonna wait around for you. I promise not to go that fast, but if you can't keep up then you're just going to have to go your own way."

"He'll keep up, Hank," Harmony said.

"Uh, Hank, can I have some more meat? I ate all you gave me."

"Jesus Christ, you did?" Hank asked.

"Uh-huh, and it was real good too. You're a good cook, Hank," Chester said, burping loudly, the sound resembling a gunshot in the dark of night. A few birds were frightened from a nearby tree and took flight.

"Thanks," Hank replied. "We can have some apples for desert, too."

Both Harmony and Chester's eyes lit up at this.

With another sigh, Hank tossed Chester some more cooked meat, the man's large hands taking the food eagerly, ignoring the scalding juices because of the tough calluses on the palms of his hands. Hank wondered if he should just hand the giant some of the raw meat instead. Why waste the time cooking it if the big lug didn't care anyway?

Chester gobbled most of the meat up in one bite, juice sliding down his chin. Harmony wiped it away with a rag she produced, like a mother would to her son.

Hank watched this silently, then placed more meat on the fire to cook. At this rate, the meat would be gone by the end of breakfast if not sooner. As he tended the fire and the sizzling meat, he gazed upon his two new companions, two strays he'd picked up along his way. Two wayward souls that would probably both be dead by now if not for his help, and he wondered the entire time just how the hell it had happened.

Chapter 13

The night passed swiftly with no issues. Hank stood guard most of the night, and Harmony had spelled him for a few hours before dawn. Chester slept like a log, a snoring one. At times it seemed the entire forest could hear him from miles around. Hank had tried to get the big lug to turn over, hoping that would alleviate the snoring, but no matter how much Hank kicked Chester to make him turn, the giant didn't so much as move an inch, nor stir.

When morning came, Hank cooked the rest of the dog meat, and between the three of them, finished it all off—Chester eating the lion's share. Then they moved out, Chester jogging behind the Triumph, Hank going a slow ten miles an hour.

No more than two hours later, Chester began complaining he was hungry.

"Harmony, reach behind and take a few apples out of one of the saddlebags and toss them to Chester," Hank said.

"I would but they're all gone, Chester ate them already," she said into his right ear.

"Shit, having Chester around is like raising a horse."

"Yeah, but a horse would be smarter," Harmony quipped.

Hank ignored her jibe. "We need to find someplace that has food or kill something on our own."

They drove some more until a small shack came into view on the right side of the road. A rough sign painted in white scrawls had the words "good eats inside." The words had been scrawled across it in a shaky hand. The word good was spelled with a *u* instead of two *o*'s, and eats was spelled with two *e*'s, and the word inside had a *y* instead of the letter *i* in the middle, so it really said, *"gud eets insyde."* But beggars couldn't be choosers, and unless Hank wanted to run around the forest searching for game, this was the only place that looked promising. Besides, you didn't need to be able to read or write to be a decent cook.

Harmony had already explained to Hank that they were out of the area she was familiar with. Now, whatever they came across was as new to her as it was to him.

The Roadster purred as Hank kicked it up to second gear and turned down the small driveway that led to the old shack. He pulled up a few feet from the door and pressed the horn twice, sending out a friendly greeting. Chester was standing right behind the Triumph as Hank and Harmony climbed off it, Hank putting the bike on its center stand. He took the key from the ignition and slid it into his pocket.

As the engine ticked softly while it cooled, Hank walked over to the front door of the shack. But before he was halfway there, the door was thrown open and an old man stepped outside, holding a sawed-off shotgun.

"Who the fuck are you people?" the old man asked, his voice hoarse from age. He stood no more than five feet tall, with wispy white hair and a beard the same color. His eyes were a deep blue, and there was a large sore on the right side of his nose. It looked like the old man had been picking at it. He was so frail that it looked like if he pulled the trigger on the sawed-off, the damn thing's kick would have thrown him back into the shack.

"Name's Hank Summers, and this is Harmony. The big guy's Chester." He lowered his voice and added, "He's a little slow but harmless if you don't mess with him."

The old man studied Hank, then at the firearms he carried. His gaze shifted to Harmony next, and though in his late seventies, the old man's libido was still intact as he licked his lips while he took in Harmony's figure. Last his eyes fell on Chester, and as the old man's head craned up to look at the big lug, his mouth dropped open, revealing the few remaining teeth still in the all-but-toothless orifice. "Jesus, Mary and Joseph, he's a big'un, ain't he?"

"That, friend, is an understatement," Hank said with a grin. "He eats like a horse, too."

"A horse you say?" the old man asked.

"Yeah, so anyway, we saw your sign about food and figured we'd come in for some."

"Well there, sonny, by those fancy blasters of yours, I reckon you got jack to pay for food and drink?"

"Depends, what are you looking for in payment?" Hank asked.

The old man spit a large, phlemy ball at his feet. "Bullets'll do just fine, sonny. How many you got?"

"Enough to pay for our meal. Why don't I wait till I see how good the food is, then we can discuss how much you get," Hank said.

The old man's face scrunched up as he considered the offer, then he lowered the shotgun, spit in the dirt, and smiled, though with no teeth it resembled a wince more than a grin. "Sounds fair to me. All of you, come on inside. I just put on a fresh pot of stew. It should be done in a bit."

With the old man leading the way, they all headed inside. Chester had to bend over almost halfway to get through the doorway, and even then he had to turn sideways or else his shoulders would have torn through the sides of the frame.

The interior of the shack looked the same as it did on the outside—worn and rundown. The floor was dirt, the walls filled with cracks that let in the outside light. There was a wooden table in the corner with six chairs. But the aroma of the cooking stew smelled delicious.

"Chester, why don't you sit by the fireplace on the floor," Hank said, knowing the big guy would break any of the chairs he sat on.

"Okay, Hank, I can do that," Chester said, and with his head bowed low to avoid hitting the ceiling, he went to the hearth and sat beside it.

"You say he's slow in the head?" the old man asked.

"Yeah, that's not a problem, is it?" Hank asked, his hand touching the butt of the SIG-Sauer.

The old man saw the movement but didn't seem to feel threatened by it. "No, it's no problem. Seen all types come through here. Tall, short, smart, dumb—you name it. Why, one time I saw a three-legged…"

"So what's for lunch?" Harmony asked, cutting the old man off, not really caring about what he'd seen or hadn't seen.

The old man blinked, losing his train of thought, and replied, "Stew with fresh vegetables." He went to a small fire pit set in the ground, a makeshift duct set over it to take away the smoke and send it outside. "I have a small garden in the back, you see. Grow all my own veggies." Picking up a spoon, he lifted the cover to a steel pot in the center of the pit and began stirring the stew. The aroma grew more pronounced and Hank and Harmony's stomachs began to growl. Chester's stomach began to growl as well, the sound overriding all else.

The old man looked up to the ceiling. "Is that thunder? Didn't look like rain before."

"That's my tummy," Chester said, patting his wide girth with a hand.

"Is it now?" the old man said. "Well, not to worry, son, the stew looks done. See, I make sure to cut the meat into small pieces, that way it cooks real quick." He gestured to Harmony. "Girl, would you please get those bowls over there and bring them here? Then I can start ladling this beautiful stew into them."

Harmony did as she was asked, and a minute later, the old man was filling the bowls to the rim with the thick stew.

Hank took one and he looked down into it. It was dark brown; he could make out carrots, onions and potatoes, but the meat was something he couldn't identify. When he was handed a spoon, he dug in, taking a few tentative bites of the meat. He wasn't sure what it was—squirrel maybe? Or rabbit? Hell, he couldn't argue whatever it was, after all, just that morning he was dining on dog. So with a shrug of *who cares what it is*, he began digging in, while beside him Chester was shoveling the stew into his mouth, the spoon and bowl looking like parts to a miniature tea set in his large hands.

Harmony took a bowl as well and began eating, the old man doing the same. Chester polished his off before most of the others had eaten a quarter of theirs, and the old man refilled Chester's bowl with a cackle. When Chester ate it all in a minute or so again, the old man cackled and said, "Maybe I should let you eat right out of the pot!"

"Would you?" Chester asked, his eyes going wide in hopefulness. His dark beard was flaked with bits of stew.

"No, he won't," Hank snapped. "Now mind your manners, Chester, or you can go outside."

"Sorry, Hank, I'll be good," the big lug said, downtrodden. He began eating the third bowl in silence and was finally slowing down some.

The old man went and sat down beside Hank. "The giant listens to you, huh? How'd you mange that one?"

Hank shrugged. "No idea. I saved him from a pack of wild dogs. Guess he likes me. Frankly, I think he'd listen to anyone who was nice to him." Hank took another bite of the stew, relishing the way the meat fell apart in his mouth, it was so tender. "This is very good. What kind of meat is it? I've been trying to figure it out, but with all the spices and the thick gravy I can't put my finger on it."

The old man shrugged, matching Hank's gesture a second ago. "Oh, whatever I can scrape up and find when I'm hunting. A bit of rabbit, deer and maybe some dog I had leftover from another meal. Those wild dogs are everywhere, aren't they?"

"Yeah, they sure seem to be," Hank said. "As a matter of fact, when I saw Chester fighting off…"

"Uh, excuse me," Harmony said, interrupting while wiping her mouth with the back of her sleeve. *Damn, that was good stew*, she thought happily. "But I need to use the bathroom."

"Out behind the house is my privy, girl, go out the door and take a left, then circle around. You can't miss it." He began to laugh and added, "A blind man could find it due to the smell."

She left the shack and walked around the house, finding the outhouse easily. When she was finished and was on her way back to the shack, she saw another small building the same size as the shack behind the outhouse, the trees all but hiding it from view. If the wind hadn't blown just the right way at the same time she was looking in the direction of the windowless building, she never would have noticed it, but some of the branches blown by the wind shifted enough to expose the faded facade. Her curiosity was peaked so she went to check it out.

The door was unlocked, and she entered slowly, her hand on her .45 in case there was trouble, but the instant she was inside she knew what the building was used for. It was a smoke house.

From where she stood, amongst the thick cloud of smoke hanging in the air, she could see the carcasses of a few pigs and goats, as well as deer, rabbit and squirrel, hanging from the ceiling in groups of four and five. It appeared the old man had every animal in God's kingdom in his smokehouse. The temperature was warm and she began to sweat, the smoke the thickest on her right. Moving there, she saw a large metal stove. It was full of woodchips, the sides giving off the smoke in an even way that filled the entire room.

She was about to turn and leave, having seen enough, when something caught her eye from behind a group of hanging animal carcasses. Her curiosity getting the better of her, she walked slowly through the hanging meat, pushing them out of her way with the tip of the gun as she walked.

Shoving the fresh and gutted carcass of a small deer aside, she stopped in her tracks at what was hanging before her. She had to blink to make sure she was really seeing what she was looking at, and as her mind came to terms with it, she felt her stomach heave, and she bent over and vomited the stew she'd just eaten across the floor, where it splashed on the compacted dirt in squishy clumps.

When her stomach was empty and she could stand again, she gazed on the carcasses before her one more time. Her stomach heaved again but this time, knowing her stomach was empty, she was able to keep her composure.

Hanging from the rafters in nice neat rows, was the meat that had freaked her out so terribly. Human bodies, gutted and drying in the hazy smoke, the heads taken off, the skin already taking on the texture of jerky.

Human beef jerky.

Long Pig smoked to perfection. She felt her stomach heave again despite herself and she turned and vomited once more. Some got on her worn shoes but she didn't care, all she wanted to do was get the taste of what she'd been eating out of her mouth.

Wiping her lips with the back of her hand, she got the hell out of there. She didn't bother to close the door behind her and the smoke began flowing out the open doorway and into the outside air.

She ran around the shack and burst through the front door, her eyes locking onto Hank the second she was inside. Hank was about to shovel another large spoonful of stew into his mouth. Harmony could see the morsels of meat on the spoon, which was heading right for Hank's mouth.

"No, Hank, don't eat that!" she yelled, dashing over to him and swatting the spoon from his hand. It flew across the shack, hit the far wall, and fell to the floor with a metallic rattle.

"What the hell, Harmony!" Hank yelled. "Why'd you do that?"

She went to him and whispered in his ear, her eyes on the old man, who was watching the scene with nervous curiosity.

"Something wrong with the girl?" the old man asked.

Hank's complexion went bone white and he dropped the bowl of stew onto the floor. It splashed everywhere but he ignored it. He'd eaten half of the large bowl and now wished he hadn't. "Tell me again what kind of meat was in that stew?" he asked the old man, his voice growing cold and angry.

"A little of this, a little of that. Meat is meat. Why?"

"Harmony saw your smokehouse."

"So?"

"She went inside," Hank said, his voice hard, his jaw taut. The two men locked eyes, and the old man realized that Hank knew what was in the smokehouse. He tried for his shotgun but was too slow. Hank lunged from where he was sitting and knocked the shotgun to the side, away from the grasping hands of the old man.

Hank pulled his SIG-Sauer from its holster and aimed it at the forehead of the old man, doing his best to focus, as he wanted to vomit desperately upon thinking what was in his stomach right now. He thought to how he'd enjoyed the way the meat had melted in his mouth, the smooth texture crossing his tongue. "Don't move a muscle," Hank warned. "Now, you have one chance to answer the questions I have for you, and if I don't like the answers, I'm gonna put a bullet through your head and toss you into your smokehouse. You understand me?"

The old man nodded slowly, his eyes locked on the muzzle of the SIG.

"Good, glad we understand each other. Now, where did you get the 'special meat' hanging in the smokehouse? Did you kill them?"

"No, I didn't kill nobody, I swear," the old man said. "I find them where I can."

"What do you mean?" Harmony asked.

"Well, you see, there's never a problem finding a few dead bodies if you travel the roads a few hours a day. Such is the state of the world we live in now, sorry to say." His voice was smooth, not trembling in the least. Hank could see the man was telling the truth, and if not, he was a damn good liar. "Sometimes they're too ripe though. One time I found a body so bloated that I…"

"Okay, enough, I believe you. Which is why I'm not gonna shoot you dead and let you smoke like the poor bastards already in there."

"So we're just going to leave now?" Harmony asked. "Just like that? You believe him?"

"Yeah, I do. You look into a man's eyes and sometimes you know if he's lying, Harmony. This is one of those times."

"Wait, what about payment? You were gonna pay me for the meals," the old man said.

"Is he serious?" Harmony asked, wanting to shoot the old man anyway for making her eat human meat…and road kill human meat at that!

"Sure I'm serious, girl. Meat is meat at the end of the day. I fed you now pay up."

Hank frowned deeply. "All right, old man, I'll pay. How 'bout one bullet in the head? Will that take care of our tab?"

The old man swallowed the lump in his throat and nodded no. "Uh, well, seems you're lookin' at it like that, why don't we say the meals are on me and leave it at that."

Chester had been standing quietly after eating the bowl of stew he'd had, hunched over, watching it all, not really taking in what was going on, though there was a glimmer of understanding in there somewhere. "Hank, was the food bad?"

Hank decided Chester didn't need to know what was in the multiple bowls of stew the big lug had eaten. It would either anger the giant or make him go nuts, either one being bad for all involved, so Hank did what anyone would do if they were dealing with a seven foot tall giant that was slow in the brainpan. He lied. "No, Chester, the food was fine."

"Okay, that's good, Hank. Can I have some more?"

Both Hank and Harmony yelled, "No!" at the same time, making Chester jump slightly from the vehemence of their tones.

"Oh, okay, I was just asking," Chester said.

"Everyone outside," Hank said, then looked directly at the old man and added, "You stay put. Don't move until we leave or you won't see the sun set tonight."

The old man nodded, not moving so much as a finger. He didn't see what was the harm in taking the corpses he found and curing and smoking them. A man had to eat, didn't he? Meat is meat as far as he was concerned. Hell, it wasn't like he was killing people that came to him and then stringing them up. Now that would be sick.

Hank got on the Triumph, but no sooner had he gotten on than his willpower let go and he bent over and vomited his entire meal. It tasted worse coming up but he felt a little better once it was out of his system.

Harmony patted his back. "Don't feel bad, Hank, I did it twice when I found out."

Hank said nothing in reply. Harmony got onto the bike and Hank kicked over the motor, then spun around and began driving away from the rundown shack.

Chester began jogging alongside, his large club swinging back and forth beside him. "Hank, you don't feel good?" he asked.

"No, Chester, I'm fine, thanks for asking."

"The stew was real good, Hank. I liked it a lot."

"That's good, Chester," Hank said, his stomach roiling again at the thought. "Now let's not talk and focus on traveling, all right?"

"Sure, Hank, whatever you say, you're the boss."

They rode in silence for a few minutes until Hank said, "You know, Harmony, the more things change the more they stay the same."

"What does that mean?" Harmony asked. "Things have been the same for almost a hundred years from what I've been told."

"Never mind, Harmony, I was just thinking out loud," he replied, and this time as they rode on, the silence lasted for hours.

Chapter 14

Thirty yards away, playing together in an open field that had once been part of a strip mall, only a few bricks and rebar left of the old buildings, were Harmony and Chester, while Hank worked on the Triumph under the shade of a massive oak tree in the glade he had parked in. Just over the rise in the hill he was next to was a small, bubbling brook that they had gotten fresh water from. The water would have to be boiled before it was consumed but it was still great for washing themselves and their clothes.

The work on the Triumph was easy thanks to the small tool kit Hank had in one of the saddlebags. The leaves of the tree were a bold green, and he had to admit that though he missed his friends back at the redoubt, he felt good, he felt *alive*.

After topping off the gas tank of the Roadster with the condensed fuel taken from one of the voluminous saddlebags, he checked the plugs and oil on the engine. The motor had been hesitating a little and Hank wanted to see if he could fix the problem. It was when he removed the last spark plug that he found it had a thick coating of carbon on it. It didn't take long to fix and soon he had the motor humming again the way it had when he'd first left the bunker.

That made him think about how valuable the bike really was out here in the world. Deciding he better protect his investment, he took some of the C4 from his supplies and began working on the bike again.

Harmony ran up to him, seeing him tinkering with the bike still and asked, "What're you doing now?"

Hank had the ignition apart, the key to the bike in his pocket. "I'm putting in an alarm system I guess, but one that's fatal to anyone stupid enough to try and steal it."

"An alarm system? You mean like when my dad would tie old rusty cans to a string and hang them around our camp so that anyone coming in the night would hit them and warn us?"

"Yeah, something like that. Only this 'alarm system' will make a hell of a lot more noise." Hank finished up and began making sure the ignition was working, only now there was a small toggle switch to the side of it. The switch was unobtrusive, and no one would think much of it if they didn't know about it beforehand. Making sure the switch was in the disconnect position, he slid the key into the ignition and started the motor on the first kick. The exhaust blew a little blue smoke for a few seconds and then it all but disappeared. Hank played with the choke a little and then smiled at Harmony, who was watching him intently.

"See, piece of cake," he said proudly while turning the throttle a little and letting the engine rev. He turned the motor off and got off the bike. "Where's Chester?"

"Oh, he's playing in the field. He saw a butterfly and he started chasing it. I told him not to, that they bite, but he didn't hear me."

"Butterflies bite?" Hank asked. "Since when?"

"Since forever," Harmony said. "My lifetime and my dad's, too. I swear Hank," she said, shaking her head in exasperation, "sometimes it's like you're from another world." She walked away to see if she could find Chester, who was picking daisies at the far end of the field.

"You don't know the half of it," Hank said under his breath. Above his head, the tree branches began to vibrate slightly but then it stopped. He barely noticed it, assuming it was some kind of animal that had made its home in the tree.

He started to pack up all his tools and gear when he felt a chill run down his back. It was the feeling of being watched, that sensation people get but don't know why; a sixth sense that most people don't even realize they have. Looking around, he saw nothing that appeared to be a danger, nor did he see anyone watching him, either man or animal. Hank turned his head slowly, letting his peripheral vision pick up on anything his direct vision might miss, but once more there was nothing in the area.

Though Hank knew to let his guard down for even a moment could mean death, as he studied the surrounding terrain, he had to let it go, as all he had was a feeling, one he couldn't let rule him. When you were always on guard and paranoid, thinking people were out to get you, though there were times it was true, there were also times when it wasn't anything more than an errant breeze.

So shrugging it off as a phantom feeling, he got back to work packing up the supplies. He picked up his automatic rifle from where he'd leaned it against the closest tree, and slung it over his shoulder, then checked to make sure his SIG and panga were where they should be, which they were.

He was about to call out to Harmony and Chester, telling them to come back so they could continue onward in search of food, when suddenly the sunlight coming through the overhead leaf canopy was blocked out in sections, like there were a hundred small shapes overhead.

Not understanding where the shade was coming from, Hank casually glanced upwards, expecting perhaps to see a weird assortment of clouds in the sky, but what he saw surprised him so much that for a fraction of a second he stood stock-still, his eyes taking in the myriad shapes perched on all the tree branches.

They were squirrels, but not like any squirrel Hank remembered seeing before sleeping for a century. He'd watched a nature show once, before the bombs had fallen, about the North American Fox Squirrel. This particular species was nearly double the size of a regular squirrel seen in most suburbs, and could grow up to as much as three pounds each in size. The heads were huge, and two of the things would have been more than enough to feed two people happily, unlike a normal squirrel, which barely had any meat on it.

The squirrels sitting on the branches over Hank, looking down at him with rapt attention, were triple in size from the Fox squirrels from a hundred years past. The ones above Hank had to be ten to fifteen pounds at least, with long razor-sharp claws and teeth honed to kill. Evidently, a hundred years of breeding had changed the Fox squirrel so that it now grew even bigger than before, and was also meaner. Nature made animals adapt to their newer, harsher environments, either that or the species would die out.

Something in the way they looked at Hank told the warrior that these squirrels weren't vegetarians, and that they were as much a carnivore as he was.

One squirrel, the size of a large house cat, was positioned directly over Hank's head. A few branches over, a foolhardy bird sat watching as well. Before the bird had a chance to fly away, the squirrel jumped to its branch and sank its teeth into the side of the bird. With a brief, frightened squawk elicited, the bird went silent as the squirrel then tore off its head and feasted on its prey. Little droplets of blood sprinkled to the ground, so tiny to be all but lost amongst the shadows and falling leaves that drifted down slowly, thanks to the squirrel knocking them off the branches.

The squirrel devoured the bird in seconds, and not full by a long shot, it turned and lunged down at Hank, its bird-blood-coated lips curling back in a growl. It shook the rest of the pack free of whatever was holding them back, and as one group they all jumped out of the tree at the same time.

Hank, seeing the danger he was in, pulled his SIG from its holster and raised it to take out the first squirrel, the one that had eaten the bird. The squirrel came down like a rocket falling from the sky, and Hank barely had time to get the pistol between him and the animal before it was on him.

The report from the SIG was almost silent, due to the fact that the squirrel had landed on the muzzle, and the gunshot was muffled thanks to its pressing, furry body. But the bullet still did its work, plowing through the little beast and out its back, right behind the head. With a hole in its body, the squirrel slid onto the barrel of the SIG, sliding down it until the fur touched Hank's fingers gripping the trigger. With half its guts blown out, the squirrel was dead before it knew it.

Ignoring the limp creature hanging off his gun, Hank shifted his aim and shot another squirrel, while darting to the side as more came down from above like German paratroopers attacking London.

He rolled across the ground, shaking loose the dead squirrel from around the barrel of the pistol, and as he came up, he found himself face to face with a hundred pairs of beady eyes.

Wondering where the hell Harmony and Chester were, he slid his sixteen inch panga from its sheathe, then crouched low and prepared for the battle of his life, one where he was severely outnumbered.

Chapter 15

The oversized Fox squirrels charged at Hank with no fear in their beady eyes, their bushy tails pointing straight up, their cone-shaped heads like arrows coming right for him.

The SIG-Sauer fired round after round, shooting the flying bodies as they came at him. One bullet took a squirrel right in the mouth, soaring down its throat and into its organs until finally exiting out its ass. With its entire internal organs destroyed from the bullet's passage, the creature dropped to the ground dead before fully landing.

But there were more, always more, and Hank shifted his aim and fired again, then used the SIG as a club to knock two more aside. He felt something biting his ankle, and he glanced down to see that one of the damn things had gotten past his guard. Lifting his foot, he stomped down hard on its head. The skull was crushed beneath his heel, blood and brains oozing out to soak into the dry ground. He kicked another one away when it tried to get at the spot the dead one had vacated.

A quicker one than the others got past his guard and jumped for Hank's throat, and only his lightning fast reflexes prevented him from getting his throat torn out by the vicious creature. At the last second, he dodged to the side, the squirrel flying past him to hit the tree. It bounced off the hard bark, fell to the ground, and renewed its attack with its brethren.

Finally, the last bullet in the SIG was exhausted. Hank dropped the gun to the ground and began swinging the panga from side to side. A squirrel would jump at him and the panga would be there, slicing the creature in half, both parts flying off in separate directions in a bloody spray. But there were always more to fight. Hank pressed his back against the tree so he didn't have to worry about getting his ass bitten, while all around him the squirrels circled. A few did ignore him and started feasting on their fallen brethren. Hank saw this briefly and thought back to the wild dog pack. It seemed everything he came across was just as happy to eat its own kind if given the opportunity.

Before he'd gone into hibernation, the world had been a dangerous place thanks to the bombs that had blown civilization to hell, but at least there had been a semblance of what to expect each day. Slavers, cannibals and radiation lepers were on the top of the list, but not giant, ravenous squirrels. In a million years, Hank never would have believed he would have ended up in the situation he now found himself in.

The panga quickly became coated in blood, as was Hank, the warrior slashing and hacking until all he saw was blood and fur. Bits of squirrel ended up on his body and gobbets of raw meat covered him from head to toe. He looked more like some kind of meat monster than a human being.

It reminded Hank of a time when he, Laurie, Carl and Stewart, along with a few people they'd met up with, had taken shelter in a cave when acid rain began to fall. The cave had been full of giant rats, and they had all fought for their lives that day. The rats had been vicious, as vicious as the squirrels easily, and though it had been hard to fight in such tight quarters, they had been victorious.

The squirrels were just like the rats, only these creatures had the advantage of being able to use the tree branches to attack from. While Hank battled those on the ground, others climbed through the tree and dive-bombed him like Kamikaze fighters.

Hank lost track of time, only the battle for his life mattering. He lost track of how many of the things he killed, as the carcasses piled up around him until they practically reached his knees.

His arms were growing tired, and despite switching the panga back and forth between the two to keep his defense fresh, he knew he was going to run out of energy long before he ran out of furry enemies. But though fatigued, he fought on, slashing bodies in half, skewering others, and gutting even more. If he fell, he would make sure there was a mound of bodies around him.

But though it felt like a lifetime since the battle had started, in fact only minutes had passed before Hank was already running on empty, due to being in hibernation and the toll it had taken on his body.

He still wasn't at his full strength yet, and wouldn't fully recover for another few days, and that was assuming he actually got to rest for a while and not continually drive all over the state of Nebraska—or what was once the former state—fighting this enemy and then another. Come to think of it, he'd never questioned Harmony on if there were any states left, whether people still called the U.S. of A exactly that, or if it had been changed over the passing decades.

And on top of not being at fighting strength anyway, he'd taken the first chance he had after leaving the old man's shack to vomit up the meal he'd eaten, as he didn't want that foul stew inside him longer than it had to be. The dog meat had been good, as were the apples, but both were long gone, and his body needed more calories than normal to make up for what it had lost in hibernation.

Add it all up and you had a recipe for a man to fall in battle long before he should. Even Hank's indomitable will couldn't fight science, and though he battled like a berserker, his arms soon began to slow, his blows not as strong. But he fought on, until a half dozen squirrels launched themselves at him and sank their teeth into his right arm as it wielded the panga. The weight of the creatures pulled the arm down, leaving Hank open to attack.

Seeing their opening, more than two dozen of the squirrels ran at Hank, climbed the pile of carcasses around him, and jumped over it, swarming over him and knocking Hank to the ground by the weight of their multiple bodies alone. The feeling of suffocating under a fur blanket came to Hank, his face becoming smothered by so many bodies he lost count.

Small pinpricks criss-crossed his body as the squirrels' claws sank through his clothes and into the flesh beneath. They were mostly just walking on him at the moment, but in a second he knew those pinpricks would get much, much worse.

And there was nothing he could do about it, so trapped were his limbs by the sheer volume of squirrels.

From a distance, someone would have seen a man swallowed by a sea of brown fur, then the fur began to slowly twitch and vibrate as the squirrels prepared to feed on their prey.

Chapter 16

No man wants to die, and Hank Summers was no exception. But as he fought the onslaught of furry critters, he knew that no matter how powerful his will, no matter how strong his body, eventually the multitude of fur-covered death would win out.

He couldn't breathe! The damn things were smothering him with their bodies as a hundred claws sank into his flesh, subtle at first, but growing stronger with each passing second.

Then one Fox squirrel shifted from off the top of his face, exposing his eyes to the air. He could see above him, and when he did, he saw a shadow loom over him and the squirrels.

Then he could breathe again, as one at a time, the furry creatures were knocked off him. An instant later, large hands wrapped around his shoulders and yanked him out of the swirling maelstrom that was the squirrel horde.

Blinking suddenly and sucking in lungfuls of air, Hank saw that he was hovering above the ground.

"Hank okay?" Chester asked as he stood with Hank in his hands. Hank's feet dangled above the ground and the warrior looked like a child being held by its father. Chester lifted his charge so he was looking directly into Hank's face. "Are you hurt?"

"I'll live…thanks to you, Chester," Hank gasped as his legs swung from side to side. Then a squirrel lunged upward at his dangling legs, its claws sinking into his left calf. Hank let out a yell and kicked the damn thing off him. "But I need your help with these things. Can you do that?"

"Sure, Hank, what do you want me to do?" Chester asked.

"Kill them, Chester, kill every goddamn one of them."

"Chester can do that easily. Just watch me, Hank," he said, and placed Hank behind him, then lifting up his giant club, Chester waded into the squirrel horde, as they jumped up and attacked the big lug, many climbing up his legs as if he was a tree.

Pulling off the rodents and slamming them to the ground, Chester began whacking the squirrels with his club.

Splat! A squirrel was flattened into a pancake.

Splat! again. And another went down, so flat it could be picked up and used as a Frisbee. Harmony joined Hank, and she tried to shoot some of the creatures with her .45, but the damn things were too fast for her, and she didn't want to hit Chester by accident. She did hand Hank his automatic rifle when she saw he had nothing to fight with, and he began shooting a few of the squirrels as well. Not that Chester needed help, but simply out of spite. The damn things had almost killed Hank and he was angry that after all he'd been through and survived, a goddamn horde of large squirrels would have been what sent him on the last train west.

Hank began firing at the Fox squirrels, shooting well away from Chester. Harmony saw this and joined in also, shooting in the same area as Hank, though any of her bullets that hit anything was pure luck, due to the fact that there were so many of the furry things she couldn't miss.

Raising his feet high, Chester brought them down again and again, squishing furry bodies under his large sandals that had been made specifically for him when he was still with his father.

Soon, the entire area around the giant was nothing but blood, guts and bits of fur, the sticky liquid squirting in and around his toes.

Chester picked up a squirrel in each of his broad hands and short fingers, made a fist, and squeezed his hands tightly. Blood and guts squirted out the top and bottom, leaving behind deflated bodies. He threw them away and grabbed some more, then he got bored so he started using the club again, which he'd put on the ground. The entire time he fought, the squirrels were climbing all over him, but he was so large they barely bothered the big lug, and in fact seeing the large squirrels next to the giant man, the squirrels looked almost normal, the proportion of giant to squirrel evening out.

But no matter how many Chester killed, there were dozens to replace the ones destroyed. Hank realized this would never end unless he did something drastic, so dashing over to the Triumph, he reached into one of the saddlebags and took out a grenade. Pulling the pin to the grenade, he held the handle tight, while running back so he was only ten feet from Chester.

To the side of the giant and the main massive oak tree, there were three smaller trees that had grown so tightly together that they were almost one tree, and because of this, the trunks were equal to the task of letting Chester use them to shield his bulk from the grenade blast.

"Chester, get behind those three trees over there!" Hank yelled while pointing to the trio of trunks. At first Chester didn't hear Hank, too caught up in smashing and squishing squirrels, but on the third time Hank yelled to the big lug, Chester heard and did what he was told without argument.

Hank was impressed by that. Anyone else would have asked why or other questions instead of simply doing what they were told.

Dropping the bloody goop that had been two squirrels from his hands as he ran, Chester darted around the trees like he was playing hide and seek. The second Hank saw Chester begin to run, he threw the grenade into the swirling maelstrom of furry bodies. No more than two seconds passed before the grenade exploded, sending bloody squirrel parts off in all directions.

Harmony wasn't near the blast radius, but she was close enough to get splattered with gore, though Hank had managed to duck behind a tree so as not to get hit with gobbets of warm meat.

The grenade did its job well, almost taking out the entire horde, and scattering the rest to the hills in panic.

Harmony stood perfectly still as the squirrels raced by her, now only wanting to escape the devastation that had ripped through their brethren. The entire front of her body was a mass of blood splatter and bits of meat. One of the squirrels' testicles was sitting on top of her head, and a particularly squishy piece of red meat was on her forehead. Hank came out of hiding to see the piece of meat slide down her nose and fall to the ground.

"Thanks for the warning," she said angrily.

"Sorry," Hank said with a grin. "I knew you weren't in the area of the blast so figured I didn't have to tell you to duck."

"Can I come out now?" Chester called from behind the trees.

"Sure, Chester, it's all clear," Hank said, now fighting the urge to laugh at a blood-covered Harmony. Maybe it was because he hadn't laughed in a while, but all he knew was that it felt good to feel jovial for a while. With so much death and destruction around him, and people constantly trying to kill him, to take what was his and make it theirs, it felt good to let his guard down, even if it was only for a few minutes.

"Well, don't just stand there," Harmony hissed as the last of the squirrels disappeared into the surrounding brush, leaving only the dead, dying, and the ones in pieces in the glade, "Come and help get this shit off me."

Hank chuckled and joined her, taking a few bloody gobbets of meat off her with tenuous fingers. "I think the only way you're gonna get clean is if you go back to the brook and wash up."

"Ya think?" she snapped irritably.

"Make sure you wash your clothes, too," Hank added as she began stomping away, her .45 swinging back and forth by her side. She grumbled to herself angrily about how all men were a pain in the ass.

"What about me, Hank?" Chester asked, standing silently nearby. Every now and then he would stomp on a twitching squirrel to make sure it was truly dead.

"You stay here with me and help me skin some of the more whole squirrels around here," Hank instructed. "There's a lot of meat on these guys, and we need more food."

"I like food, Hank," Chester said, grinning widely. With his face covered in blood, as were his clothes and beard, he looked like a serial killer who had gone on a killing spree.

"You and me both, pal," Hank replied, then gathered up some decent-sized squirrels and handed them to Chester. "You know how to skin these, right?"

"Sure I do," Chester said. "Dad taught me." He looked on the ground and then picked up a rock the size of Hank's fist. The rock had a sharp tip. Sitting down on a fallen long, Chester placed the carcasses before him. His strength was so much that he easily used the rock to slice into the belly of the squirrels, to then simply rip the fur off in one long pull, leaving the meat exposed. Next he sliced the stomach and chest open and pulled out the entrails and organs. Upon seeing that Chester knew what he was doing, Hank got to work on his own pile of carcasses. When they finished there would be more than enough to last for days, even with Chester's massive appetite.

They worked for a while, the two not talking, just concentrating on skinning and gutting the carcasses. Finally, Hank looked up and said, "Harmony should have been back by now. It doesn't take that long to bathe and wash clothes."

"You want I should go check on her, Hank?" Chester asked.

"No, Chester, I can do it. You keep cleaning the ones in this pile and then find some more that look good." He stood up, wiping his bloody hands on his pant legs. He would need a bath too when he was done, to wash the blood as well as clean all the small cuts he now had thanks to the squirrels' claws. Chester would need a good dunking, too.

"Okay, Hank, I can do that."

"I know you can, Chester. You're a good boy."

Chester beamed with happiness, proud of himself.

Once more Hank found it amazing how such a giant brute of a man in appearance could really be so gentle in reality. But he'd seen the inner rage Chester had firsthand as well as his docile side.

Grabbing his automatic rifle, Hank headed off to see what the hell was taking Harmony so long.

Chapter 17

Harmony trudged over the hill and to the brook, grumbling the entire way. If there had been any danger around, she probably wouldn't have known about it until it was too late. She barely glanced at the burned-out strip mall, and if someone had been in there waiting to jump her, she never would have seen them coming.

Upon reaching the brook, she pulled off her clothes, dropped them at the water's edge along with her .45, and slid into the water. After dunking her head below the surface and rubbing her face and hair with the palms of her hands, she went to her clothes and began washing them by swirling them in the water. Bits of flesh and blood came off and floated away. The clothes would be stained, as she had no soap to get them out, but the material would still be a hell of a lot cleaner than it was before she began.

Finishing, Harmony laid the clothes out on a few rocks right at the edge, the .45 too so it was closer, then began swimming. If she had to be in the water then Harmony figured she might as well enjoy it. The water was a little cold but it was still refreshing. Many streams were radioactive or filled with sludge and other nasty things, but Hank had checked the brook with a badge on his chest and had told her that this particular brook was clean. She figured it was anyway. Though out of the immediate area of her roaming grounds, she was still close enough to her home to know that the area she was now in wasn't contaminated.

Now, go west where multiple bombs had gone off a hundred years ago and that would be a different story. There, the sky wasn't blue it was a dark purple, with thick clouds of radiation that constantly poured death down on the already destroyed land. She'd heard stories ever since she was a little girl about the strange and horrifying creatures that roamed the blighted lands of death. How humans, filled to the brim with rad poisoning, actually lived in the dead zones, somehow building up a tolerance to the radiation, though living lives that to her seemed worse than Hell itself. How their offspring were twisted, malformed things that barely resembled human beings. How sometimes they escaped the rad pits and crossed over to where the land was still healthy and the people weren't dying of sickness. These were the tales she'd been told to make her behave and go to sleep when it was bedtime, or else the things in the night, in the dark zones, would come and take her back to their lair of radiation-filled death.

But it was a beautiful day and the sky was clear, so she pushed the dark thoughts from her mind and enjoyed the time alone she now had. Though she missed her family terribly, if there was one thing that had been instilled in her since the first day she could walk, it was to take life as it came, and no matter what happened, if you were alive, rejoice and be glad.

Her eyes were closed and she was humming a song her grandmother had taught her, as she swam gracefully around the brook. Casually opening her eyes to see where her exact location was, she let out a gasp when she found that she wasn't alone.

"Well, well, lookee what we got here," a man's voice said upon seeing he was discovered.

Two men in their late thirties, wearing filthy clothes, their bodies even filthier, were gawking at her with mouths hanging open and guns in their hands, the weapons hanging casually so that the muzzles were pointed at the ground.

Realizing they were staring at her nakedness, she covered her perfect breasts with her arms and glared at them angrily. Standing up, the water came to her belly button, her toned, flat stomach in full view. At seventeen and at the peak of her flowering, she was a picture of loveliness, one any man would admire if given the chance.

"Who the fuck are you two? What do you want?" she demanded. Her eyes glanced over to her clothes and her .45, all of it on the rocks where the clothes were drying more than ten feet away. The .45 was too far to reach. She knew that before she was halfway to it, the men would shoot her if they wanted to. But by the way they were looking at her, she had a bad feeling they wanted a lot more than simply killing her.

"Oh, I think you know what we want, little lady," the first man said, wiping his runny nose on the back of a grime-encrusted sleeve. He was covered in filth, with a thick black beard and a deep scar running down the left side of his face. "Me and my brother are gonna have a good time with you. Right, Robby?"

"Hell yeah, Bernie," the second man replied in a hoarse voice. "We gonna have a good time with you. Gonna split you wide open. For sure." To emphasize his point he grabbed his crotch and licked his lips.

"I know, right?" Bernie added. "Shit, man, just look at those sweet tits. Gonna wrap my mouth around those titties and suck like I was a newborn."

"I want to fuck her in the ass, Bernie. Can I, please?"

"Sure, Robby, I don't see why not," Bernie said, feeling magnanimous about it all. "You can fuck her anywhere you want. But that's after I'm done with her first." He glared at Robby, making sure his domination over the second man was complete. Robby looked down and nodded, signifying that their pecking order was intact.

Robby took a step closer to the brook's edge, the battered hunting rifle held in his hand coming up, the muzzle pointed right at Harmony breasts. "When we heard an explosion, never thought in a million years we'd find something as sweet as you," he said.

"Now, come on, girl and get out of that water. Me and Robby need to be serviced and good."

Harmony could see the man had a hard-on through his baggy pants and she shivered in the water. "Can I get my clothes first?" she asked sweetly. From where the men were standing, her .45 was hidden from them by a larger rock than the one the gun was on. If she could get over there she might have a chance. Even if she took one of them out it was better than nothing. She didn't want to die, but she accepted the world she lived in, and if you were going to die than it was at least bearable if you could take your enemy with you. To put them off guard, she dropped her arms and exposed her breasts to them. The water chilly, both her nipples were standing at attention. The men's mouths fell slack yet again. "Please, I really could use my clothes back," she said in a soft voice, almost purring.

For a few seconds, Bernie stared in amazement at the vision of loveliness before him, but he quickly shook his head as if breaking himself free of a spell. "No, fuck that. Where you're goin' you won't be needin' clothes."

"Yeah," Robby added. "Me and my brother are gonna fuck you till you can't stand any more. Damn, girl, what a fine piece of ass you are."

Bernie slapped Robby in the back of the head. "Shut up, you fool, let me do the talkin'." He had never fully taken his eyes off of Harmony and now he focused his complete attention on her. "Enough stallin', bitch. Get over here or I'll shoot you dead and fuck your corpse, though I'll admit, a warm body is still better than a cold one. But I'll take what I can get."

"I'm not going anywhere with you assholes," she snapped, crossing her arms over her breasts again. Robby looked sad when that happened as his eyes had been glued to her chest the entire time.

Bernie sighed. "Fine, we can do this the hard way." He slapped Robby in the head again, but this was so he had his brother's attention. "Go and get her outta there. You can slap her around some if she fights, but try not to bruise the merchandise too much. If we keep her lookin' good, we can sell her on the slave market once we're bored with her."

"Okay, Bernie," Robby said and trudged into the water, heedless of his clothes. With the exception of rain, it was the first time the clothes on his back had touched water in over a year.

Harmony turned and tried to reach her .45, but Robby was on her in a flash. She fought to free herself but the man was strong. Only because she was naked, her skin slippery from being wet, stopped the man from grabbing and holding her, to then haul her out of the water with ease. Harmony screamed for help but knew she was too far away from the glade where Chester and Hank were for them to hear her. She was about to be kidnapped and used as a sex slave for the rest of her life and there was nothing she could do to stop it.

"Quit strugglin', girl, you're just makin' it harder on yourself," Bernie called from the bank. He had a grin on as he watched his brother wrestle with the young nymph, and he rubbed his crotch even more when he caught flashes of her inner thighs as she kicked and fought off Robby. The pubic hair at the junction of her thighs was a light blonde, the same color as her hair, and looked as soft as feathers.

In the heat of the fight, Harmony couldn't hear a thing, so the first inclination she had that the situation had gone in her favor was when Robby's head suddenly exploded, as if dynamite had been shoved into his skull and ignited. As the head vaporized and bits of blood and bone sprayed off in all directions to sprinkle the surface of the brook, the report of the gunshot that had done the deed came to her ears an instant later.

"Harmony, get the hell down!" Hank screamed from the opposite shore as he began firing at Bernie, who ducked for cover behind a fallen tree.

The headless body of Robby slid under the water; fish appeared, to begin feeding on the bits and pieces. The corpse floated away, caught in the gentle current.

Bernie began firing at Hank, who ducked down, bullets ricocheting off the boulder he was crouched behind. Hank wished he could have taken out both men at once, but there was only time to get one before the advantage of surprise was lost.

Harmony dropped down into the water and swam for the far shore, knowing she needed to stay hidden if she didn't want to get shot. Bernie saw her drop away and he fired a few shots at her, deciding a corpse was better than nothing compared to losing her completely. "You shot my brother, you son of a bitch! You'll pay for that with your head!"

"Well, that's more than your brother can say!" Hank quipped from across the brook. "Seems he doesn't have one any more!"

"You no-good fucker!" Bernie screamed and then popped up and fired twice. Hank waited for the man to shoot, and then he returned fire. His first bullet went wide but the second clipped Bernie in the shoulder. The man fell to the ground, rolling back and forth. Searing pain filled his shoulder and blood was already pooling under his mud-caked jacket. He tried to lift his arm but it would barely move. Knowing the fight was over and he'd lost, he rolled over and crawled away, to be lost in the brush a second later.

Hank stayed low, watching the location of the shooter, but when the man didn't pop back up, he wondered if he'd killed him. But then the sound of an engine floated on the wind, to be lost a second later. Whether it was Bernie escaping or another partner was unknown.

Hank waited another thirty seconds, and when no shots sounded, he slowly raised his head. His back itched from where he expected a bullet in the face, but he knew the man was already gone and he was worried over nothing. When no shots sounded, he stood up, and just as he expected, there was no barrage of gunfire from the opposite shore. "Okay, Harmony, looks like the coast is clear," Hank called as he went to the shore to greet her.

She'd been hidden between two rocks near the edge, about six feet from her clothes. Now she swam to them and grabbed them, then stood up and walked out of the water with no shame at her nudity. Hank averted his eyes out of respect, though he did manage to catch a brief glimpse of her nude form. He admired what he saw; she was achingly beautiful.

Harmony grinned to herself as she dressed. She had known of her beauty by the time she was twelve and had learned how to use it to her advantage a year later. But Hank was something else. So far he had made no advances on her. It was a relief in a way, but now she'd started to feel unwanted. All men wanted sex, and surely Hank was no different. Sure, he was much older than her, but he was handsome and his body was all muscle, sculpted from the hard life of living on the road. The more she'd thought about it the more she began to realize she wanted him. But that was for a later time, right now they both needed to deal with the situation at hand.

"You all right?" he asked.

"Yes, thanks to you, Hank. I don't want to think how things might have ended up if you hadn't shown up when you did."

He snuck a peek to see she was about dressed and he raised his head and looked full on at her. "I thought you were taking too long so figured I'd come and check on you."

"Well, I'm glad you did." She bounced over to him, and on tip-toes, reached up and kissed him on the cheek. "Thank you for that.

You saved my life…again." The .45 was in the small of her back between the waistband of her pants.

He grunted. "Seems like I'm making a habit of that, isn't it?" He gestured with the muzzle of the rifle to the opposite side of the brook. "Let's go back and get Chester, then we'll pack up all the meat and our gear and head over there."

"Why?" she asked.

"Because I want to know for sure if there's a dead man lying on the ground over there or not."

"I could swim over there." She began pulling off her shirt, which was barely dry.

"No, don't bother. I don't want you going over there alone. We'll all go. Besides, if he's dead, there's no rush."

"And if he's not? If he's only wounded and dying slowly?" Harmony asked with wide eyes.

He shrugged. "Same damn thing to me."

Chapter 18

When Hank and Harmony returned to the glade, Chester was finishing up skinning a squirrel. Before him was a large pile of meat. Flies buzzed around the meat happily. In fact, there were so many flies around that if they stayed for another half hour, there would be nothing but flies.

"I did good, huh, Hank?" Chester asked, proud of his skinning.

"Sure looks that way," Hank said then pointed to Chester's mouth and beard. "But it also looks like you've been eating as much as you've been cleaning. Am I right?"

Chester hung his head low. "Yeah, sorry, Hank. I was hungry."

"It's fine, pal, there's more than enough anyway. We can only take so much with us." Then he had a thought. "Chester, if we can make some kind of sack, could you carry the meat in that?"

"Sure I could. That would be easy."

"Good, then that's what we'll do. Once we're away from here we'll set up camp, get a fire going, and cook all the meat—just like we did with the dog meat."

"Only this time hopefully it'll last a little longer," Harmony added, gesturing to Chester, who was slurping down a piece of squirrel meat.

"Don't hold your breath," Hank replied.

They got to work packing up their gear. Hank took out a tarp from one of the saddlebags and this was used to pile the meat onto. Once that was done, Hank folded the corners, tied it together with some rope, and Chester picked it up and tossed it over his shoulder. He looked like a bizarre Santa Claus, but instead of toys he had a dripping sack full of squirrel meat.

"We need to reach the other side of the brook, Chester," Hank explained to the big lug. "But I need to get the motorcycle across. I have an idea how to do that with your help. You game?"

Chester nodded happily, pleased to be needed.

"Good," Hank said and got on the Triumph, then waved Harmony to do the same. "Let's get moving."

Hank started the motor to the Roadster on the first kick. He spun it around and drove the way he and Harmony had just come from the brook. Chester jogged right behind them. When Hank reached the edge of the water, he gestured for Harmony to get off, then he did the same. He gestured to Chester to come over, and when the giant did, Hank pointed to the bike and to the far shore, right where the body of Bernie should have been.

"Carry *this* over *there*," Hank instructed, pointing to the bike and the opposite bank. "But before you do, put down that sack of meat and jump in the water and wash up. You're filthy."

Chester nodded, placed the meat and his club on the ground, and jumped into the water.

"Wash good, too," Hank called.

Chester did as he was told, rubbing his face and scrubbing his beard with his massive hands. Hank pointed to the top of Chester's head and he washed there. By the time the big lug was finished, there was a wide area of red around him. But the brook had a gentle current and it was already dissipating as the giant exited the water. The body of Robby was long gone, the current taking it further downstream.

"You look a million times better," Hank said when Chester exited the water.

The big lug's clothes were still stained with blood in places, but now it was more of a pink color.

"Okay, now take the bike over to the opposite side, and be careful. If you drop it in the water it'll be ruined." Hank glared at Chester. "You understand me, right?"

"Sure I do, Hank. The motorbike needs to stay dry."

"Exactly."

Chester picked up the Triumph as if it was nothing but a child's toy, then he walked into the brook and crossed it. He had to hold the Roadster high over his head, but he managed to make it all the way across without slipping or dropping the bike. When he reached the opposite side, he set it down and waved to Hank and Harmony. "I did it!" he called, beaming with pride.

"You sure did," Hank called. "Now come back and get the sack of meat. Leave the bike there." Chester waded back into the brook, crossed it, and came out sopping wet but smiling. He picked up the meat and was back into the brook a moment later. "Okay, now it's our turn," Hank said.

"I don't know why I bothered trying to dry my clothes," Harmony said.

With their weapons held above their heads, the pair crossed the brook. They had to swim in the middle but they managed to reach the other side without dunking their guns. Climbing out of the water, Hank slung his rifle over his shoulder but held the SIG in his right hand as he crept over to where Bernie had fallen.

Though he expected to find a body, all he found was a patch of blood in the dirt and scuff marks where Bernie had dragged himself into the brush. "This way, Harmony. Looks like he's wounded," he called, following the trail. "Chester, you stay here and guard the bike and gear."

"Okay, Hank."

"And don't eat all the meat," Hank called back, stopping Chester as he was about to reach into the sack and pull out a juicy piece of raw squirrel.

Following the scuff marks in the dirt, Hank and Harmony came out of the brush to see the area was empty.

"Look there," Harmony said, pointing to tire tracks that led away.

"Looks like an ATV," Hank said, seeing the tracks and more blood splatter in the dirt as well.

"A what?" Harmony asked, not understanding the name.

"A three-wheeled motorcycle. Like a tricycle but with an engine," he explained. "It has one wheel in front and two in back for stability. It's called an ATV."

"Oh," she said. "I swear, sometimes you say the strangest things."

"We need to follow him and find the bastard."

"Why?" she asked. "He's gone; we won't see him again."

"How do you know for sure? Harmony, if there's one thing I've learned is that you don't leave an enemy alive if you have a choice. He could circle back at anytime and try and take us when we're not expecting it. Hell, he could go back to wherever he's from, gather a posse, and have them on us before we know what's happening."

"I didn't think of that."

Hank didn't reply, not seeing a reason. He walked thirty feet or so, seeing that the trail ended at a cracked and weed-infested blacktop. If they were going to catch Bernie, they would need to use the Triumph. Upon returning to Harmony, he said, "Come on, he doesn't have that much of a head start. If we move fast maybe we can catch up to him before nightfall."

"Yeah, that's if he isn't too far from home," she added.

"Good point, but let's deal with one thing at a time," he said, his face hard.

Together, they ran back into the brush to retrieve the Triumph, and Chester as well.

Chapter 19

The highway was a cracked mess, huge sections missing. Neglected for a hundred years, there were places where the entire roadway was nothing but weeds, Kudzu as tall as man or taller.

Hank drove the Triumph in and around the chunks of asphalt, and when it was impassible, Chester carried the Roadster over the mess until it was clear for Hank and Harmony to ride again.

It was apparent to Hank that over the decades there had been flooding, the rushing water washing away the road until there was nothing but craters filled with scummy water.

"You know, a hundred years ago there would have been hundreds if not thousands of cars and trucks on roads like this everyday," he told Harmony as he weaved his way over the bumpy terrain. He could see why Bernie was using an ATV, for nothing on four wheels could have managed to go far before needing to stop, the driver then having no choice but to continue on foot.

"I don't believe you," Harmony scoffed. "Thousands? That's impossible. There wouldn't be enough fuel to run them all."

"Oh but there was," Hank replied. "See, there were giant refineries all over the planet, some as far away as the Middle East, that took the oil from the ground and made it into gas."

"Now I know you're lying," she said. "Because if that were true, then how did they get the gas from way over there to here?"

"By using fuel trucks, pipelines and tankers to name a few."

"What's a pipeline?" she asked.

"Never mind," he said. "I was just making conversation to pass the time."

"If it's all true what you tell me, where did you learn about all of this stuff?" she asked, interested. "You seem to know a lot about how things were back before things changed."

Hank decided the truth wasn't something she would believe and he didn't feel like trying to convince her; the last time he'd tried she'd thought he was joking, so he said, "I like to read a lot. I read about it in a book I found."

"My family owned some books from the old days," she said.

"Oh really? What happened to them?" he asked.

"We had a bad winter, and when we needed things to burn, the books were the first to go."

"That's too bad," he said.

She shrugged, Hank feeling the gesture on his back as she pressed up against him, as well as her breasts. "Not really. They were just some stuff about how to fix plumbing, grow flowers, and another was how to build shelves and furniture."

"Those sound like they would come in handy."

"Not really," she said. "All the men learn from an early age how to do things like that, and some of the women, too. Plumbing isn't something we had anyway. We had an outhouse like everyone else around us."

"I see."

"Besides, not many of us could read so all we did was look at the pictures."

Chester was running alongside the Triumph, his huge legs eating up the terrain easily. Hank glanced at the big lug and was amazed to see that Chester was barely breathing hard, nor was he sweating. A tinge of jealously filled him and he pushed it down.

Chester was half his age, and though he had Down's syndrome, was in almost perfect physical condition. It reminded Hank of something his mother used to say. *God gives with one hand and takes away with another.* Chester may have been a powerful man, but his brain was defective. Still, whatever the reason, Chester seemed to be able to make do with what God had given him and he always seemed happy, though oblivious of his true surroundings. In a way, Hank envied the big lug for that. Sometimes knowing too much wasn't a good thing.

"Hey, Hank, I found another drop of blood!" Chester yelled, clapping happily.

Hank slowed and stopped the Triumph beside Chester, who had run ahead of the Roadster. Hank had explained to Chester how the blood drops were a trail they needed to follow. Chester had good eyesight and had no problem spotting the small droplets scattered in a long line in the cracked and broken pavement. A few times Hank had thought he'd lost the trail, that perhaps Bernie had turned off the main road, but then Chester had waved from fifteen or twenty feet away and pointed down at his feet.

"Great job, Chester," Hank said, patting the giant on his massive arm as thick as Hank's thigh. "How's that sack of meat doing?"

Chester swung the sack around and dropped it on the ground. "It's okay. Can I have some? I'm hungry."

"Sure, go ahead, dig in," Hank said with a wave of his hand.

"Oh boy!" Chester yelled as he slid his hand into a small opening on one side of the sack. The opening didn't look that new and Hank had a feeling Chester had been sneaking snacks when Hank wasn't looking.

"You guys want some?" Chester asked through a mouthful of raw meat. He stretched out a hand overflowing with meat, his short fingers trying to contain it all. Harmony looked the other way and said, "No thanks. I prefer it cooked."

"Yeah, me too," Hank added.

Suddenly, Chester cocked his head to the side, as if he was listening for something. His mouth slowed its chewing as he concentrated.

"What's wrong?" Hank asked. "You hear something?"

Chester nodded and Hank turned off the engine to the Triumph. Sure enough, now he could hear what Chester had picked up on first. Engines, and from the sound of it, more than one. Glancing to the left and right, he picked the left and gestured to Chester to follow him. Starting the Triumph on the first kick again, he mentally praised the Roadster for being so reliable and then drove off the road and into a copse of trees, Harmony holding onto his waist so she didn't fall off.

Chester followed, and as Hank and Harmony got off the Triumph and hunkered down, Chester stood tall, still chewing on what he had in his mouth.

Hank reached out and grabbed Chester's shirt, pulling the big lug down to the ground, saying, "Get down or you're gonna be seen, damn it."

"Sorry, Hank, I didn't mean nothing," Chester said, now sad.

Hank was holding his automatic rifle in his hands, about to use the scope to see down the road and who was coming. "It's okay, Chester. I'm sorry I snapped at you. It's just that we don't know who's coming, and it could be bad men."

"Bad men?" Chester asked. "I hate bad men. They're not nice."

"You can't argue with him there, Hank, sometimes he knows exactly what to say," Harmony whispered beside Hank, her .45 gripped tightly in her right hand.

Hank glanced at her, seeing her stern face, her blonde hair. God, how she reminded him of Laurie. That sent a pang of loss over missing Laurie through him. He pushed it down deep. Now wasn't the time to be thinking of Laurie. She was safe in the bunker, sleeping. He was the one out on the side of the road with a special needs giant and a wayward seventeen year old.

The engines grew louder until finally the first vehicle came over the rise of the highway. It was a motorcycle, but as for the make and model, that was lost to the annals of time passed. The bike had been repaired with so many different parts to make it all but unrecognizable as a motorcycle, with the exception it was on two wheels and had the general shape of one. The rider looked like something out of the old 1980's apocalyptic movies Hank used to watch when he was a kid.

Covered from head to toe in radial tires for armor, the rider wore a hockey mask over his face. His gloves had spikes sewn into the knuckles, and the tips of each boot had long, three inch spikes as well. Anyone getting too close to this fellow would be in for a world of hurt, Hank thought.

The next vehicle was an ATV, the sides of the tires covered with steel plates to protect them from being shot out. The rider wore chain mail and what looked to Hank like medieval knight armor, no doubt looted from some museum decades ago.

Five more vehicles followed, each an amalgam of a motorcycle or an ATV in some way. All the riders wore similar attire, and all carried a firearm in some capacity.

Hank pulled his eyes from the group of marauders, and his mouth fell open at what was still in the middle of the road, almost directly across from where he and the others were hiding.

It was the meat sack, left on the highway by Chester, who had been in such a rush to follow Hank into hiding that he'd left it behind. And if that wasn't bad enough, there were a few bloody footprints leading right to their hiding place, the prints lightening as Chester made each step, until by the time they reached the copse of trees the prints were all but faded to nothing.

"Shit," Hank hissed, knowing it was only a matter of time before they were found. The gang was already too close for Hank and the others to move. If they did, they would be seen immediately. All they could do was wait and see what happened next.

Chapter 20

The first vehicle in line slowed to a stop at the sack of meat, the rider getting off his motorcycle. Looking around the area, and expecting an ambush, he raised his hands for the rest of the gang to stop a ways back.

Pulling his sidearm from its holster on his hip, the man studied the trees and brush that lined both sides of the old highway. The only sound was the purring engines that waited just down the road for the 'all clear' from the man.

A full two minutes passed with the rider standing in the middle of the road, his gun slowly swinging from left to right as he waited for something to happen.

Hank thought either the man had courage or was a fool. Unknown to Hank, it was the rider's job to draw out an attack, but the man wasn't even the least bit concerned. He and his people ruled the entire area with an iron fist for miles in every direction. They worked for the baron and no one would be stupid enough to fuck with them—not if they wanted to live anyway.

The rider opened the sack of meat and pulled out a handful with a yell of excitement. It was fresh. Sniffing it, he detected nothing wrong with it. He assumed someone had been carrying it, had seen him and his men coming, and had dropped the sack and high-tailed it into the treeline.

That was when the rider saw bloody footprints on the ground. They started from the sack of meat, where blood had dripped out the bottom to coat the road. Someone big had stepped in the blood to then track it across the pavement. Near the edge of the cracked and sun-faded asphalt, the bloody prints were all but gone, as the blood wore off with each step. But it was enough to see the exact location where the owner of the meat had left the road.

Raising his hand high, he lowered it fast, which was the signal for the rest of the gang to join him, and that the area was safe. Engines roared and tires burned rubber as the ATVs and motorcycles practically flew across the road, all eager to reach the point-man and see what was going on.

From within the trees, Hank watched the rider intently, knowing that if he or the others tried to get up and leave, the rider would have spotted the shift in the shadows and known someone was there. Chester had been the wild card, but he had been a trooper. He'd knelt down and stayed that way the entire time.

But when Hank saw the rider step away from the meat sack and begin walking along the road, his head looking down, Hank craned his head forward and realized that the rider had discovered the bloody footprints also. That was when Hank knew the jig was up, that their hiding place was about to be discovered.

Hank waited until the rider was only ten feet from where he was crouched, then he stood up, and before the rider could swing his gun at him, Hank shot the man in the chest.

The bullet hit the man directly over his heart, shattering ribs before, plowing into the heart, destroying the muscle as the round exited the torso, leaving behind a fist-sized hole in the man's back. The rider stood absolutely still, not quite understanding that he was dead, but still hadn't fallen down yet. Then the legs gave out and he collapsed, a pool of urine already spreading out from within his pants as his bladder let go in death.

After that, Harmony joined in, shooting at anything that moved. Hank shifted his aim and began firing at the other marauders, but the men weren't peasants who shivered and ran away at the sound of gunfire. These were hard men that had killed more people in their lives than should be allowed. As the first rider slumped to the pavement, the others in his gang were already returning fire at Hank's position using semi and automatic weapons.

"Get down!" Hank yelled, grabbing Harmony by the back of the neck and practically slamming her face into the dirt. It was a good thing, too, for the instant he pushed her head down, bullets flew past, so close she could hear the whine of the bullets' passing.

A barrage of gunfire made them all hunker down as close to the ground as possible. Behind Hank, Chester yelled in fear as only inches above him, the trees beside the big lug were chewed up and spit out, sending splinters off in all directions.

Hank managed to return gunfire sporadically, and he knew for sure that he'd shot at least three of the men. One of those men had been Bernie. Hank spotted the man's clothes and recognized them as the same as the enemy at the brook. Bernie hadn't been shooting though, but he'd kept poking his head up to see what was going on. Hank had waited for just the right moment, then had shot the man right between the eyes when he'd stuck up his head. Though a waste of a bullet, Hank felt some joy at knowing he'd finished the job started at the brook.

Then he had to hit the deck once more, as the onslaught of bullets coming at him was too strong; he spent most of the next two minutes eating dirt, praying the men didn't decide to shift their aim a little lower or that they had a grenade launcher. The thought of them sending a grenade to explode in the spot the three friends were hiding in wasn't one Hank wanted to consider.

"We need to get the hell out of here!" Harmony yelled, her voice muffled with her face in the dirt.

"No shit," Hank said, but before he could say more, the gunfire suddenly stopped

"It stopped," Harmony said, describing the obvious.

"Yeah, but the question is, why did it stop?" Hank received an answer a moment later when footsteps from behind caused him to spin around, the rifle muzzle of his H&K leading the way.

"Move one more inch and you're fucking dead," a cold voice hissed, followed by the cocking of a shotgun.

Harmony spun around, her .45 before her. She probably would have taken a chance anyway and tried to shoot the two men standing there with shotguns aimed at her face, but Hank reached out and slapped the .45 down. "Don't do it," he said. "There's no chance."

"But I could of…"

"No," he said sternly. "If you'd tried you'd be dead right now."

"Fuckin' A," the second man said. "And that would be a waste of a Grade A piece of ass."

"All three of you, come out of there," the first gunman said, using the barrel of the shotgun to gesture for them to exit onto the road. Now Hank understood why the gunfire had ceased. It was so the two men could flank the area and not risk getting shot by their own men.

Chester looked like he was going to erupt into violence, and no doubt he could easily kill the two gunman, but there were still another half dozen on the road with weapons aimed at them. Chester looked at Hank before doing anything, and Hank shook his head, locking eyes with Chester. Luckily, the big lug understood, and he lowered his fists and let his shoulders slump a little.

Once out on the highway, the rest of the men surrounded the three friends and quickly stripped them of their weapons, which were gathered and taken to one of the ATVs for transport.

"What about the big fucker?" one of the men asked the others. "Do we take his club with us, too?"

"Nah, it's just a big stick; toss it away," another man said, who Hank assumed was the leader. He had bright white bleached hair and a long scar ran down the left side of his face. The man that had asked the question took the club—which he needed both hands to hold and even then could barely lift it—and he walked a few feet and dumped it in the dirt on the weed-infested shoulder of the road.

"Hey, look what I found?" another man said, wheeling the Triumph from out of the bushes. Hank studied the Roadster, seeing that the bike had made it through the onslaught of bullets unharmed.

"Another bike, good," the leader said, glad at the find. "We can take it back to Lincoln with us. Baron Steele will be pleased." He looked over the three prisoners. "Two for the slave pits and one for the whore house. Not a bad find to come across. Shit, I'd give Bernie a bonus if the dumb fuck wasn't dead. But that's good, saves me jack that I now don't have to pay him." A few of the other men laughed at that. He walked over to Harmony and cupped her chin with his hand. "Open your mouth, bitch." At first she wouldn't comply, but when the man began to squeeze, she capitulated. "Nice teeth, looks good. Gums are clean, too." He squeezed her left breast. "Nice and firm here, too. I just may have to ride you myself before anyone else does." He glanced at his men. "Then my men can have some fun with you. It's a long way back to Lincoln, and tonight when we make camp it'll give us all something to do."

"Fuck you," she hissed. "Any man comes near me and I'll bite his dick off!" Harmony yelled.

The leader slapped her across the face with the front of his hand. Harmony reeled from the blow, but other than a red spot that was already fading, she was fine.

"Next time you'll get the back of my hand," the leader hissed. "Don't fuck with me, bitch. You can come back to Lincoln a little messed up. A beauty like you, no one will mind a few scrapes and bruises." He sneered. "I know I wouldn't."

Hank had stood silently by, watching, though it was a battle to do so. But he knew if he tried anything he'd be shot before he could get three feet. His mind was working as well, trying to figure out how to escape, but nothing was coming to mind. Chester was already being chained up, and the thick links wrapped multiple times around him, was more than enough to hold the big lug.

Then an idea came to Hank, so he said, "She's a virgin, you know. Aren't they worth more?"

The leader of the marauders turned and walked over to Hank. "What did you say, asshole?"

"I said the girl's a virgin."

He laughed and so did the rest of the men. "Oh please, you expect me to believe you haven't tapped that piece of ass every night for a month?"

"Well, I haven't. Never touched her," Hank replied, locking eyes with the man.

The man stared into Hank's eyes, looking for a lie, but eventually he glanced away and shifted his gaze back to Harmony.

"Is what he says true?" he asked Harmony.

It wasn't true. A year ago she and a boy from town had snuck off into the woods to be together. It had hurt at first, but once the initial pain had gone away, she'd enjoyed it. She'd never seen the boy again but she still remembered that experience with fondness. Some girls in her town had been roughly taken their first time, and others had been taken by their own fathers, so she cherished her memory that she had chosen the time and place to lose her virginity. Still, now wasn't the time for sharing, so she replied, "Yes I am. I…I've never been with a man before."

The man studied her face for a second, as if he was trying to detect if she was truthful, then he clapped his hands and said to the men gathered around, "No one touch this girl. You hear me? If she's a virgin she's worth her weight in jack back in Lincoln." Then he turned and glared back at Harmony. "We'll have to wait till we get back to town. Once there she'll get checked out to know for sure. If she's not, she'll regret ever making that claim." The evil grin on his face as he stared at Harmony told her he was utterly serious. "Okay, get the prisoners on some three-wheelers and let's move out. Time to head back to town."

There was a flutter of activity as the men began herding Hank, Chester and Harmony over to a set of ATVs. Each had a driver, and the prisoners would be placed on the back seats.

Harmony's hands were tied and she was made to get on the back of an ATV with a fat man for a driver. Chester was put on one by himself as there was no room for both him and the driver. But Chester didn't get to drive the vehicle. Instead it was connected to another with rope so that it could be towed.

Chester remained silent, only doing what he was told. None of the marauders noticed he had Down's syndrome, assuming the big lug was simply taciturn. Besides, Chester being so huge, and towering over the other men, no one wanted to make eye contact with him, despite the men being armed with guns and Chester helpless before them, such was the giant's imposing stature.

Then it was Hank's turn to be tied up and placed on an ATV. So far there had been no chance to escape, and Hank was beginning to feel that there would be none. These men were professional coldhearts, and they had all the bases covered to keep their prisoners in line.

As a man began tying Hank's hands together with rope soiled with dried blood from previous prisoners, Hank spotted one of the marauders messing around with the Triumph. The key had been left in the ignition by Hank. The man got onto the Roadster and prepared to start the motor and drive the Triumph back to town with the others. But as he reached down and turned the ignition key, he didn't see the small toggle switch beside it. With a flick of the wrist he turned on the ignition, and then promptly exploded in a massive explosion of smoke and fire as the C4 Hank had planted there as a safety feature erupted, the gas tank and all the munitions in the saddlebags catching an instant later.

The fire-blast rolled across the highway, taking out another four men and sending the rest sprawling to the ground from the shockwave. Hank was ready for the blast, however, and he grabbed the man who had been about to tie his hands and spun him around so he was facing the explosion, his back to Hank. As shrapnel ripped through the air, pushing Hank and his human shield to the ground; nothing touched Hank, and as the fireball and debris faded away, Hank rolled the man off him to see that his face and the rest of his body was nothing but a bloody mishmash of meat and bone. Hank had been close to the blast, and if not for using the man as a human shield, no doubt he would have been killed, too.

Chester and Harmony had been further away, with men and vehicles between them and the explosion. They were shoved to the ground from the shockwave, but other than a few scrapes from flying shrapnel that had gone a little farther than the blast radius, they were unharmed. But they were too far away for Hank to reach them, as already the men that had only been stunned were getting to their feet, looking around in wide-eyed amazement at the carnage before them. One man at the epicenter of the blast was disintegrated, only his boots left on the road, sliced off at the ankles. The feet were still in the boots and the ankle bones still smoked from where the blast had severed the rest of the man.

Knowing he had seconds to make a decision on his next move, Hank realized the only thing he could do was escape, then try and return and find Chester and Harmony and rescue them. But if he tried to get to them now and they all made a break for it, they would never make it before either being gunned down or chased and re-caught.

The man dead at Hank's feet had been carrying a shotgun, and Hank grabbed it and slung it over his shoulder, then jumped onto the ATV he'd been about to be placed on. He started the engine and drove off, using the other vehicles as cover. No one noticed him, all too dazed to do more than stare in shock and horror. Most of the men couldn't hear, their ears ringing from the blast. Hank made eye contact with Harmony from across the highway and he saw the look on her face. It was one of betrayal, for she believed he was leaving her to a fate worse than death. Chester spotted Hank and he waved to him, not understanding what was going on. But Hank had said to be good, and not to try and kill the bad men, so Chester was doing what he was told.

Hank's gaze locked with Harmony briefly and he wished he could tell her what he was doing, that he would come back for her, but he had to escape alive first. It was their only chance. But then he was past her and into the trees, the ATV like a living beast beneath him as he rolled and bounced over bumpy terrain. One gunshot sounded but whether it was at him or just a misfire from the blast, he would never know.

He drove for more than a mile before he even took a second to glance over his shoulder. When he saw nothing behind him, not even a dust cloud, which would be a sign of possible pursuit, he slowed and finally came to a stop.

For what it was worth, it looked like he'd escaped.

But now he had to make it to Lincoln with no food or water, and only a shotgun. Once there, he would have to find Harmony and Chester, free them without getting caught himself, and then finally, all three of them would have to get out of town without being killed.

Shaking his head at the daunting task before him, he spun around and began heading back to the highway and the location he'd just escaped from.

Chapter 21

As Hank drove back to the highway, a voice in his head suggested he turn back to the bunker. He didn't have to go after Harmony and Chester, he owed them nothing. In the world they lived in, they were used to people looking out for their own interests.

But then another voice overrode the first one, the *ying* to the first's voice's *yang*. This one said he had no choice, that by saving Harmony and Chester's lives before, they were now his responsibility. It was no different than if Carl, Stewart or Laurie were in need of rescue.

It was an easy choice for him to make however. Despite all that had happened, he felt himself growing close to Harmony, and Chester was like a big puppy dog. He debated if he should return to the bunker, wait for the others to awaken, and then with their help try and rescue Harmony and Chester. But that would be weeks, and who knew what would be happening to the pair in the meantime.

No, it had to happen now, and fast. Hank knew the best time to rescue them would be immediately, before they were put to whatever gruesome tasks would be their lot.

When the highway was in sight, Hank parked the ATV and went the rest of the way on foot, as he didn't know what to expect. It had been over a half hour since he'd escaped, and the marauders might still be there, searching for him, even waiting for the exact thing he was doing now.

Before he reached the road by pushing through the trees and brush, he could detect the odor of blood, offal and fire. When he was twenty feet from the road, he stopped and listened, straining his hearing to pick up anything amiss, such as the roar of an engine or a raised shout. But there was nothing.

He waited for another five minutes for any sign the men were still on the road, then he readied the captured shotgun and moved closer, so he was in the exact same place that he, Harmony and Chester had been using to hide in before being captured.

He peered through the brush to see the highway, but there was nothing moving with the exception of a few scavengers feeding on bits of meat lying in the road. That was good enough for Hank, and he stepped out of the treeline and onto the asphalt almost dead center of where the Triumph had exploded. There was a dark black spot and some of the pavement was missing at the epicenter of the blast, and from there the scorch marks on the ground spread out in a rough circle. After that he came across body parts and bits of flesh and bone. The scavengers had already done a good job of cleaning the road of meaty debris, and the half dozen wolves and dogs that were still there didn't seem interested in Hank in the least. After all, why fight for your meal when there was one lying all across the road?

That was fine with Hank. If they left him alone he would do the same to them.

Spent shells littered the ground as well, left over from the marauders weapons. Hank kicked some away with his feet, and the tingling brass caused a few scavenger heads to pop up. But when they saw there was no danger, they went back to feeding on the gobbets of still-moist flesh spread everywhere. One wolf was worrying at a boot, trying to get the foot still inside it.

There was nothing here of use. He was about to turn around and return to the ATV, where he would then follow the road until he could find a map or someone who could tell him where the hell Lincoln was compared to his location, when he saw a wolf over to the far side of the treeline, on the opposite side of the road. The wolf's body was half in and half out of the brush, as if it was trying to get something. But each time it tried the animal would jump back, like it was startled, but it would quickly return and try again, repeating the same action once more.

Curious, Hank went over to investigate, and when the wolf saw him, it lowered its head and began to growl, the meaning clear. *This is my meal; get the fuck out of here.*

Hank leveled the shotgun and said, "Fuck off or I'll turn you into ground chuck." He only had a few shells for the shotgun, and he didn't really want to waste one on a wolf, especially as he didn't know what was in the brush. For all he knew, it was nothing but a rabbit, or a piece of a body part that had been blown there. But it was worth a look before he left.

The wolf growled louder, telling Hank it wasn't about to back down, so with no choice, Hank fired the shotgun at almost point-blank range. The report echoed over the road, chasing the other animals away. They knew what that sound was and they weren't going to be next. Besides, they could return to the road later and finish up eating after Hank was gone.

The wolf's head evaporated under the pellet blast, and its brain was turned to mush for those pellets that went through the eyes and into the skull cavity. After falling to the side into the weeds, the wolf's legs still twitching, Hank grabbed the carcass by its tail and pulled it away from whatever it had been trying to reach, leaving a bloody trail in its wake as it was pulled across the pavement. He left the carcass in the middle of the road—more fodder for the hungry masses.

Returning to the spot the wolf had been so interested in, Hank used the shotgun to push the weeds out of the way. He was shocked to find a man lying there—or what used to be a man. It was one of the marauders, there was no question about that. Hank lowered the shotgun, knowing there was no threat from the half-man before him. Hank was about to turn away when the man's eyes suddenly snapped open, the lips parting. Like a zombie, the man moaned and wailed before saying, "Kill me, please. For the love of God, kill me."

"Jesus Christ, you're still alive?" Hank gasped as he stared down at the mangled form of the man. "That's impossible."

The man had been thrown across the road and into the brush, where he'd been left for dead by his pals. He had no arms, both limbs blown off in the explosion of the Triumph. The heat had been so powerful it practically fused the wounds as soon as the arms were blown off, though blood still seeped out in small spurts. But that wasn't all the damage the man had suffered. One leg was missing at the knee, the other one was still there, but was only hanging by a thread of flesh and muscle, tendons stretched out like elastics. The poor bastard's stomach had been sliced into by shrapnel so that his intestines had popped out of him like a joke snake in a false can of peanuts.

It seemed impossible that the man was still alive, but there he was, moaning softly, his head shifting slightly from side to side. He was in terrible agony, there was no doubt about that, and the side of Hank that showed mercy wanted to kill the guy on the spot. But he needed information first.

"Kill me, *pleeeasse*," the man whispered, bloody bubbles forming around his mouth.

Hank knelt down next to the mangled form, the shotgun in his hand. He saw a sidearm and a hunting knife strapped to the man's torso, and he quickly took them for his own. There was a spare clip for the pistol on the man's belt as well, and a second later it was Hank's.

"I'll kill you, pal, but first you need to tell me something."

"Anything…just...kill me. God the pain," the man said, his voice rising and falling in agony.

"My friends were taken back to Lincoln. That's what I heard before I got away. I need to know how to get there from here. No funny business either. You tell me straight or I'll leave you to wither away. The wolves will be on your ass as soon as I leave, too. I figure you've still got some time to die, despite your injuries."

"No, no, I'll…I'll tell you," he whispered and quickly told Hank how to get to Lincoln from where they were. It wasn't hard, Hank learned, and other than taking one turn off the highway fifteen or so miles down the road, he would be there in an hour, maybe even sooner given the speed of the ATV.

"But be careful by the Saline…Saline…" the man drifted off, falling in and out of unconsciousness.

"The what?" Hank asked, grabbing the man's shirt and shaking him. "Tell me! The Saline what?" The man opened his eyes from the shaking, but Hank saw that they were glazed over. He was still alive but wasn't seeing clearly.

The time to get information from the man was over; he was close to death, but Hank made a promise and he would stick to it. Hank used the guy's own hunting knife and slit his throat. Blood spurted from the gash in his neck, and as Hank stood up and walked away, the man was quickly boarding the last train west, his blood soaking into the already moist ground from blood previously spilled there from the guy's countless wounds.

Hank left the road and went to the ATV. He climbed on, then spun it around and drove back onto the highway. At least now he knew his destination clearly and had added a pistol and knife to his arsenal. It wasn't much but it would have to do.

Chapter 22

The ATV Hank drove was a fickle bitch, and it stalled more than three times. The last time it happened, Hank thought the machine was done for good, but on the last try before the battery would have given out, the engine chugged to life, belched a cloud of thick black smoke, then began to idle out and become smooth.

As he drove down the road, the land opened up so that there was nothing on either side of him but flatness; he truly accepted without question that he wasn't in his own time, that he truly was living in a new century.

For one thing there were no buildings, only the remains of buildings, and where once green signs with white words that declared where you were and going to on America's state highways could be seen constantly, now there was nothing but a few jagged posts, where the signs had been cut down to be used for scrap or building materials.

Every now and then a car or truck was on the side of the road, but it was nothing but a hulk of rusting metal, everything that could be salvaged long gone. Sometimes animals were using the vehicles for homes, and where the engines used to be, now there were birds or skunks or any number of other creatures taking up residence.

He ran out of gas at the edge of a stretch of denuded land just after taking the turn-off from the main highway onto a smaller road; Hank knew from the dying man's directions that he only had a few more miles to go before reaching Lincoln. Letting the ATV roll for as long as it would, when it finally came to a stop he got off it and pushed it off the road so it would be hidden. It bounced and jumped down the slanted shoulder before rolling onto its side. But Hank didn't see it happen, he was already walking down the road, keeping to the shoulder in case he had to get off and hide if someone appeared.

After about a mile he saw that the dirt road twisted to the north, and that instead of staying on it, he could cut across the flat land and pick it up again. Wanting to save time, worrying about what might be happening to Harmony and Chester, he walked off the highway and into the brush, then began making a straight line to meet back up with the road. He figured it was probably safer to cross the flat area than stick to the road, too, as there would be less chance of him coming across people. At the moment, anyone he came across was an enemy until proven different, though he'd found out even before waking in this new world how that same advice was worth its weight in gold, or whatever the locals used for money nowadays.

The area he was crossing had once been the Saline Wetlands, but now, after climate shifts thanks to the bombs of a hundred years ago, the area was nothing but dry land similar to a desert.

His boots crunched under the dry sediment, and he kept careful watch all around him, but with the land so open, nothing could sneak up on him. As he walked by a small hole no larger than three inches, a Salt Creek Tiger Beetle poked its head out to investigate. Its antenna shifted back and forth before it came out some more. Before Hank went to sleep for a hundred years, the beetle had been rare in Nebraska, but with the reduction of man in its habitat, they had quickly begun to thrive, until there were not just thousands but millions of them. Normally growing up to 0.5 inches, the one that came out of its hole was at least three inches and change, its coloring a dark brown to match its landscape. The originals of a century ago had been metallic brown with green undersides, but the one that scuttled out of its hole had learned to use camouflage as a weapon, and was a light brown to match the ground. Soon, more were coming out of their holes to see what had been foolish enough to come into their territory. Not that they were complaining. It was the only way they got food, for there were always animals that would wander onto their land in search of food, only to become what they sought themselves.

In a matter of a few minutes, there were over a hundred beetles spread out across the ground, Hank none the wiser as he walked along. He glanced over his shoulder now and then to see if he was being followed, but the beetles blended in so well with the terrain that he didn't see what was going on only fifty feet behind him. Oblivious to the danger, he strolled onward, his eyes creased from the harsh sun.

Soon there had to be a thousand beetles covering the ground like a blanket, their brown color allowing them to blend in perfectly. From above, it would have looked like the ground was undulating, flowing like water, but from six feet off the ground it was barely discernable.

The beetles began to flank their prey, slowly moving on Hank's sides to surround him in a circle of death, their long feelers picking up his scent. They had hunted the same way thousands of times before and the animal had never been able to escape.

Boulders of different sizes were scattered across the land, and the beetles swarmed around these, as if they were the Red Sea being parted.

Hank stopped and wiped the sweat off his forehead. Before him, scattered across the land, were the dried and bleached bones of countless animals, the meat long stripped away. Whatever had fed on these poor beasts had left absolutely nothing behind. Hank wondered how they had all gotten there but it was only idle curiosity.

He turned and glanced over his shoulder yet again. A battle-hardened warrior, he knew to not constantly check your surroundings meant death eventually—if not today, some other day.

It was what gave him a fighting chance when other animals hadn't been as lucky. Looking back, he spotted the ground moving, the thousands of beetles coming right for him. His eyes went wide in abject terror, knowing immediately that this enemy wasn't one he could fight with a gun. His eyes went to the left and right, and once more he saw the ground shifting and heaving as the beetles came closer. Turning, he began running for all he was worth, but quickly saw that he was being flanked on both sides.

Leveling the shotgun, he fired a blast at the ground when the beetles closed ranks. The pellets destroyed a hundred beetles easily but there were thousands more to replace them. Hank was amazed as he ran, his eyes taking in the beetles. They were huge, three inches at least, some even bigger, which was something he'd never seen before. One thing he'd learned since leaving the bunker was that creatures grew larger now, thanks to fewer humans to slow down the creatures' development as well as residual radiation that had mutated them over a hundred years.

His boots crunched on the beetles as he ran, and he knew if he slipped and fell for any reason, it would be his last. They would be on him in seconds and there would be no escape. With his hands out and to the sides, he ran and balanced himself as best he could. The beetles began crawling up his legs, and he had to brush them off while running. If he stopped he would be swarmed as well. He was now running on nothing but beetles, each step crushing them under his soles, the feeling like stepping on discarded peanuts shells. He fired a few more times before him with the shotgun, but as soon as the pellets were gone, the beetles swarmed in and filled the spot, writhing and crawling over their dead brethren. Some fed on the dead ones but most wanted the warm meat and soft flesh that was Hank.

A large boulder was nearby, and Hank ran for it, jumping onto it. But as soon as he did, the beetles began crawling up the boulder's sides. Knowing he had to keep moving, he began hopping from rock to rock, praying he wouldn't get to one that was too far away.

He did this for five full minutes, and was soon huffing and puffing from the exertion. On the last jump he almost didn't make it, and he knew fatigue was setting in. That was when he spotted the slow stream off to the right. Turning, he lunged for the next boulder, landed hard and rolled off the top, but at the last possible second managed to throw out a hand and grab the far edge and halt his fall. The beetles were already climbing onto the boulder, and Hank let out a yelp when he felt some of them crawl on his hand, still attached to the boulder. A few took tentative nips at his flesh but Hank stopped them when he yanked his hand back and flung off the damn things.

Standing up, he brushed off the beetles that were on his pants and jumped for the next boulder—which was the last one left to use. The stream was still another fifty feet away, and he would have no choice but to make a run for it. Hell, he didn't even know if water would stop the giant beetles. Not that he had many options.

With a yell to psych himself up, he jumped off the rock, landed hard, and fought the impulse to roll on the ground to take up the force of the landing. Instead, his legs took the brunt of it and he felt something pull in his right leg. Then he was off, running for the stream as the beetles lifted their heads, their feelers calling out to Hank, wanting him to stop, to lie down and let them feed.

Jut before Hank reached the stream, he slipped on some of the beetles after crushing them, their guts making the rocks beneath them slippery. Hank went down hard onto his back, and for an instant he was dazed, but all he had was an instant as the beetles immediately swarmed over him.

He wanted to scream in horror but he kept his lips clamped shut, for to open them would allow some of the beetles to crawl into his mouth. He didn't want to think about that, how they would slide in and down his throat, then into his stomach, eating their way out before the acid therein could kill them, their hard shells allowing them to survive far longer than they should.

Covered in beetles, their feelers caressing his exposed flesh, their mandibles clamping on his skin, Hank found the will to stand up, and though blinded thanks to the beetles covering his face and closed eyes, he stumbled in the direction he believed the stream to be. The beetles pushed on his eyelids, wanting Hank to open them so they could get at the moist orbs within, but he refused. They tickled his nose and ears, but were far too large to get in easily, though with time they would burrow into his skull. But that would be after he was killed and lying prone on the ground.

Hank wanted to scream in revulsion as the beetles went under his clothes and pushed on his skin, but he held fast, knowing to open his mouth would cause far more problems than if he kept it closed.

He didn't even know if he was going the right way, and for all he knew he'd been turned around and was going back the way he'd come. But there was no choice in the matter. He stumbled forward like a zombie, the beetles tripping him up and threatening to make him fall again. He knew if he went down again there would be no getting up. His skin was on fire from all the tiny pinpricks as the beetles sampled their food, but Hank kept right on going. He was so wrapped up in his own world of terror and pain that he didn't even realize it when he fell face first into the stream after running out of solid ground.

For a few moments he sank into the water, which was no more than four feet deep, but then he snapped out of it and his hands went to his face and he started slapping it, knocking the beetles loose. Once pulled free, the current took the little bastards away from him, their bodies turning and tumbling in the water. They wouldn't die in the water but they were done with the hunt.

Hank finished wiping his face and head, then slapped his neck to clear out more. Coming up out of the water, he opened his eyes and began punching his body, crushing the beetles that were under his clothes. He took off his shirt to save time and killed the remaining ones under his pants, the BDU's so damn loose that there had to be a dozen of the foul things between the material and his legs.

Eventually he got them all and he floated there, just glad to be alive, then he began to swim away from where he'd fallen into the water. When he looked over at the shore, he saw thousands of beetles lined up, all climbing over one another. But they didn't like the water and weren't about to dive in to try and reach their prey. Somehow, this animal had outsmarted them and their feelers were held high in anger, their mandibles opening and closing, as if they could make the prey return to them.

Hank continued to swim away, ignoring the annoyed beetles.

Soon, the information that the prey had escaped was transmitted to the thousands of beetles covering the ground and slowly, they all began to return to their burrows in the ground. They were frustrated that food had been within reach and had slipped through their mandibles, but in time more creatures would come, thinking the nearby stream was available, and once they had gone too far to escape, the beetles would be there to take down the prey and feed once more.

Chapter 23

Hank floated a quarter mile before coming out of the stream. His face and arms were covered in small red marks from where the beetles' mandibles had bit him. Sitting on the edge of the shore, he inspected his shotgun and pistol, not happy with the dunking both had taken. Chances were that now when he needed to use them, they would misfire. The first thing he needed to do was acquire more weapons.

From where he was, he could see the remains of Lincoln, so he gathered himself and set off once more. As he trudged closer, he saw that the original capital of Nebraska was far from its former glory, and now resembled a burned-out husk.

Though Hank would never know for sure, to him it seemed that a bomb had gone off far too close to Lincoln. Whether a missile had been sent to Lincoln on purpose to destroy America's farmlands, or simply had been an error in navigation, the end result was the same. The city had taken a blast that had blown off the tops of buildings, destroyed windows, and set fire to more than half the city. Even to this day Hank found it amazing how there were parts of America that looked like rubble turned over while other parts were virtually untouched, though the population still found themselves on their own with the collapse of the government.

The sun was beginning to set and Hank realized he'd been fighting and running for the entire day, which was why he was so exhausted. He was hungry, but at least he'd had plenty to drink, thanks to the water from the stream. He'd consumed it without boiling it and he prayed the water was okay or else he would get such a case of diarrhea he'd wish he was dead. Or worse, there was something in the water, such as a parasite, that was already working on his insides, eating him from the inside out. But he couldn't think of that now. He'd had no choice in the matter. Even if he'd had a way to make a fire, there was nothing to boil the water in. So far he felt fine, which was a good sign. Bad water didn't waste time letting you know it was 'bad' water.

With night falling, the sky had shifted in color here as well. Gazing upwards, Hank could see the bathing rays of the purple and reddish moon pushing their way down to earth, a thin haze of radiation that circled the planet high in the Van Allen belt. Hank glanced at his radiation badge, seeing it was moving out of the green, but not so much that it would be a threat to his survival. Whatever missile had exploded a century ago hadn't been nuclear, which was a bonus for the population, but despite this the devastation was still evident.

With night fast approaching, Hank was able to make better time on his way to the outskirts of the city, as he didn't have to be worried about being spotted by a roving patrol or a wandering traveler.

Before Hank realized it, he was standing in what was once a city street in the vast capital of Lincoln, Nebraska. He didn't know where he was exactly, as there were no signs denoting it, but he did see faded signs on some of the surrounding buildings. The choice to keep on going and enter the city was an obvious one. Somewhere in the sprawling rubble that was Lincoln he would find Chester and Harmony.

With the shotgun leveled before him, Hank walked down the street, keeping to the middle in case of an attack. Vines and weeds covered most of the outer facades of the buildings, kudzu everywhere like a living carpet, and not one window was intact; some had small trees growing out of their slanted roofs or shrubbery poking out of foundations as well, where seeds had blown to then take root in the powdery substance that had once made up the foundations of the buildings. Doors were hanging from their frames at odd angles, some doorframes missing the doors entirely; the wooden doors had probably been scavenged long ago to be used as fuel to burn or for building supplies. Three and four-story structures peered down at Hank, most nothing but empty husks, the scorch marks on their facades from long ago, the masonry cracked and crumbling, and turning to dust. The few faded signs Hank could read hung above the stores: **JOE'S HARDWARE, SISSY'S BEAUTY PARLOR**, and **MOM'S BBQ: TAKEOUT OR DINE IN**, and a **7-11** were some of the stores he recognized at having uses he was familiar with. Others had signs so weathered from age he couldn't make them out, and the insides were so looted and destroyed to be unrecognizable.

He could smell cooking smoke on the wind but it didn't seem close by. Still, it made his stomach rumble.

He'd covered about a half mile, still seeing the same sign of debris and devastation, when he heard something scuttling to his right. The moon was out in full and the light was enough to see shapes, but not enough to discern actual faces. Leveling the shotgun at the shape, he held fast, and was more than slightly surprised when a cat popped out from between two piles of boulders. It was a mangy thing, with matted fur and an ear missing. It was a scrapper. Hank could see that immediately. It was big, three feet long at least, and he could add another foot with the tail, and it stood two feet high from paws to remaining ear. The cat held a dead rat in its mouth, the rat also of decent size. The cat hissed at Hank, then growled low in the back of its throat, before spinning around and taking off in the opposite direction. Hank lowered the shotgun a little. Finally, something that didn't want to kill him.

He continued on, deeper into the city, seeing the same type of devastation on each street. But he didn't know where he was going and knew he needed to find out soon, or else he could wander through the wasteland of Lincoln for days, if not weeks.

The sound of shifting rubble came to him again, and he casually turned around, expecting to see the shape of the cat again, but his eyes went wide when he saw that it wasn't the cat at all, but was an animal nonetheless.

The biggest wolf he'd ever seen was standing no more than thirty feet away, its teeth bared, its haunches raised for attack. Its muzzle was stained with dark blood, signifying that it had fed on something already. But whatever it had partaken of had been the appetizer. Hank was going to be the main course.

The damn thing had to be seven feet long and four feet high. When Hank glanced down at the shotgun in his hands, and then the pistol in his waistband, and then not even knowing if the weapons would fire, he felt quite inadequate to the task at hand, which would be to kill the wolf.

The wolf walked a few feet and stopped, its fangs gleaming in the moonlight, its eyes creased in murderous hunger. It was going to attack at any moment. Hank looked over his shoulder to see if there was somewhere he might be able to run to in the hope of escaping the devil beast, but there was nothing but darkness wreathed in shadows all around. He could try to make a run for it, but if he picked the wrong way, ended up in a blind alley that had been blocked with rubble or some such thing, he would quickly find out what it felt like to be steak tartar.

Movement before him made his attention focus back on the wolf. It was moving again, a few steps at a time, but slowly it was picking up speed.

"Oh shit, this isn't gonna be good," Hank muttered as he raised the shotgun.

Like it was shot out of a cannon, the wolf suddenly went into action, charging full speed at Hank, who held off shooting, knowing he needed to wait for the last possible second. The closer the beast was the more damage the pellet blast would do to it—or so he hoped.

But despite this, the chance that the blast would be enough to stop the rampaging wolf was small, and he knew his luck had run out. This was how Hank Summers was going to die, mauled to death by a wolf in the remains of a once great city. Laurie and the others would never know what happened to him either, they would wake to see his hibernation chamber empty, find the note, but he would never return.

When the wolf was no more than ten feet away, Hank squeezed the trigger on the shotgun, knowing he only had one chance. By the time he fired and the shotgun erupted with flame and death, the wolf had already made it another four feet. The blast took the wolf in the face, but the beast managed to turn its head at the last second, the brunt of the barrage of pellets striking on only one side. Still, that eye was pulped into a soupy mess of ooze and half its face was blown off, peeled back to expose the muscle and tendons beneath.

Hank saw this in the briefest flash, one of those *'blink and you missed it'* kind of deals. Then the wolf was hitting him in the chest and he was being forced backward and to the ground. Snarling filled his world as teeth snapped at his face. Hank thrust the shotgun up and under the wolf's chin, keeping it at bay but just barely. The wolf's hind legs tried to scratch at Hank's crotch, wanting to gut him and thus take the fight out of its prey.

Hank wanted to reach down and grab the hunting knife he carried, but if he so much as lessened his grip on the shotgun with both hands, the pressure and weight of the wolf would do him in. All he could do was hold the beast at bay, and wait until his strength waned, which wouldn't be long. Fatigued already, battling a wolf three times his size wasn't high on his list of things to do today.

Suddenly, the wolf began to jump and twitch, stopping its onslaught cold. Hank could feel thuds hitting the wolf's body right through its fur, and he wondered what the hell it could be. Buried under the wolf's chest, he could see nothing of the outside world, his world now nothing but fur and blood.

It took him a full five seconds to realize that the wolf wasn't trying to kill him anymore, that it was just dead weight lying on top of him. At first he wasn't sure, but he doubted it was a trick. A wolf wasn't that smart nor would it risk being harmed by playing dead. Slowly, Hank used the shotgun to shove the wolf off him. It took all he had left, the carcass now nothing but dead weight, but he bucked his hips and managed to shift it enough so that it rolled to the side a little. Then he slid out from under it. Lying on the ground, sucking in air, amazed he was still alive, his eyes were closed as he breathed deeply.

Finally, after seconds passed, he opened his eyes to see he was surrounded by a dozen women, all in different attire, their faces hard and not at all inviting to outsiders such as Hank. One wore what looked like an old wedding dress, cut and chopped so it could be worn easier. Another wore army fatigues, another a jogging outfit, ripped and torn at the seams. The rest wore similar outfits, all modified to make them usable in a harsh environment, where running and fighting were a necessity. All were armed with crossbows, bows, and knives strapped to their bodies, some on hips and some across their chests on small slings. Most had their hair cropped close to the skull, but one or two still wore it long, though it was tied up in ponytails.

Glancing over at the carcass of the wolf, Hank saw that it had been riddled with more than a dozen arrows, which were what had killed it and had saved him.

He was about to open his mouth to tell the women thank you for saving his life, when a shadow moved out of the corner of his eye. Craning his head around so he could see up and behind him, he just had time to see the fist-sixed rock coming straight for his forehead, and the woman holding it, her face one of hatred and showing absolutely no mercy.

Then there was only darkness.

Chapter 24

Slowly, pain blazing in his head, Hank opened his eyes. At first he was disoriented and didn't understand anything he saw, then he realized he was upside down. Craning his head forward, he looked up to see that he was tied to two poles that had been made to look like an X. But what was worse, he was naked, not a stitch of clothing on his body.

When Hank squinted his eyes, his forehead felt as if something had dried there, and he didn't have to give it much thought to know it was probably dried blood—his blood when he'd been whacked with a rock.

Looking around some more, he found that he wasn't alone. There were three X's, one on each side of him, and all were occupied. But unlike Hank, the other X's only held corpses, some looking like they had been there for days if not months. They hadn't died easy by the looks of them either. What was the most terrifying thing was that each man had had his genitals cut off and then stuffed into their mouths, to then bleed out slowly. Not a very pleasant way to go, that was for damn sure.

Turning his eyes away from the macabre scene, he let his head hang down and he gazed off over the rooftop. The world was upside down, but he tried to make sense of what he was seeing. He was on a rooftop to one of the apartment buildings that still stood, in the far west corner, the X's lined up along the roof's edge. Before him was an empty, rooftop pool, the depression now used for living and cooking by the looks of it. Because the X was elevated slightly, he was able to peer down into the pool. There he saw a fire blazing, the depression of the pool allowing the flames to remain hidden from anyone on the ground who might be searching for survivors.

As he watched, three women were skinning the wolf Hank had battled. The inner organs had already been removed, and as he watched, they took the carcass and placed it on a mesh wire that was then wrapped all the way around the carcass. Next they brought it to a pile of rocks at the deepest part of the pool that smoked and glowed. Hank figured out that they were cooking the wolf like the Hawaiians would a pig, by placing it under rocks and wet leaves and allowing it to smoke for hours. Only there were no palm tree leaves in Nebraska so the wet blankets had to suffice instead of leaves.

Once the wolf was placed on the rocks, fireproof blankets soaked in water were draped over it to allow the wolf to steam. Buckets of water sat nearby to keep the blankets wet when they began to dry out.

More women were moving around, doing different chores. One woman took the inner organs of the wolf and began cutting them into smaller pieces, then dropped them into a pan of water so it could be boiled to make a stew of odds and ends. There were canned goods there, too, but the labels were either missing or so faded that what was in the cans was anyone's guess. Besides, the canned goods were over a hundred years old. It was a gamble they still were edible at all.

Watching these women go about their business, ignoring Hank, he thought that they reminded him of the fabled race of warrior women called Amazons. One of the women glanced over at him, and when she saw Hank looking around, she yelled out, getting the other women's attention.

Four women separated from the crowd and approached Hank, who could only look helplessly back at them as they surrounded him. Not knowing what to say, Hank tried to smile, but when his head began to pulse in agony, he stopped. "Who are you people and why did you capture me after saving me from that wolf?" he asked. He figured they weren't cannibals or they wouldn't be cooking the wolf, which was a small load off his mind. But then again, he had corpses on either side of him with no genitals, which didn't bode well for his future.

"You know damn well who we are, *man*," one of the women spat at him. She was beautiful, with long raven hair and tan skin. Her skimpy clothes did nothing to hide her athletic body, nor did it hide the obvious scars made from a whip.

"Ah, no, I really don't," he replied. He felt like a piece of meat as the women glared at him. But though most seemed to look at him with hatred, there were a few that let their eyes play over his body, admiring his manhood, his tone stomach, muscular thighs and arms. These women licked their lips with lust.

"Bullshit!" the raven-haired beauty yelled. She jabbed a finger at Hank. "You were sent by Baron Steele to find out where we were so you could report back to him, and he could send his guards and kill us or worse, drag us back to his brothels and whore houses to once more become sex slaves."

A few other women yelled at this, waving fists at Hank, wishing him to suffer as he hung on the X.

"No, I wasn't, I swear," Hank said, doing his best to stay calm, despite his precarious position. "I've never met the baron you speak of and in fact, I'm trying to save my two friends that some of his men captured this morning."

"You lie!" another woman screamed. "All men lie to get what they want. Well, no more. Now we're the ones who are in control. Am I right?" she said to her fellow warriors, who all cheered and screamed, hooting and hollering.

They were getting worked up into a frenzy, and Hank didn't like where this was going, not one bit. He yelled as loud as he could, "I'm trying to save my friends! Harmony and Chester. Harmony is seventeen or so with long blonde hair and Chester is a giant of a man with a thick black beard. I swear, I don't know this Baron Steele, but if I come across him and get the chance, I'm gonna put a bullet right between his eyes for what he did to me and my friends!"

The raven-haired beauty heard Hank's words and she considered them. While the others were calling for Hank's blood, she waved over another woman, then raised her hand for all to be silent. As if a switch had been pulled, all stopped chanting and yelling as their leader requested.

Hank blinked in amazement. It felt like he was on some tropical island, and had discovered a lost tribe of Amazonians who had then captured him like in a bad jungle movie.

"Brenda," the leader said to the woman she'd called over. "Today you watched the baron's men bring back prisoners, didn't you?" She knew this to be true after she'd received Brenda's report earlier that afternoon, but she now asked for the benefit of the other women.

"Yes, Sharona, I saw a small convoy returning with two prisoners."

"Then tell everyone what you told me. What did those two prisoners look like?"

Brenda gazed at each of the warrior women, who all stared at her intently. Sucking in a deep breath so she could project her voice, she said, "One was young with blonde hair, the other was a man, a giant, with a thick black beard. Both were tied up."

The other women began to talk amongst themselves. Brenda was one of them; they all believed her implicitly, and if what she said was true, then the man they now had wasn't one of the baron's men at all.

"Kill him anyway, he's still a man!" a woman screamed and a few more joined in.

Sharona raised her hand to quell them before they became too rowdy. "No, we aren't killers of the innocent, be they man, woman or even animals. We kill to survive, and only kill those who seek us harm. To do more would make us as bad as the baron and his men." She pointed to Hank. "This man isn't our enemy and is actually as much a victim as we are."

"That's true, I am so a victim," Hank said, trying his best to get them on his side. Blood filling his head was making him woozy, and he had a feeling he was going to pass out soon if he stayed in this position for much longer.

"So what do we do, Sharona?" an Amazon asked. "Do we set him free? He knows where we live; he could betray us."

"I wouldn't betray you, I swear," Hank said, getting in a few words while he had the chance. "I have no reason to. I just want to save my friends and go back to where we were before they were captured."

"You wish to save them by yourself?" another woman asked. "That would be suicide."

"Maybe, but I have to try. I don't leave friends behind, not when there's a chance to save them. What if it was me who'd been captured? I sure as hell would want to know that my friends were gonna try and save me."

"I've heard enough," Sharona said. "Cut him down, clothe him, and bring him to my tent. Once there I'll learn more about him and his friends."

A few women protested, but Sharona raised her voice, cutting them off, "Enough, I am the leader here and I've spoken. Besides, if what he says doesn't pan out in the end, despite what Brenda saw, we can always put him back up again." She sneered as she said the last part, looking right at Hank, who tried to smile again but failed miserably.

Chapter 25

Twenty minutes later, Hank found himself taken down off the X—to his ultimate joy—dressed, and placed inside Sharona's tent on the far side of the rooftop. No other Amazon lived near her, so considering the tent was on a rooftop, there was actually a modicum of privacy. No one was close enough to hear them talk, nor would anyone dare to intrude on their leader without permission.

Sharona had given strict orders not to be disturbed. She told her officers that she wanted to interrogate Hank some more, and didn't want any distractions.

Hank was leaning back on a bed of pillows, the ten-by-eight foot wide tent not large enough for tables or chairs, just pillows and blankets.

"I have to tell you something, Hank," Sharona began, sitting with her legs stretched out before her a few feet from Hank.

"What is it?" he asked.

"I was impressed with the way you stayed calm earlier. Most men would have been whimpering and begging for their lives."

Hank flashed her a sly grin. "Well, Sharona, I'd be lying if I didn't say it crossed my mind once or twice."

"I see," she said, moving so she was sitting closer to him. She poured him a cup of homemade wine and handed it to him, then poured one for herself. She sipped it first so he knew it was safe. "You know, it was fortunate that Brenda spotted your friends, or else you'd have been dead by now. We always love a good kill before a feast."

"I'm glad Brenda saw what she saw, too," he said. "Why did she see them at all?"

"Let's just say that I like to keep an eye on the comings and goings of Baron Steele." When Hank said nothing in reply, she continued. "Baron Steele believes in the old ways of slavery. Everything he has is built on the backs of others. Myself and the women with me are all escaped slaves from his whore houses and brothels. The first slave to escape was years ago, and after that woman got away, she stuck around close by, and when another managed to get free, the two joined up. Soon, others got away, too, but the chances are slim to escape alive. For every woman that escapes, fifty are hunted down and killed. Most just accept their lot in life and don't even bother fighting back. But a whore's life can be measured in months, and hardly ever a year. So to stay is a death sentence anyway. All the women in town know about us, and if they can get away safely, they know we'll find them and give them a place to live. But the baron is always trying to find our camp, and he sends out patrols. We find the patrols and kill them first, then we put them on display for all of us to see so we don't forget what we're fighting for. Sometimes he lets a woman escape and sends a tracker to follow her in the hopes of finding our camp, but once more we've always been there, and then the hunter becomes the hunted."

"So he's never found out where your camp is at any given time?" Hank asked.

She shook her head. "No, if he had, then myself and all my women would be dead." She sipped her wine. "Besides, we move around in case one of us ever gets caught and gives up our location under torture. I doubt any one ever would, not after all they've been through, but better safe than sorry, as my grandmother used to say."

They talked some more, about who Sharona was and how she'd ended up as a sex slave. Hank was prodded to tell more about himself, but each time he managed to deflect the questions back to her. He didn't want to even try to get into the whole 'slept for a hundred years' thing.

By the time they were done talking, Sharona had agreed to lead Hank to Baron Steele's encampment, to free Harmony and Chester, and perhaps kill the baron as well.

At midnight, voices called out that the wolf was ready to be eaten. Everyone, with the exception of the women on guard at the edges of the rooftop, gathered around the bottom of the pool as the wolf was taken out of its smoker and placed on a makeshift table consisting of a door and concrete blocks.

Sharona stood behind the wolf as if it was a podium, and looked on the faces of her tribe. As her stern gaze fell on each of them, the Amazons went silent, knowing their leader was going to speak.

"My friends," she said, her voice strong and full. "We've been through countless hardships, and many of us have died in the battle to survive, but despite this we still stand strong." Cheers erupted and she waited before speaking again, the power of her voice quieting the women down. "Now we stand here with a man, who is not our enemy, but is our friend. He too has suffered loss from the baron and his guards when his traveling companions were captured. He managed to escape and was on route to finding the baron when the wolf came upon him. The same wolf that has killed many of us, and though we've tried, it has always escaped us. Till now. This man stood against the wolf and fought it alone, and though it took him down, it wasn't before he wounded it gravely and in the fight, allowed us the time to finally put enough arrows into the beast to kill it. So now we stand here, about to feast on the meat of the very beast we've fought countless times, and now it's us who are the victors!" Once more cheers erupted. When it began to subside, she added, "Tomorrow I leave with this man to guide him to Baron Steele in the hopes of finding his friends. He has given me his word that if he has the chance, he will kill Baron Steele with his own hands. That's enough for me. I'll need four more warriors to come with us in case we're ambushed along the way. Do I have any volunteers?"

Without a second's hesitation, a woman stepped out, then another, then two more. Each of them was strong and beautiful, as were all the women Hank had seen thus far. Even some that had been scarred somehow, whether by the baron or from fighting in the streets of the devastated city, were still attractive. All were lean, due to their living environment, with full breasts and shapely hips. But then, they had all been used as sex slaves, and usually only beautiful women were picked for such a terrible task.

"Excellent. My four fellow sisters, I thank you for volunteering. We leave at first light tomorrow, but tonight, we feast on the meat of our fallen enemy!" she screamed, raising her fist into the air, the other Amazons doing the same. Soon, they were gathering in a line as other women who did the cooking came out and began carving up the wolf. Hank took a healthy portion as well. Sharona said he deserved it, for without his aid the wolf never would have been taken down. He had simply said thank you, not wanting to get into how the wolf had been about to gut him and that he hadn't had much of a choice in the matter.

He ate until he was so stuffed he could barely walk. With a full stomach, he found he couldn't keep his eyes open. Sharona took him to her tent and laid him down to sleep.

"You're safe here," she whispered into his ear as he drifted off to sleep, the instant his head touched the pillow it rested on. "No one would dare harm you while you're in my tent."

He heard her words as if she was far away, and truth be told, he was too exhausted to care one way or the other. Besides, if Sharona had wanted him dead, she'd had plenty of opportunities before he'd passed out in her tent.

"You see," she said while brushing Hank's hair as he slept. "Some of the women here have their own ideas on how I should lead. Every once in a while I have to beat one down to maintain my control over them." She smiled while she touched his hair, her eyes then sliding down his body. "You know, Hank, you're a handsome man, and from what I saw when you were naked, I have to admit I was impressed by your ah…stature."

Hank groaned in his sleep, then turned over so that he was facing away from her.

"Perhaps later, after you've rested a bit," she said, then she left the tent to continue the festivities. As she exited the tent, she pulled one of the Amazons close to her. "Guard my tent. No harm will come to the man inside, and it'll be your head if it does. Do I make myself clear?"

"Yes, Sharona," the guard said, and though dejected that for her the fun was over for the night, she obeyed her leader implicitly. She owed Sharona her life, for it was Sharona that had saved her when she'd escaped from Baron Steele.

Inside the tent, Hank slept the sleep of oblivion. If a bomb had gone off, devastating the already destroyed city, he wouldn't have known until he awoke the next morning. He was exhausted, both mentally and physically, and as he fell deeper into sleep, he dreamed of Harmony and Chester, of how they must be suffering, and it was all because of him.

Then Laurie appeared, wearing nothing but a gossamer gown that was see-through. Her long blonde hair was blowing in the wind, and she went to Hank, who was lying prone on a bed of silk sheets. They kissed tenderly, their lips locked in passion. Then, slowly, with a hint of a smile on her full lips, Laurie began to slide down Hank's body, kissing his neck, chest, before going lower. Her tongue caressed his flesh as she went ever lower, her hot, moist mouth pausing to tickle his belly button. He told her stop, that it tickled, then gently gave the top of her head a shove to make her go lower. His manhood was so hard he could have cut diamonds with it, and he was anxious to have her take him in her mouth, which she did a moment later. He gasped as the feeling of warm-wetness seemed to envelop his entire body. At that exact second, his entire being was focused on his manhood. Slowly, then faster, Laurie began to slide her mouth up and down, mimicking the feeling of intercourse. Hank could feel himself about to orgasm, and he grabbed her head hard and thrust himself even deeper down her throat. She didn't gag but instead accepted him fully, taking him in deep so that the tip of his penis touched the back of her throat. Then he felt himself releasing into her, and she took it all, greedily swallowing the entire emission.

Breathing heavily, Hank slowly opened his eyes inside the tent, for the moment thinking he was with Laurie, though not knowing exactly where the bed might be. There was a dull gloom in the tent, but as his eyes slowly focused, he realized where he was and that the woman sliding back up from his waist to kiss him softly wasn't Laurie but was Sharona. She licked her lips as she nuzzled his neck, her naked body warm against his also naked body. How did he become undressed? But then he'd been so exhausted when he'd fallen asleep that he probably wouldn't have known if he'd been tossed onto a horse and sent across the state on bareback, lying on his stomach the entire time.

"I…" he began, but Sharona placed a hand to his lips.

"You don't have to thank me, my love. I wanted to do it?" she whispered into his ear.

"No, it's not that," Hank said and then stopped, trying to come up with the right words to say. He didn't want to insult her, but he also didn't want to have sex with her either. He'd been asleep, he hadn't known what was happening. "I have someone waiting for me and I love her deeply. Sharona, you're beautiful and if I wasn't attached I would love to be with you, but I don't want to be unfaithful to my woman."

"How touchingly noble," she said and kissed his neck. "But I don't care who you have waiting for you. I take what I want Hank. If you're willing that's all the better, but I don't care whether you are or not. If there's one thing I've learned is to take pleasure from life when you can, for tomorrow you may be dead."

"Fitting words, but that's not how I want to live. You said you hate all men, if that's so how do you explain this?" he asked.

Suddenly, Hank felt something cold pressed to his neck, directly over his jugular. It didn't take him long, even in his drowsy state, to know she had placed a knife to his throat.

She slowly raised herself so she was on an elbow. "Hank, look at me."

Hank carefully turned his head to the side so he was eye to eye with Sharona.

"You owe me your life. Do you deny this?"

"No," he said simply, not wanting to move. Even the slightest pressure would cut his skin and the artery beneath.

"That's good, I'm glad you agree with me. To answer your question, yes we hate men, but that's not to say we still don't find some—how should I say it—value in them. Those men on the X's you saw? Many of them pleasured some of my women before being put there. Not such a bad way to go I suppose, yes? But you see, when they laid with us it was *we* who were in charge, not them. The same goes here, with us. You will fuck me, Hank, or else you won't be alive to see the sun come up. Do I make myself clear?"

"Yes," he said flatly, his jaw clenched in frustration.

"Good," she replied and slid her hand down to his manhood. She began to caress his balls and rub him again, her fingers knowing exactly what to do. In a matter of a minute he was semi-hard and quickly rising to the occasion. Not that anyone could blame him, technically it had been over a hundred years since the last time he'd had sex.

Without removing the knife from his throat in case he was lying, she slid on top of him. He could feel the hotness between her legs as she sat on his chest, then an inch at a time, she slid her butt down his body until his manhood was pressed against the crack of her ass. Skilled in the art of lovemaking, she began to slide her ass up and down, rubbing him and getting him hard once more. When she was satisfied with the results, she lifted her hips and came down on top of him. Hank gasped as he felt his member surrounded by warmth, and she squeezed him tight inside her. She was talented in how to use her internal muscles, and she quickly had Hank gasping for release a second time, but she knew how to stop him, caressing him and squeezing him until he was at the point of thinking he would explode like a grenade if he didn't get release.

She leaned over and pressed her full breasts into his face, demanding he take each nipple and suck them, lick them, love them. He did as he was told, and though he might have been forced into the act, deep down he had to admit it wasn't total torture. Sharona was an incredibly beautiful woman with a body to match, and though he would have declined her offer if given the choice, at the end before he orgasmed for the second time, he found himself lost in the moment, entirely turned on by the rapturous woman riding him in the throws of passion.

"Yes, Hank, do it now! I want to feel you come inside me!" Sharona screamed, as she relaxed her vaginal muscles and released him so that he found himself pumping his seed deep inside her. She screamed in passion and the knife dropped from her hand to fall to the pillow. She tossed back her head and with her mouth wide open, as she orgasmed as well, her entire body shaking and twitching, her eyes rolling up into the back of her head as her eyelids closed halfway. Then she fell forward onto him, and as they lay there, Hank's flaccid member slid out of her amidst his seed, which seeped out of Sharona and onto his thigh. She ignored it, basking in the afterglow of sex.

"That was incredible, Hank," she said, her voice hoarse. "Your woman is very lucky." She kissed him gently on the lips one last time, then rose, wrapped a gown around her, and left the tent. As Sharona exited, she paused and said over her shoulder, "Thank you for that. You can go to sleep now. I promise you no one else will be bothering you this night, including me. I'll wake you before dawn so you can eat and prepare to head out." Without waiting for a reply, she was gone.

Lying very still on the pillows, Hank stared at the opening in the tent Sharona had left by. "Ah well, what a man must do to help his friends and stay alive," he muttered. Missing Laurie and wishing it had been her body he'd made love to, he turned over and went back to sleep, even more exhausted than before.

This time, he didn't dream.

Chapter 26

The next morning, an hour from sunrise, with just the hint of dawn touching the sky, Hank, Sharona and four Amazons set out for the baron's encampment. All six of them were dressed in what Sharona said people in the city wore, so that once inside, they would blend in. Gone were the garb of warriors, and now the women wore capes and old, but well-maintained clothes, all taken from the men they had killed—all those foolish enough to do the baron's bidding and try to find the Amazon's camp. Hank spotted a few faded bloodstains on the shirts the women wore, as well as stitched-up tears, the stains so deep into the material that washing hadn't gotten them out; he didn't ask about them.

While they walked, Sharona explained about how years ago, Baron Steele had taken twenty square blocks and had made them his. The perimeter of the area was surrounded on all sides by a wall made of detritus. Anything from old cars to pieces of buildings had been piled twelve feet high to keep out trespassers; guards walked the perimeter, making sure the area stayed secure. But Sharona said that it was really to keep people inside, not out.

The baron had a massive stockpile of gasoline and oil, which was how he managed to keep all his men in line, for the man who owned fuel owned the world. Thanks to Steele, generators ran in select buildings, giving light and heat. He also owned a small collection of cars and motorcycles, which his men used to go out on patrol, to find more slaves to bring back to the city. Steele had adopted the Roman way of using slaves to make his city run. Everything from cleaning the outhouses to disposing of the dead fell to slaves. Without slavery, his city would have ground to a halt years ago.

There were only two classes of people living inside the walls of the city, those with wealth and those too poor to afford food each day, and who had to do anything to survive. But compared to slaves, the poor ones lived like kings, for they were still free. If caught in the act of committing a crime, more often than not it was an excuse to sentence that man or woman into slavery, so most knew not to get caught, for sometimes crime was the only way to survive, whether it was stealing a loaf of bread or siphoning a precious quart of gas from a car left alone for too long.

Then there were the women forced to become sex slaves, where the worst debauchery imaginable was done upon their persons. Most whores lasted a year if they were lucky, then they either caught a fatal disease or were killed by one of their Johns. Those few that made it for more than a year, but became too worn out to be wanted, were then tossed to the guards to play with until the time when they were finally killed.

Hank listened intently, his anger growing with each passing second. To think that Harmony was in that cesspool made him want to run ahead and save her. But he knew that was foolish. The only way to succeed would be by stealth.

Hank gripped the shotgun tighter, looking forward to using it on the first guard he came across. He wore a bandolier filled with more shells for the shotgun across his chest, and on his hip was the pistol taken from the dead marauder, as well as the hunting knife.

All his weapons had been returned to him by Sharona, who had seen to their cleaning and oiling. Then she had given him more ammunition, as well as another automatic rifle that he slung over his right shoulder by its strap. The gun had been taken from one of the men the Amazons had killed when the man had come searching for their camp. The AK-47 was worn and aged but it was still serviceable, despite a hundred years of use. Almost every part of the gun had been replaced at one time or another, and not one part of the gun resembled another, even the metal was different colors. It actually barely looked like an AK anymore, with so many parts that had been added and swapped out over the decades. Hank had tried it before leaving the Amazon camp, and despite its look, the gun did work well, and best of all, it didn't blow up in his hands the second he squeezed the trigger.

They walked for more than two hours, ending up on the north side of the city. Finally, before they rounded a burned-out husk of a brick building, Sharona raised her hand to stop Hank and her Amazons.

"We're here," she said flatly. "Around this corner is a part of the wall where there's a breach."

"And you know this how?" Hank asked.

"An escapee from a week ago. She was caught a mile from our camp but lucky for her some of my warriors were out hunting and they heard her screams for help. My women killed the four men that were following her and brought her back to our camp."

"What else is there to hunt in the wastes of this city?" Hank asked.

Sharona shrugged. "Mostly rats, snakes, birds and wild dogs. Sometimes cats as well." She looked directly at Hank, their eyes locking. "Now wait here for my signal, then you and the others follow."

Before Hank could say more, she had turned the corner and was gone. Hank peeked around the corner of the building to see Sharona dashing across the open area that had once been a street, but was now covered in dirt, rocks and debris. She made it right up to the wall without getting spotted by the guard, who was walking lazily along the perimeter, ignorant of the Amazon leader's passing. Sharona had informed Hank that the guards covered the entire wall, each one owning fifty feet. They would walk back and forth, changing up their routine, but Sharona knew from many escapees that the guards became lazy, and by this were predictable.

But Sharona wasn't waiting for the guard to reach the end of his section. She hid below the wall, letting the natural protuberances hide her lithe form, and when the man passed by where she was below him, she used a rope with a hook and threw it at him. The rope caught the man in the leg, then wrapped around twice before the sharp point on the hook sank into his leg. Before the guard could cry out in pain and sound the alarm, however, Sharona yanked on the rope as hard as she could, pulling the man off the wall. The guard found himself flying through the air, then his face came straight down on the top of the wall, crushing his nose and knocking him unconscious. Sharona dragged the body off the wall, where it tumbled to the ground to land in a limp heap. Using a large hunting knife, she slit the man's throat, then rolled him as close to the wall of debris as she possibly could. Satisfied, she began moving again. She reached a place where Hank could see her, and quickly waved to him and the other four Amazons to join her.

With Hank in the lead, one at a time they dashed across the open area, to quickly press their backs against the wall. When the last Amazon had made it safely, they followed Sharona down the length of the wall until she stopped before an old and rusted husk of a car. Only the frame remained, the inside and out gutted so bad that the car resembled the carcass of a dinosaur. At one time the interior of the husk had been stuffed with items such as old TVs, rocks, and anything else the wall builders could get their hands on. But it had all been painstakingly removed so that now there was a five foot tunnel that led into the city. Hank saw some discarded items to the side, where Sharona had taken them out. These items were stuffed inside the car normally, and though looked solid to a cursory glance, were removable.

"This way," she whispered, and was the first through the gap, followed by Hank. As he entered the cramped space, a creak sounded from above his head. He tried not to think about the countless tons of debris packed over him, and how the roof of the car was rusted and pitted from decades of acid rain. Imagining being crushed alive, or worse, trapped under tons of rubble, wasn't the way he wanted to start the day. But it only took seconds to traverse the gap, then he was standing under the open sky on the inside of the perimeter wall. Right behind him, silent as cats, came the other four Amazons.

"We need to go to the far side of the city," Sharona told Hank. "That's where they keep the slaves. We should have at least two hours before an alarm is raised when they find the dead guard upon changing shifts, that is unless he's discovered sooner by accident."

"Then let's stay hopeful no one comes around to check on him," Hank said.

Sharona nodded in reply, and waved for him and the rest to follow her once more.

The sun had risen and the city was bathed in morning light, but the guards on watch would be at the end of their graveyard shift, tired and sleepy, thinking about nothing but breakfast and a warm bed.

Clinging to what shadows remained, the rising sun banishing them for another day, the six intruders in the city crept slowly along. Ten minutes passed uneventfully, though there was a time when a man appeared, walking down a path between the rubble. He never knew that six people had weapons aimed at him, and as he scratched his ass with his right hand, sniffed, and spit, the audience was there, ready to kill him if they even suspected he had seen them. But the man continued onward, and disappeared around a corner, never knowing how close to death he was.

Soon, they reached a wide-open area that had once been a park of some kind. Off to the right, Hank could still see a few protuberances jutting out of the ground, the remnants of a Jungle Gym or the mounting brackets to a slide, the metal harvested long ago for scrap.

Sharona pointed to the far side of the park, where they needed to go to next. "We go together, I'll take the lead," she whispered.

On the count of three, they broke cover and dashed across the park, the denuded ground, a hundred years ago, once containing lush green grass. They moved like the wind, and Hank was feeling optimistic they were going to make it to the far side without being seen by anyone, when suddenly twenty men stepped out from hiding in the exact location the six warriors were heading, all with guns leveled and ready to fire.

"Shit, it's a trap!" Sharona screamed, sliding her crossbow out from under her coat and aiming it at the first man she saw. "Don't let them take you alive! Kill as many as you can!" she shrieked and fired her bow, the shaft slicing through the air to strike a man in the center of his chest. He flew backwards and fell onto the dirt, his mouth opening and closing as he struggled to deal with the agony of dying.

Hank looked around for cover but saw none. They were in a Deadman's Zone, nothing on either side for fifty feet but tiny pieces of rubble that wouldn't protect his head. On closer examination, he spotted marks on the ground where larger debris had once been, but now had been removed, leaving behind the outline of the debris. The trap had been sprung, with the targets having nowhere to seek cover, nowhere to hide.

"Don't kill the lead woman and the man, the baron wants them alive!" someone yelled out along the enemy lines.

So Baron Steele wanted Hank and Sharona alive. That was good for them but not for the other four Amazons. "Sharona, fall back to the others, we need to protect them!" Hank yelled.

But Sharona heard nothing but the blood boiling in her ears. She had been caught in a trap and the guards of the baron were right before her. She fired again at the guards, shooting another man in the thigh, then she rolled to the side, reloaded, and was up firing again.

Hank unslung the AK, leveled it, and sent a burst at the men, making them duck for cover. The shotgun was useless at such a long distance and he was glad to have the AK.

Someone grunted from behind him. Hank glanced over his shoulder to see one of the Amazons down on the ground, a spreading red spot on her shirt right between her breasts. Then to his left another Amazon went down. Seeing her mate go down, the third Amazon went to her friend, only to be gunned down a second later.

"Shit, we're dropping like flies!" Hank yelled and sprayed another tri-burst at the men. But the guards were under cover now, and after appearing to show their strength, had quickly darted behind objects placed there for just that reason. Old cars, a pitted jersey barrier, and steel girders placed one atop the other, were some of the items used for cover. Hank had to admit the kill zone the men had set up was damn good. The only reason he and Sharona were still standing was because someone over there didn't want them dead.

The fourth Amazon was shot down, taking a bullet to the throat. Hank went to her and crouched down, cradling the woman in his arms. Blood spurted from the wound each time her fading heart beat, and Hank could see there was no way to staunch the flow. Even if a medic had been nearby and this had been a Twentieth century war, the odds the woman could have been saved would have been one in a million. Hank could only hold her as the light went out of her eyes. He closed her eyelids and stood up, sending another spray of gunfire at the enemy, though not really caring where the bullets went.

The gun shots suddenly ceased and Hank and Sharona stopped firing as well, so that silence reigned over the kill zone.

"Drop you guns and surrender!" a man's voice called out.

"And if we don't?" Hank replied.

"You see that tin can by your feet?" the man asked. Hank glanced down to see the crushed and flatten soda container of a hundred years ago. Hank nodded, knowing the man could see him. No doubt there were either binoculars trained on him or some kind of a sniper's rifle.

A single gunshot sounded, and an instant later a bullet landed no more than an inch from Hank's left boot, exactly where the can was. A neat hole was left in the can after the bullet's passing.

"Does that answer your question?" the man called.

Hank grinned. "Yeah, I guess it does." He leaned closer to the Amazon leader and said in a low voice, "Drop your weapons, Sharona, they got us cold."

Sharona turned to face Hank. "Are you mad? Do you know what they'll do to me if they take me alive?"

"I have an idea, but as long as there's breath, there's hope. You can't do a damn thing if you're dead."

Another gunshot sounded. The bullet struck directly between the two warriors, kicking up some dirt when it hit the ground.

"Last warning!" the man called. "Put down your weapons or we take you down the hard way. We don't have to kill you, you know. A couple of arm and leg shots would do the job just as nicely."

"He makes a good point, Sharona," Hank said. "They don't have to kill us to capture us. They can wound us so we can't fight back. Don't be foolish, we need to surrender."

Sharona's face was set tight, her jaw clenched, as she looked down at her four fallen Amazons. After ten seconds that seemed to last an hour, she raised her gaze and locked eyes with Hank. "You can do what you want, *man*, but I'll die before I let them capture me."

Spinning on her heels, she darted off to the side, weaving back and forth as gunshots began to sound. Hank could only watch as Sharona raced for freedom. Bullets churned up the dirt at her feet, but she managed to avoid being shot. She was almost to the end of the park when a bullet caught her in the left shoulder. It sent her flying forward to land face first on the ground. Hank stared at her still form, not knowing if she was alive or dead.

The bullets stopped as well, the guards waiting and watching. Tense heartbeats ticked by—a minute, then two minutes. Finally, the man that had spoken to Hank sent out three guards to retrieve Sharona's body, but as the men set out, Sharona suddenly jumped to her knees, then her feet, dashing once more for the end of the park and freedom. As she ran, she held her left shoulder with her right hand, blood spurting between her fingers. Another volley of gunshots sounded, but Sharona reached the edge of the park and a pile of rubble just as the bullets would have reached her. Darting around the rubble, the bullets only clipped the corner of the pile, sending rock and pieces of concrete off in all directions.

Hank was glad to see Sharona make her escape. It was bad enough that four Amazons had already given their lives in his foolhardy attempt to free Harmony and Chester; it wasn't fair if Sharona died, too.

Upon seeing she was gone, the three guards on their way to Sharona changed direction and ran over to Hank. Once they reached him, Hank relinquished his weapons and was taken into custody. His hands were bound with metal straps, so there was no way to cut them even if he was lucky enough to get the chance. Once more he was a prisoner of Baron Steele, only this time there was no exploding motorcycle to give him a chance to escape. This time they truly had him.

With a rough shove in the back with the butt of a rifle that almost sent him sprawling in the dirt, he was forced to walk, the guards surrounding him on all sides. One wrong move and he would be shot, and like they said, not all gunshots had to be killing ones.

"So much for my heroic rescue attempt," he muttered while thinking of Harmony and Chester.

Chapter 27

The black cloth bag that had been placed over Hank's face was removed, bright white light blinding him for a few seconds. The guard that had removed the bag walked out into the hallway after taking it off. Hank struggled to focus his eyes, to see where he was, but his vision wouldn't cooperate. He tried to raise his hands but they were secured to the table or gurney or whatever the hell he'd been put on. His feet were also tied down, as well as his torso, so that he couldn't move at all.

Time was hard to keep track of, but if he had to guess, he would say almost three hours had passed since he'd been captured. Then he'd been shuffled around the city, taken from one place to another for God knows why. The entire time his head was covered, so that he had no idea where he was in the city, or even if he'd gone anywhere at all. For all he knew, he'd been taken around the block a few times, as the cloth over his face made his movement impossible to fathom. He'd been interrogated multiple times, men yelling at him, demanding that he give up the location of the Amazon's camp, but he refused to answer. He made up a story that the women had captured him and forced him into the city, but the interrogators knew Hank was full of shit and told him so. Other than a few punches to the face and gut, they didn't get very rough. Hank found this odd, but he wasn't complaining.

When his vision finally cleared, he saw that the reason he wasn't tortured before was because they had a special place for that, the place it seemed Hank had ended up. His eyes darted every which way at once, trying to take in the horror house he now found himself in. He tried to crane his neck forward, but he was strapped down so tightly it hurt to move his head. Still, he tried, wanting to get as much information as to where he was as possible. He was naked again, and he wondered why everyone thought it was amusing to have him that way.

The large room was Spartan, nothing but naked walls on all sides. The walls had once been painted brown, but now they were covered in dried splatter of what had to be blood and other body fluids, all splashed there when past prisoners had been tortured. On the far wall was a rack of tools, each one more horrifying to look at when under the assumption that they were used to do harm to the human body. Some weren't even torture implements, but simple construction tools, but used in the wrong hands, or in this case, 'skillful' hands, these work tools could be even worse than the actual torture implements made for the job of causing human suffering. There was so much to see; too much if Hank had a say in it. Spread out across the room, were other, larger, torture devices. Each one had an occupant.

To Hank's left stood a naked man with just his head stuffed into a metal box. On the outside of the box, steel spikes were visible, and each day the spikes were hammered in a fraction of an inch. Eventually, the spikes would impale the man's brain from all sides, killing him. Hank could see the man was still alive, the chest rising and falling slowly. His upper body was covered in sticky blood from where it dripped out of the right corner of the box. A pool of urine was at his feet and a dark brown sludge ran down his inner thighs. Blood was there as well

On Hank's right was another man, this one with his body inside a coffin-like box, but with the head poking out the top. What was inside the iron maiden were more spikes, and by the way the man stared off at nothing, told Hank he'd been there for a while. Blood pooled on the floor after seeping out of the box.

The worst of the lot was a nude man hanging over a plastic barrel. The barrel was full of acid, and each day the man was lowered an inch. From the first day, when his toes had gone in, the acid had eaten away at his body, until now, the man was gone from the belly button down. The worst part of it all was that the acid cauterized the wounds it made each time the man was dipped lower, so that though missing his lower half, he was still alive, if just barely. He had no stomach but then he wasn't going to be eating anytime soon. His face was curled into a rictus of death, the man pretty much insane from the constant pain. Hank saw the poor bastard's eyes and all he saw was madness therein.

Another man chained to the wall was devoid of skin, the skinning knife used off to the side, set there for when the torturer returned. The man hung by his arms, looking either dead or unconscious. Then he twitched and Hank realized the poor sap was still alive. With his nerve endings exposed to the open air, it must have been a living hell every second that passed.

The last torture device was a simple wooden table. The 'rack,' where the hands and feet were tied to a spool, and a crank at the end of the rack by the poor bastard's feet, pulled his limbs apart slowly, stretching the muscle and tendons. The pain was beyond description, and if the crank was turned enough revolutions, eventually the man would be drawn and quartered. This man was naked as well.

"Jesus Christ, nice place you boys have," Hank said as he looked out at the other suffering men. "Any of you guys still alive?"

"I'm still here," the man with only his head sticking out of the iron maiden said. "But I wish I was dead. The pain, it's so much, throbbing, pulsing. I want to die. The spikes are everywhere, impaling me from chest to toe. I'm pretty sure some of my organs have been punctured." He began to cry. "You'll wish you were dead too soon enough."

"Me too," came the muffled voice of the man with his head in the metal box. "The spikes are in my eyes, my cheeks. I'm blind.

The next time they hammer the spikes in deeper I think one's going into my right ear. There's one in my left already so I can't hear you too good. I'm deaf in that ear, though for some reason there's a ringing that won't go away."

"The guy hanging over the plastic barrel. Why isn't he dead yet?" Hank asked. "And what the hell did he do to deserve that?"

The man in the iron maiden glanced at the hanging half-man and he actually smiled, though it was barely seen and more of a grimace. "Him? Oh, it don't matter what he did. The baron might put someone in here for stealing bread or for reneging on a bet. See, he likes to see people tortured; the sick fuck gets off on it. I heard stories that he has his whores whip him, candle wax on his dick, the whole thing. He's a sick bastard the baron is." The man locked his gaze on Hank, lying prone on the table. "What about you, new guy? Why are you here? Never seen you before in town."

"That's 'cause I'm not from town," Hank said. "The baron's men caught me after me and the women I was with killed a bunch of their men. They want to know the location of the camp of women that took me in, but I won't tell them. So I ended up here I guess."

All the men that were able began making sounds of pity to Hank. Which given their present predicaments didn't bode well for Hank's future. If these guys felt bad for him, just what the hell was the baron going to do to him?

"Shit guy, I feel sorry for you.

"You poor fuck, it's gonna be nasty," another said.

"Glad I'm not you," the man on the rack added, as he was now awake.

Footsteps sounded down the hall and all eyes became downcast, as if there was something interesting on the floor. The men went silent as well. A few seconds later, two men entered the room. One was the guard, but the other was a lanky fellow with dark black hair and tattoos covering every inch of his exposed body and face, with piercings anywhere someone could think to put them. He wore a business suit a hundred years out of date, but the suit had been modified. It had no sleeves and he only wore the jacket, no shirt. On his exposed skin, his torso was nothing but black ink in a thousand different pictures such as skulls, naked women and words scrawled across his flesh. He resembled a rock star of old, only with a much meaner face. The man stopped right before Hank's table, at his feet, so that Hank had to crane his neck upwards to see the man.

"Nice outfit," Hank said sarcastically. "You gotta give me the number of your tailor."

Baron Steele grinned at Hank's remark, but it wasn't because he was amused, it was because he knew he held all the cards. "I heard you're a funny guy," he said. "Go 'head, make your jokes, maybe even have a few laughs, 'cause soon you're gonna be screamin'."

"We'll see about that," Hank replied. "I have a high tolerance for pain. After all, I've seen your get up and I'm still not laughing."

"Enjoy it while you can, asshole. We'll see who laughs last. You know, you can save yourself some heartache and just tell me where the whores' camp is."

"Why? Because when I do you'll set me free with a pat on the back and a hearty thank you?" Hank scoffed. "Please, we both know the only reason I'm still alive and not in a slave camp is because you need information from me."

"Yeah, that's mostly true, but I'm not worried. Sooner or later you'll talk. They always do." He glanced around at the other suffering souls. "Am I right, fellas?" No one replied. "I said, am I right, fellas?" This time there were some grunts of ascent from the others. Baron Steele walked over to the hanging man, careful not to get too close to the acid. "Hey, asshole, I asked you a question," he hissed, while gazing up at the face of the dying man.

Hank watched as well. Slowly, as if the effort was the hardest thing the guy had ever done, the half-man opened his eyes. The orbs were glassy, unseeing, and Hank wondered if the man saw what everyone else did. Like a mechanical part in desperate need of oil, he moved his head up and down, agreeing with the baron.

"Good, that's what I thought," Baron Steele said. Turning, he walked over to Hank again, but as he did he picked up two small wooden boxes from a side table. The boxes were about a foot long and six inches wide, with straps and a belt buckle on each one. Hank couldn't figure out what the hell they were for. They reminded him of wooden shoeboxes actually.

"My men did ask nicely before they brought you here, to my playroom, but you refused to talk," Baron Steele said as he opened the boxes and placed them onto Hank's feet. "So now you get to feel some pain."

"Oh really? What're you gonna do? Give me a pedicure?" Then his joking stopped and his eyes widened as the boxes were fitted on his feet. As the boxes were closed and the straps engaged, the first hole in the buckle was used. Suddenly, Hank felt pressure on the soles of his feet, and what felt like a hundred sharp needle points pressing into his tender flesh. He was amazed by how much it hurt, especially because the needles hadn't actually penetrated his skin but were only pushing against the first layer of skin. But a quarter ounce of pressure would be all that was needed to sink the tips of the sharp needles into his feet. He didn't want to think about that, not one bit.

"Ah, I can see you're already enjoying my little box of pain, huh?" Baron Steele said as he walked up so that Hank only had to turn his head slightly to see the man. "Tell me, Hank," —he'd learned Hank's name during the interrogations, though that was about all Hank had given his questioners. "Did you know that the feet have the most nerve endings in the entire body? Yes, it's true, I learned about it in an old book scavenged from the rubble of a building about five miles from here." He moved back down to Hank's feet. "But maybe you don't believe me. Here, let me prove it to you." He reached out for the left foot, undid the strap, then cinched it to the next hole in it, buckling it once more. As Hank gasped in agony, the baron went to the other foot and did the same. When he looked back at Hank's face, he saw exactly what he expected: a man in great pain. But he was impressed that Hank hadn't let out a scream yet.

Even when using only one hole in the strap, most men were howling in pain and begging to tell the baron anything he wanted to know, or would just make something up, just please stop the pain.

Hank was in a world where only pain existed. Though the needles had barely penetrated the soles of his feet, they had broken the skin, and it felt like his feet had been dipped in acid or were roasting over an open fire. It was all he could do not to scream, and he feared he was about to pass out. He tried to arch his back from the agony but couldn't and fought to stay sane. Maybe that would be a good thing. The sweet vastness of oblivion, a nothingness where pain didn't exist.

"How's that feel, tough guy?" Baron Steele asked with an evil grin of a cold-hearted killer. "Doesn't tickle, does it."

Hank had no quip this time; his teeth were grinding together as he fought to keep his screams in his head. He knew it would only give the jerk satisfaction, and he'd be damned if he would do that.

"Huh, don't have a wiseass crack to toss at me now, do ya, asshole," the baron laughed. He moved so that he was by Hank's head again, and leaned over so that their faces were only inches apart. Hank could smell the odor of onions and bad meat on the baron's breath, the foul scent so strong it burst through his pain.

"Jesus, pal, use a Tic-Tac, will ya?" Hank gasped through gritted teeth. "Your breath stinks like road kill."

The baron ignored Hank's jibe and said, "The best thing is the deeper I put in the needles, the more it'll hurt. We can go at it for days, hell, even weeks, as long as I keep you fed and hydrated." His face disappeared and a second later Hank felt the needles go in some more, one foot then the other. In actuality, the needles were barely in a quarter of an inch, but to Hank it felt like they were in so deep they were going to come out the tops of his feet. "So you think on that shit for a while, tough guy. I'll come back tomorrow and we can have another talk about where the sluts' camp is. Till then, let's see if you can get a good night's sleep." He turned to go but before he did, he gestured to the guard while speaking to the entire room. "And I haven't forgotten about the rest of you assholes," he said to the suffering men. "Have them dipped and hammered some more as well," he told the guard.

With a flurry of the tail of his suit jacket, he strolled out of the large room, much like a rocker leaving the stage of a sold-out concert.

The guard got to work, first dipping the half man into the acid half an inch, then going to the others and banging spikes into heads and bodies, then skinning the man in the corner some more, and finally finishing up by cinching the wheel on the rack a quarter turn to stretch the victim's limbs some more.

Screams filled the entire room, but Hank didn't hear any of it.

He was dealing with his own shit at the moment.

Chapter 28

Hours later, Hank thought he'd fallen into one of the seven layers of Hell. His feet were the only thing he could focus on, and though he still hadn't screamed, thick tears ran down the sides of his face to pool under his head. He was in utter agony, and though at first his iron will to remain silent was firm, with each passing second he began to doubt himself. How much can a man take, how much pain, before he gives up? No man could go on indefinitely. When all you have is your inner suffering, eventually everyone gives in, whether that's a day, a week, or even five years later, but sooner or later, you simply wanted the pain to end, and how you make that happen was irrelevant.

Some of the other prisoners were moaning softly, their wails and pleadings to be killed adding to Hank's own misery. If this wasn't Hell, then he didn't know what was.

The solid-wood door to the room was suddenly thrown open and in walked the guard, a playful gleam in his eyes. "It's time for some fun, fuckers," he said through a mouthful of yellow teeth. "Time to bring some pain into your miserable lives."

One at a time, the guard began making his rounds; a slice here, a crack there, a turn of a wheel over there, until the wails and moans had been reinvigorated.

Then it was Hank's turn. The guard walked over to Hank and leaned down over him. Hank fought to keep a straight face, though he could do nothing about the tears or the pool of them under his head. But he still locked gazes with the man, remaining as defiant as humanly possible.

"What about you, huh?" the guard asked Hank. "You ready to talk yet?"

Though his voice was a little shaky, Hank managed to level it out as he said, "I'll make you a deal, asshole, I'll talk when you take a goddamn shower, which by the looks it will be never."

"Oh, a tough guy, huh? Well, we'll see about that." The man went to Hank's feet and tightened the box one notch on each belt. Hank's mouth fell open as unbearable agony flooded his mind. He wanted to open his mouth as wide as it would go and scream to the heavens, to bellow out how much he was hurting, but instead he clenched his jaw and smiled, and through gritted teeth said, "It tickles."

The guard barked a short laugh, knowing Hank was full of shit. He returned to standing beside Hank's head, then leaned forward so that he was only an inch from Hank's face. Though in utter agony, Hank could smell the foul odor of the guard's body. The man hadn't bathed in a month, if not longer, and he was as rank as a human being could get.

"Soon you'll be begging to suck my cock if for only a minute of me taking the pain away," the guard said. "I can, too, I can loosen the straps at any time. But not yet, you still got some fight in you. I'm gonna make you suffer some more, then when I put my cock in your mouth, you're gonna gobble it up like it was the best thing you've ever had."

Until the instant he did it, the idea hadn't come to Hank, but as the guard taunted him, his nose bobbing only inches from Hank's face, the urge to tear off that nose flooded his mind. Before the guard realized what had happened, Hank craned his neck as far as it would go, lifting his head up. He only managed to raise his head a few inches, but that was all the space he needed to reach the man's nose. Teeth open wide, Hank clamped down on the tip of the guard's nose, and like a dog working at a tasty bone, he snapped his head to the left and the right, tearing the tip clean off the man's face. As Hank let his head fall back to the table, he spit the nose off to the side. It flew five feet through the air before landing on the floor, rolling another foot and remaining still. It wasn't there for more than a second before a juicy rat darted out of a hole in the wall, scooped up the tasty morsel in its mouth, and scampered back into the hole to enjoy its nighttime snack.

As the guard lurched backwards, screaming, his hands going to his face, Hank laid back with a satisfied smile. The smile was coated in blood, red covering his white teeth, and he spit out the foul taste of blood, the iron and copper flavor making him want to retch.

Though the act might get him killed just a little faster, Hank didn't care. He felt good, felt happy, despite his throbbing feet. All around him, the other victims laughed and hooted, making fun of the guard. The man with the box of spikes on his head was calling out, wanting someone to tell him what had happened. Even acid guy was smiling, though it looked more like a grimace.

"Shut the fuck up, all of you!" the guard yelled, touching his nose tentatively. The blood had already slowed and he saw that he still had a nose as he inspected his face; only the tip was missing. Shit, for a moment there he thought Hank had torn off the whole goddamn thing.

The victims refused to stop laughing, and Hank saw that a lot of it was really forced, that the last thing the men wanted to do was laugh. But still, they did their best to act jovial, like they weren't all slowly dying, and instead were all sitting around a table at the local bar having a drink together.

"You fuckers are gonna pay for this; especially you!" the guard shrieked, his finger pointing at Hank accusingly.

Hank made a face that said, *Who, me?* and the guard only became more enraged.

"As soon as I get cleaned up I'm coming back. Then you're all gonna see what pain is." With the men laughing and taunting him some more, the guard left the room to wash his face and get his nose bandaged.

No sooner did the man leave than the laughter stopped, like a switch had been pulled.

"You know," the man in the iron maiden said to Hank, "He really can make you suffer more. I'm sorry to say that when he comes back you're going to regret that act of defiance."

Hank tried to shrug but couldn't, so he said, "Maybe, but for the rest of that guy's life, whenever he sees his reflection, he's gonna think of me."

"Well, keep that in mind when he's torturing you even more," the man scoffed.

The room fell into silence after that, with exception of the occasional moan or someone pleading to be killed, to let their misery end. Hank lay with his eyes closed, feeling the blood dry and crust on his mouth and chin. In many ways it was more of an annoyance than his throbbing feet, like when a person had to scratch but for some reason could not. Deep down, he had to admit he wasn't looking forward to the guard's eventual return, and now that he had time to reflect, perhaps biting off the guy's nose wasn't the best idea in the world. But he had to admit, it had felt damn good when he'd done it.

The room was wreathed in shadows by the time the guard returned, which had to have been a few hours by Hank's guess. It was hard for him to keep track of time when all he had were the moans of his fellow victims and his own internal suffering.

A gasp by the man in the iron maiden—who faced the door by coincidence—caused Hank to turn his head to see what the man had seen.

The guard had returned, his body mostly hidden in the gloom of the room. A bandage was on his nose, the white of it sticking out amongst the shadows, and in his right hand he held a whip with a nasty-looking barbed tip on the end. When that sucker hit flesh, the pain would be excruciating.

"Now we'll see who's laughing," the guard growled, but before he took a step into the room, he suddenly went stiff, his back arching so that his posture was perfect. It seemed off because he'd always walked slumped over slightly, his shoulders drooping, but now his shoulders were perfectly upright, his back so perfect a ruler could have been pressed to it with no space between ruler and man.

The seconds ticked by and the guard didn't move, which seemed odd. Finally, Hank said, "So get on with it then, you asshole, what are you waiting for?"

The guard didn't reply. Hank was about to send another taunt his way when the guard slumped forward to the floor, like he'd gone to sleep.

"What the hell?" Hank said, not understanding what was happening.

But then it all became clear when a woman entered the room, stepping over the fallen man. In her right hand she held the knife she'd used to stab the guard in the back, the blade sliding into his heart. Blood dripped from the knife to splatter onto the floor.

"How come every time I see you you're naked," Sharona said as she stepped over to Hank, a wry smile on her full lips. She wore the garbs of a street whore, right down to the garish makeup. Her raven hair was gone, cut close to the scalp. Hank had to admit that in her getup, he barely recognized her as the woman he'd first met as the leader of the Amazons.

"Guess you're just lucky," Hank replied. "But do me a favor and take those goddamn boxes off my feet right now, will you?"

"Of course, my love," she said with a grin and went to his feet. Hank held back the scream as the boxes were jiggled. "Careful, damn it, there's needles inside jabbed into the bottom of my feet."

She nodded. "I've heard of this place but never seen it until now. How horrible it all is."

"So sorry if we've offended you, lady," the man in the iron maiden said. "We'll try to die less horribly for you."

"No, you don't understand," she said. "That's not what I meant at all."

"Forget him, Sharona," Hank said. "He's just cranky 'cause he has spikes running up his ass."

Sharona blinked at that, taking in the coffin-like box with a new perspective. "I'm sorry to hear that. Though most men are foul beasts, I know that not all are."

"God, that feels better," Hank said as Sharona took off the second box. Sitting up, he crossed one foot over his knee sideways so he could inspect the bottom of his foot. He was amazed to see only tiny red pinpricks, and only a few showed any signs of bleeding. The damn needles had barely penetrated his skin, but to him it had felt like inches had been shoved deep into his feet. It went to show how when you couldn't see the pain bringer, how an imagination can run wild.

"Can you walk?" Sharona asked.

"Yeah, I think so, just give me a second."

"We don't have a second," she replied. "Hank, I had to kill three more men getting up to this room. I hid the bodies but eventually someone's going to find out they're missing, even at this late time of night."

"What time is it anyway?" he asked as he slid off the table, and with her help and by holding the table, managed to stand upright. It hurt like hell, but the longer he stood, the better it felt.

"It's almost morning. If we escape while it's still dark we'll have a better chance of it."

She spotted a shelf at the far side of the room, filled with clothes and other items taken from former victims. Hank's clothes were there as well. She grabbed them and quickly walked back to him, handing the clothes over, as well as a pair of boots she thought would fit him.

"Thanks," he said and quickly dressed. There were no socks, and sliding his wounded feet into a pair of boots that weren't his own wasn't a good feeling, but he gritted his teeth and made due. It hurt to walk but he could tell almost immediately that given time he'd be back to normal. Though he wouldn't be doing any sprints anytime soon, he could get around well enough.

"Good, now that you're dressed, let's get out of here," she said hastily.

"Wait," the man in the iron maiden said. "You have to kill us all before you go."

"What?" Hank said in shock.

"You heard me," the man said. "We're all dying here, there's no hope for us. But you can give us sweet release and at the same time thwart Baron Steele from getting his satisfaction from us."

"That's true," the man with his head in a box said, though the voice was muffled. He knew Hank was free by what he'd heard. "I'm blind and deaf in one ear. What kind of life can I have? Kill me, kill us all!"

"Kill us all!" the rest began to chant. Even acid guy began to say it, as did rack guy and skinned guy. "Kill us, kill us! Kill us all! Please!"

"They have a point, Hank," Sharona agreed. "They're already dead, but they just haven't stopped breathing yet. It would be a mercy to end their suffering."

Hank sighed, his eyes going to each man. All made eye contact—except head in the box guy. He couldn't obviously. Thinking back to how he'd been tortured and seeing the dire straits the men were in, he had to agree that the prisoners were right. Still, he didn't like what he was about to do.

"Give me your knife," he told Sharona, who handed it over without a word. "You sure about this?" Hank asked as he stepped into the center of the room. "I could set you all free and from there…" He trailed off, knowing what he said was foolish.

"Just do it already," the man in the iron maiden said. "Let me have peace finally." He was crying, though whether it was because he was about to die or because he was *happy* he was about to die was unknown, and Hank wasn't going to ask.

Hank looked at the mockery of human life surrounding him one more time, and then with smooth steps, he crossed the few feet separating him from the man in the iron maiden, and before the man could tell him thank you, Hank slid the knife across his throat, making sure to go deep enough so that there would be no way he could survive.

Blood geysered from the wound as the man's eyes rolled back into his head. He would be dead in seconds. Hank was already moving, however, and reached the man lying prone on the rack. With one smooth plunge of the knife, he stabbed the man in the heart. He was dead before Hank pulled the knife out. Then it was on to the man with his head in a box. He too got a knife to the heart to end his suffering fast. The skinned man was standing tall when Hank reached him, using whatever was left of his energy reserves to go down like a man. He pushed his chest forward so that Hank had an easy shot at his heart, and a second later was hanging from his shackles, dead.

Last was acid man. Hank couldn't reach him so he had to get a chair and stand on it.

Acid guy was weeping softly, saying a prayer to God. "I'm ready, do it before I change my mind," he said in a whisper.

Hank reached up and slit the man's throat, then had to jump back and off the chair as the blood splattered into the acid to make it pop and hiss. Hank didn't want to get any of the stuff on him.

Upon Hank going back to join Sharona, she nodded. "Now they're at peace. That's really all you could do for them."

"Yeah, I guess so, but though they were mercy killings, it still feels like murder."

"Well, it's not." She grabbed his arm and pulled him along. "Now we must go. We've been lucky so far but that luck is going to run out soon. I know where your two friends are being kept. I made sure to find them before coming here."

Hank's eyes lit up with relief. At last, some good news. He leaned over and kissed her and she took the kiss, sliding her tongue into his mouth, her passion rising with each touch of their lips. He hadn't planned on giving or getting such a passionate kiss, but he went with it, not wanting to upset her. Soon he would be leaving to return to the redoubt, if all went well, and he hoped it wouldn't be an issue. As independent as Sharona was, she was still a woman, and women had trouble sometimes letting go or became too attached despite knowing it was a 'no strings attached' relationship. But one thing at a time; first they needed to escape the city.

With Sharona leading the way, they left the room, crept down the hallway, and were soon outside, where they quickly blended into the night, while back in the torture chamber, only the drip, drip of spilled blood echoed in the room.

Chapter 29

Hank blinked as he stepped outside, seeing it was early evening. Time had held no meaning within the torture chamber, and he'd been inside, being tortured, for a full day and most of the night.

As soon as Hank and Sharona exited the building, they began running down the street, Hank gritting his teeth as he did, due to his aching feet.. While they ran, Sharona explained how she'd found out where Harmony and Chester were being kept.

Harmony was in a whore house on the west side of town. The name of the place was the Gold Rush, and it was here that Harmony would spend the rest of her life, however long or short it ended up to be.

Chester was in the slave quarters, locked in a first floor room of a corner apartment building, in what was once called Arnold Heights before the bombs fell. Though all the windows were barred, Chester was so strong he could probably just batter his way out through one of the exterior walls, but with no one to instruct him, he was obeying the guards in charge of the slaves.

No more than ten minutes after leaving the torture chamber, a loud church bell began to ring out, carrying to all parts of the city. Minutes after the bell began to sound, groups of the baron's men started moving through the city in the hunt for the escaped prisoner—namely Hank, as no one knew about Sharona. The bodies Sharona hid had been found, and now Baron Steele was aware that Hank had escaped, too, but he also knew that Hank was still in the city—somewhere.

So even though it was night, the city was as busy as ever, and Hank and Sharona found themselves constantly having to hide or risk discovery from search parties.

"I haven't had a chance to ask you yet," Hank said as he and Sharona stood in an alley, waiting for a group of armed men to pass. "Why did you come back for me, anyway?"

She shrugged. "The way we came in was blocked off again so there was no way for me to get out of the city. See, anyone coming or going has to go through the main gate, where they're given the once-over. So I figured I had a better chance of getting away if I had you with me."

He grinned. "And here I thought you were falling in love with me."

She was standing in front of him, and now she turned to the side so she could look right at him. "Oh, please, don't think you were that good, Hank. You were a distraction last night, nothing more."

He had to admit that his ego got deflated some after hearing her reason for saving him. Still, he could deal with it. "Well, thanks anyway for coming for me, whatever your true reason was."

"Okay, it's clear, let's go," she said and they began moving once more.

But no sooner did they begin walking than a complement of Baron Steele's men came marching down the street. Hank and Sharona ducked into an alcove to a building and pressed tight against the wall, the shadows hiding them from view.

"We can't keep this up all night," he said. "There's too many damn people in this city looking for me—us—that we need to hide from."

"What do you suggest?" she asked.

"We need a distraction, something that'll keep not only the baron's men busy, but everyone else as well. That way no one'll notice us in the chaos."

"I'm all for causing some mayhem, Hank, but what can we do? We don't have any weapons other than the knife I had on me," she said. "I had to get rid of my crossbow. Carrying that in the city would be like a target on my back to Baron Steele's men."

An ATV drove by along with three men running beside it, and that gave Hank an idea. "Sharona, the baron has lots of vehicles, am I right?"

"Yes. Why?"

"Because those bikes and trikes need fuel to run. I suspect Steele has a place he parks all his vehicles, and to make things easy he has to keep his gas reserves close by."

Sharona instantly knew what he was getting at. "You want to blow up his fuel storage?"

"Sure. We can set that giant bomb off with nothing but a match, and the entire city will have to deal with the inferno. Then in the craziness we can get to Harmony and Chester, take out whoever's there with them to free 'em, and then get the hell out of Dodge."

She looked confused. "I don't understand. Where's this Dodge you speak of?"

"Never mind," he said with a wave of his hand. "It's a saying before your time."

"Then how do you know it?" she asked, prodding.

He ignored her question and pointed to the empty street. "Come on, it's clear now' let's get moving to the motor pool."

"The what?" she asked.

"The place he parks his cars and motorcycles."

"Why didn't you say that in the first place?"

"I did." He grunted in frustration. "Look, can we please focus on the task at hand, namely staying alive?"

"I'm not the one who keeps talking in a strange way," she said.

He sighed but didn't respond to her, hoping that would end it. This time with Hank in the lead, they stepped out into the street, making their way down the sidewalk and close to the buildings, so that if anyone went by they could hopefully find a place to conceal themselves within the shadows.

With Sharona giving directions, they soon arrived at the perimeter fence of the motor pool and fuel dump. They had needed to hide a few more times as they made their way to the place, but each time they'd remained undiscovered. Knowing he'd need a way to ignite the gas, Hank had seen a lone man walking down one of the streets, a homemade, lit cigarette hanging from his mouth. Hank had jumped the man and dragged him into an alley where Sharona was waiting. After knocking the man unconscious, Hank searched the guy's pockets and was pleased when he found an old and battered Zippo lighter with the faded Marine's emblem etched on one side.

"Someone should have told him that smoking is bad for his health," Hank had joked upon finding the lighter. Unknown to Hank, the old relic of a bygone day was worth more than gold and had been the man's prize possession.

"Why would it be bad for his health?" Sharona asked, confused.

"Oh, never mind. Forget I said anything," Hank said, exasperated.

The perimeter fence was six feet high, chainlink, and topped with barbed wire. There was debris everywhere, just like in the rest of the city, so Hank found a tarp that had more holes than material, but still would be serviceable for the use he planned for it.

With Sharona keeping watch, Hank tossed the tarp over the barbed wire, then climbed over the fence himself. His feet gave him some trouble and he winced, but he was no stranger to pain, and if anything it kept his head clear. It was hard to believe that just that morning he'd been with Sharona at their camp, and now here he was, about to blow up a fuel dump, the bottom of his feet feeling like pin cushions.

"I'll be right back," Hank said in hushed tone to Sharona, their eyes locking through the links in the fence.

"I should come with you."

"No, I won't be long. This'll be easy." He turned and was off, hobbling on his aching feet. He reached a one-story building and slid along the wall until he'd reached the corner, and after peering around the edge, he saw it was clear and took off running. It was more of a half-jog thanks to his sore feet, but it got him where he needed to be. It wasn't hard to find the fuel storage area; all he had to do was follow the odor of gas.

He snuck around another building, then darted behind an old pickup truck that had seen better days. Making sure it was clear, he slowly crawled over to a stack of empty, fifty gallon steel barrels. The tops were open, and the second Hank reached them, he could smell gas coming off them. But it was only residual, the barrels empty. There were no torches burning in this area, the baron smart enough to know how easy his reserves could ignite, but there was light cloud cover and the moonlight was sufficient to navigate by.

Hank spotted more barrels piled five high across the lot he was at the edge of, and after making sure it was clear again, he dashed across the lot, making it to cover only a second before a sentry appeared, who was doing his rounds in a lazy circle around the inside of the perimeter fence.

If there were any more sentries Hank didn't see them. He figured Baron Steele didn't think he needed a lot of men guarding his fuel reserves. After all, the gas was deep inside the baron's camp, and no one got that far without him knowing about it, with men everywhere walking the streets. From where Hank stood, he could still hear the church bell ringing, but it was so far away that the sound was muted. If that bell stopped, it would mean it was because the escapees had been found, so he planned on making sure the bell rang forever.

His eyes scanned the barrels of fuel, taking it all in, trying to figure out the easiest way to set it all off. Sure it was simple, but if he didn't want to get caught in the blast himself, it became just slightly more difficult.

What he basically needed was a timer, some way to delay the explosion so he had a chance to get away. It didn't take him long to come up with something, however, and a few seconds later he was digging a hole in the ground about ten feet from the barrels.

The dirt he was digging in was saturated with gas and oil as well, and he knew that would only help his cause.

The hole was about a foot deep and a foot wide when he finished. All around him was trash, and he quickly gathered a small amount of paper and other items that looked flammable. Then he put it all in the hole and lit it with the help of his new Zippo lighter.

The trash caught easily, and in half a minute there was a nice little fire going. The instant Hank knew the fire was going strong, he stood up and went to the first barrel in line. Picking up a small piece of grime-covered rebar about six inches long, he used the end that was the sharpest and jabbed the barrel. The second he did, gas spurted out, but Hank was already moving over to the next barrel. He did this to three more, the elapsed time no more than thirty seconds, then he was running back to the fence and a nervous Sharona.

He was only a feet away from the fence when a man shouted, "Stop right there or you're fucking dead!"

The voice brooked no argument, and Hank had a gut feeling that if he didn't do as he was told, he was about to get real dead. He stopped running and stood there, while inside his head, a timer was counting down.

"Turn around, now!" the voice demanded.

Hank did as he was told. Before him, was a man in his late thirties with long brown hair and a dark complexion. He held a battered rifle in his hands, but though battered, it looked like it would still kill a man just fine.

"Who the fuck are you? What are you doing in here?" The sentry demanded. "No one's authorized in here without the baron's permission and I sure as shit know you don't got it."

Hank said nothing, knowing he had to run down the clock for just a few more seconds. The man was no more than twenty feet from the barrels of fuel, Hank was more like thirty. Hank didn't know if he was far enough away to be safe, but at the moment, he didn't really have a choice. All he could do was wait.

"Come here, now," the sentry demanded.

Hank shook his head. "Sorry, pal, I can't do that."

The sentry blinked in surprise. "You what? Listen, asshole, if you don't get your ass over here in one second I'm gonna shoot you in the fucking head."

Another sentry appeared from the left, and he joined the first one. This guy was short and fat with a beard that had the remnants of his last ten meals in it.

"What's going on here, Briscoe? What you got?" the fat man asked.

"Found an intruder, that's what," Briscoe said.

The fat man got a better look at Hank. "Hey, I think this is the guy that escaped the baron's playroom. I think you caught the fucker. Holy shit, you're a rich man, Briscoe. Baron Steele offered a shit load of jack for whoever found this guy."

"No shit? There's a reward?" Briscoe asked, but he turned his head to look at the fat man, and when he did, Hank dropped down flat on the ground, covering his head with his hands, his face buried in the dirt with the aroma of gas and oil. When Briscoe's gaze snapped back to see Hank, he saw him lying flat on his stomach. At first it didn't make sense, but because the prisoner wasn't doing something aggressive and in fact was being submissive, Briscoe didn't shoot Hank. But when he saw that Hank had placed his hands over his head, like he was protecting his face from something, that made the sentry even more curious.

"Hey, do you smell smoke?" the fat man asked Briscoe as he looked around. It was subtle, the odor, and it barely touched his nostrils, but he was pretty sure he could smell smoke. That was never a good thing when you guarded a fuel dump.

Meanwhile, behind the two sentries, the barrels of gas were still spitting their fluids, and as the gas saturated the ground, eventually it began to run off, and a small stream began to form. The little stream meandered across the dirt, following the contour of the ground until finally reaching the hole with the fire in it. The instant the gas reached the hole and the small fire, the fumes erupted, igniting the stream and taking the flames across the ground to the barrels.

Then the darkness was pushed back as the entire fuel dump ignited in one massive, glorious fireball.

Briscoe and the fat man never knew what happened. One second they were standing with guns aimed at Hank, who to them had dropped to the ground for some odd reason, though Briscoe figured the man was just surrendering, and the next second, the two sentries were enveloped in a growing fireball that rose a hundred feet into the air, turning the night into day for a few seconds before the initial blast faded, leaving behind a roaring inferno that had plenty of fuel to feed it.

The two sentries were incinerated instantly, as the fire shot outwards in all directions. Hank was just at the edge of the explosion, but he still felt the heat as tongues of flames licked at his body, only the fact that he was flat on the ground saving him from being roasted along with the two men.

The fine hairs on the back of his neck and his arms were burned off from the heat. The reaching flames only lasted for a moment, then retreated, like the hand of the devil reaching out from Hell and upon catching nothing, returned from whence it came.

Hank's ears were ringing, and he shook his head to clear it. Suddenly, from all around him bent and twisted steel barrels began falling from the sky, the eruption of the blast sending them flying off in all directions.

Getting to his feet, which felt like he was standing on needles still, which was a phantom pain from when he was tortured, Hank began running for the fence, as all around him twisted and warped metal barrels plummeted to earth, most of them on fire with whatever residual fuel was still stuck to them. If one landed on him directly, the impact would either gravely wound him or outright kill him, no doubt flattening him into a bloody mishmash of flesh and bone.

He ran in a zigzag maneuver, which seemed odd given that where the barrels landed was anyone's guess, and he might be in more danger than if he was moving in a straight line.

His hands over his head, as if that would help, he ran for his life. Behind him, the flames began to spread as the wind caught the inferno, and hot ash drifted off in all directions. Wherever a piece of ash landed, soon a small fire was beginning, to then become larger.

"Hurry, Hank!" Sharona yelled as she waited for him at the fence. When she'd seen the sentries she'd hidden, but now had reappeared.

Hank lunged for the fence, his hands grasping the links as he pulled himself up and over the fence, the tarp barely protecting him from the barbed wire. No sooner did he drop down off the top of the fence than a burning barrel came plummeting down, landing where Hank had been a second ago. The fence was crushed under the weight of the barrel. Sharona began slapping Hank's back, hard. He looked at her, not understanding why she was hitting him.

"I was putting out a small fire on your shirt," she explained.

"Oh, thanks," he replied, looking over his shoulder to see a black smudge where his shirt had been burned slightly.

The wind shifted and the odor of burning gasoline filled the air, making Hank and Sharona cough.

"Come on, that should keep everyone busy for a while," he said, fighting the urge not to cough.

"That's some distraction," Sharona said. "I just hope you don't manage to burn down the whole city."

"Would that be so bad?" he asked. "From what you've told me and from what I've seen for myself, this place could use a good cleansing."

"Come to think of it, no, I guess it wouldn't."

With the flames surging higher, and smoke billowing out to blanket the city, they ran off to free Harmony.

Chapter 30

"This is the place," Sharona said.

She and Hank were standing outside a nondescript building ten blocks away from where the gas fire was raging out of control. The bell still rang out, too, but now the sounds of people yelling and screaming was added to the mix. Hank's 'distraction' might have worked too well, and once Harmony and Chester were rescued, the four of them might have a big problem with fleeing the city if it was wreathed in flames.

But one task at a time. First they needed to save Harmony and Chester before concerning themselves with leaving the city.

"Okay, let's do this," Hank said, and with him in the lead, they walked up the stairs and entered the establishment. At the door he said, "You stay here and keep watch." She nodded and he went inside.

The place had once been a normal apartment or condo, but had been turned into a whore house. After Hank entered a small foyer, he walked down a thin hallway from the front door, and stepped into a large living room that was now filled with four couches, one for each wall. On the couches were women, all in different states of dress or undress. More than one eyebrow went up at the sight of Hank entering the room. Off the living room was another hallway, where there were bedrooms for the girls to take their men. Hank looked at each of the women, not seeing Harmony. "I'm looking for a young girl named Harmony. She has blonde hair and if I know her she's been a real pain in the ass since arriving. Do any of you know where she is?"

"She's in the last room on the right, handsome," one of the women said, pointing to the hallway. "She's exactly what you say she is; which is why she's getting taught some manners."

Hank was about to ask the woman what she meant when a large brute of a man came barreling down another hallway off to the right from where Hank was standing. A curtain covered the hall, which was why Hank hadn't seen it. But he heard the footsteps and the roar of anger as the bouncer for the whore house ran at him with his arms held wide to grasp Hank and crush him.

Hank spotted the man coming at him, and saw that he was double the size of Hank. This wouldn't be a fair fight so Hank needed to level the odds in his favor, fast. Spinning around, Hank reached out and picked up an overflowing glass ashtray sitting on a beat-up coffee table. As the bouncer came at him, Hank threw the ashes in the tray at the bouncer's face, thus blinding him.

The man kept running, and only stopped when he ran straight into the wall, leaving a large dent in the already-chipping plaster. Wiping his eyes to clear them, he spun around, his teeth bared in anger. "You're fucking dead, little man. You hear me? *Dead!*"

Hank had no doubt that if the bouncer got his hands on him, the boast would come true, so Hank crossed the few feet separating him from the bouncer and went in for the killing blow without so much as one word of warning.

Hank did a running kick, and when he reached the bouncer, he slammed his right knee up into the man's groin, the blow so strong it lifted the bouncer off his feet an inch.

The bouncer screamed long and loud as his testicles exploded into a sticky paste of skin and fluids, which began to drip down his legs and soak into his pants.

As the bouncer came down off his toes, Hank slammed his left elbow into the man's throat, crushing his larynx, windpipe, veins and arteries into a mass of blood and shattered bone.

The bouncer grabbed his throat with both hands, trying to force air into his lungs, but it wasn't going to happen. Spitting blood and gasping for air, his face turned red, then purple, as he suffocated. Already dying, he slumped to the floor with his back pressed to the wall, coming down with his knees up by his chest. Slowly, his head slumped forward onto his knees, and to anyone seeing him for the first time, they would have thought he was sneaking a nap in the corner.

Hank saw a handgun in the bouncer's pants' waistband and he took it. Popping the chamber of the revolver open, he found it was loaded, all six rounds ready to be fired. Though old, the gun looked like it had been taken care of and the odor of gun oil could be detected.

Returning to look at the women, who hadn't moved a muscle, Hank singled one of them out by pointing the gun at her. "Are there any more here like him?" He gestured to the bouncer.

The woman shook her head no. "He was the only one."

"Good. Show me where Harmony is—now!" he yelled.

The woman jumped up and ran down the hall, Hank right behind her. She pointed to a door at the end, like he was told seconds before. Kicking the door in, Hank stepped inside with the revolver leading the way.

Lying on a full size bed was Harmony. She was clothed, but from her situation that was about to change quickly. At the foot of the bed stood a man in his fifties. His pants were down by his ankles, his manhood standing at attention. It was pretty damn obvious what was about to happen.

"Who the hell do thing you ar…" the man said right before Hank shot him twice in the chest. The man was thrown back against the wall, to then slide down it, leaving a trail of blood on the grime-coated plaster.

"You okay?" Hank asked.

"Am I okay? No, I'm not okay. That asshole was about to rape me! It's about damn time you got here," she snapped as she stood up and fixed her clothes. She was wearing a Catholic girl school outfit. It wasn't perfect to Hank's pre-bomb memory, but it was close enough, especially having been made by a seamstress using old pictures for a reference.

"Nice outfit," Hank grinned.

"Shut up," Harmony snapped, then walked past him and out into the hallway, where she stopped to look back at him. "Well, are you coming or what?"

"Yes, ma'am," he said and followed. He was walking more easily now, the bottoms of his feet almost back to normal.

Harmony was waiting in the living room for Hank when he arrived. Once more he made eye contact with each of the women on the couches. "All of you, listen up. The city's burning and the guy who kept you here's dead." He pointed to the dead bouncer. "So I suggest you grab what you can and get the hell out of Dodge."

When he saw they didn't understand the reference he grunted in frustration and added. "Out of town. You all need to get out of town."

"Ignore him," Harmony said to the women. "He says weird stuff like that all the time."

Footsteps from the front door caused Hank and Harmony to turn to see Sharona standing there.

When Sharona saw Hank she said, "We got company outside. Two men, armed. I'm pretty sure by the way they were walking towards me that they plan on coming in here."

"Okay, both of you, get over there out of the foyer," Hank instructed.

"The what?" Sharona asked.

"The goddamn hallway! Get out of the hallway," he snapped. This shit was getting old.

Sharona took Harmony by the hand and the two women joined the other women in the living room. Hank stood six feet from the front door, which was open. A handful of seconds ticked by, and no one appeared. Hank was about to tell Sharona that maybe she'd been wrong, when two shadows darkened the doorway.

Both men were young, mid-twenties or so, and both were armed with rifles and pistols, the first man also wore a large Bowie knife on his belt. They were talking quietly together, and Hank managed to hear a few snippets before the men had fully entered the apartment. The words pertained to how the baron wouldn't miss them, and how they could get in a 'quickie' before anyone would know they were gone.

Hank gave the men time to get all the way inside, and before either man could react, Hank fired two shots at the first man's chest, and as he went down, he fired twice more into the second one's chest. What bullets were the killing shots wasn't known, but something internal was struck that was fatal. Both men collapsed to the floor, their mouths opening and closing like landed fish.

Hank was already moving towards them, kneeling down and taking away their weapons. Sharona and Harmony were there right behind him, making sure the men were staying down as they were stripped of their accessories. Hank tossed the revolver he'd taken from the bouncer away. It landed in the corner of the hall-way. It was empty and he didn't have time to search for more rounds. Better to take fresh guns and move on.

"You girls ready?" Hank asked as he checked one of the rifles. Sharona had the second one and Harmony took one of the pistols. Hank had the other pistol and the Bowie. Sharona had a knife as well.

"Sure are," Harmony said. "Let's go get Chester and get the hell out of his damn place."

"I hear that," Hank said and led them to the front door. After peering outside and seeing no one was waiting to shoot his head off, he descended the stairs and stepped out onto the street. The air was filled with smoke, and people were running every which way. Chaos was in full swing.

"Which way to Chester, Sharona?" Hank asked.

"That way," she pointed, after getting her bearings. "It's about four blocks."

With Sharona now on point, they began to jog. People moved out of their way when they saw their guns, and so far none of the baron's men had been sighted. Hank was glad for that. He didn't feel like getting into another gun battle. He wanted to find Chester, steal a car, and leave this cesspool of a city behind.

They were three blocks into their journey when Hank stopped and stared at three of the baron's men coming their way. Sharona saw them, too and wanted to hide, but Hank shook his head no.

"You want to fight them?" she asked. "Why the hell would you want to do that?"

"I have my reasons," Hank said and leveled the rifle he was holding at the three men. "I got the one in the middle," he said. "Sharona, would you take the one on the left and Harmony, take the guy on the right. On my signal, fire."

Both women nodded and they lined up side by side.

The three men were moving quickly, not really looking around at where they were going, but when the three people lined up before them, their eyes went wide and they began to yell.

"Now!" Hank yelled. He fired directly at the center man, the first bullet taking the guy in the throat. The gun sight was too high, Hank found out, so he adjusted his aim and fired again. The next shot took the man in the chest, just a little below his heart. But the damage done was still more than enough to kill him. He flew backwards from the impact of the round and landed hard on his back. His eyes stared up at the dark sky as blood pooled out around him.

Sharona might have favored a crossbow but she knew how to use a gun as well. Her bullet took her target in the face, right between the eyes. The man was dead with half his head blown out before he hit he ground.

Harmony had a more difficult time. She hesitated, and it gave the man she was supposed to shoot time to dart for cover. She fired at him, only managing to clip him in the shoulder before he was lunging for cover behind crumbing stone stairs. He was lost in shadows a heartbeat later.

"Shit," Harmony spit, knowing she'd fucked up.

But when the man popped up to return fire, Sharona swiveled with her waist and shot the man in his right eye. The guy's head snapped back and he collapsed to the ground, dead.

"Thanks," she told Sharona, who nodded in reply.

Anyone on the street was running to escape the gunfight; they didn't know what was going on and they didn't want to know. In no time the street was empty. The church bell still rang in the distance.

Hank ran over to the man he'd killed, kneeling down by his side. Careful not to get his pants in the man's blood, he began stripping the body of weapons.

Sharona was there a moment later, with Harmony right behind her.

"You want to tell me why we just shot three men for no reason when we could have let them go past us?" Sharona asked. "Not that I mind of course, but what was so damn special about these three?"

"Not all three," Hank said. "Just this one." He was checking the dead man's weapons: a Heckler and Koch G-12 automatic rifle, a SIG-Sauer-226 pistol with holster, and a sixteen inch panga and sheath. When he was satisfied with the condition of the weapons and panga, he began arming himself with them. "I thought these were lost forever when the baron's men took them from me out on the highway. I guess as soon as they were brought back here someone handed them out to this guy." He pointed to the dead man. "From the looks of the guns, they haven't even been fired. They still have the same rounds in them when they were taken from me."

"I'm so glad you have your toys back," Sharona said. "But we're asking for trouble being out in the street like this, especially when we're standing over three dead bodies."

Hank grunted in agreement. "Take anything of use from the other two and let's get going."

The corpses were quickly stripped of anything that might come in handy, then they were off again, Sharona once more in the lead. Hank had to admit to himself that he felt damn good about having his weapons again. It made him feel like he could take on the entire city single-handedly.

Half a block from where the three bodies were left, they came across a street vendor. The man was pushing his cart as fast as he could go, wanting to get away from the encroaching fire. As he passed Hank and the women, Hank's stomach began to rumble. The man sold some kind of meat on a stick and the marinade he used was heaven to Hank's nostrils.

"Hold up, I need a second," Hank called out.

"Again?" Sharona said, aggravated, her hands on her hips in obvious annoyance. Hank raised a finger to her, the 'one moment' gesture, then he ran after the vendor. Sharona and Harmony watched Hank talking to the vendor, who didn't want to talk but wanted to run. Finally, Hank handed the man one of the acquired pistols he'd gotten in payment, and the man gave Hank a large pan full of meat on a stick. Hank smiled, took the meat, and retuned to the woman.

"Sorry, but I haven't eaten in like forever. I'm starving. When that guy ran by us and I smelled the aroma, well, it was all I could do not to shoot him and take the stuff that way."

At first Sharona looked angry, but when the scent hit her nose she too felt her stomach rumbling. They had set out from the Amazon's camp that morning and now it was almost morning of the next day. Twenty-four hours without eating; they were both starving, but had been too busy surviving to think about food.

Now, though the danger was still present, it wasn't breathing down their necks. Sharona sighed and took a piece of meat, biting into it happily. Hank was already on his third piece when Harmony stamped her feet in impatience. She'd already eaten at the whore house. Whores needed to be well fed, so they had their strength for the task of fucking and sucking. She'd been lucky. The man Hank had killed would have been her first *date*, so though her time had been unpleasant in the city of Lincoln, it hadn't been anything that would haunt her dreams.

With Harmony watching impatiently, Hank and Sharona gorged themselves on the tasty meat.

Chapter 31

Chester was locked in a brick building with bars on the windows. Inside were multiple rooms that had been transformed from office space to holding rooms for the slaves.

Hank was out of patience by the time they reached Chester's location. He and the women had been in three gunfights since he'd eaten something, and each time they'd barely come out the victors. Then add in the cloying smoke that was filling the city in thick clouds of noxious fumes he'd been breathing, and all he wanted to do was to get out of the city and never come back.

There was a small, four-by-four inch sliding trap in the metal door about head height. It was the kind of thing speakeasys had used when accepting passwords before letting people into the underground, illicit bars. Leaving the women to wait on the street, Hank walked right up to the door and knocked like he belonged.

The trap door slid open. "Yeah, what do you want," a gruff voice said through the small opening.

Hank replied by sticking the muzzle of the SIG-Sauer into the face of the man and squeezing the trigger one time. The 9mm round went into the man's face just below the nose, entered his mouth, and rebounded off his back teeth before shooting straight upwards and blowing off the top of his head.

Hank lowered the pistol and shot the lock out, then kicked the door in, charging inside as the door struck the back wall and rebounded.

Two more slavers were inside and to the right, in an office-type room set aside for them. Yelling loudly, they jumped in their chairs, where they were playing poker around a small, circular table. The men reached for their guns, which were on the table, but Hank shot each man twice in the chest, sending them falling over backwards to land hard on the floor. Both men were dead with shattered hearts before they hit the floor, such was Hank's skill as a marksman.

He waited in the doorway to the office, making sure no one else appeared and tried to shoot him. When ten long seconds had passed with him holding his breath, he was confident there was no one else to deal with. Moving down a long corridor, he glanced left and right into the rooms there. Each one had the original door removed to be replaced by a metal barred door similar to what would be found in old prison cells. Inside each room were upwards of ten to twenty men, all crammed in so that as they laid down to sleep, they were touching one another, head to feet and vice versa. The only toilet facilities were a couple of buckets that were in the corner of each room, and by the looks of them, the buckets hadn't been emptied in a while. Hank wondered how men could let themselves be treated this way. After all, if they'd rebelled, the slaves would have been able to reclaim what was taken from them by sheer numbers alone.

Sure some would die, but they would die like men. Better to die like a man than live like a dog. But then Hank didn't know their life stories, or how long they had been in captivity. Still, he knew if he'd ended up here, he wouldn't have given in so easily.

"Chester, you here?" Hank called out as he moved from room to room. The men in the cells were rousing, due to all the gunshots and yelling. There were thick padlocks on each door and Hank wasn't keen on trying to shoot the locks off. The damn things were so heavy that the bullet would probably just ricochet off and kill him. Then an idea came to him and he turned and went back to the three dead slavers. He found what he wanted on the second corpse in a front pocket of the man's pants, then he returned to the cell doors and began unlocking the padlocks. By now most of the men were awake and many were close to the cell doors, as they tried to see what was happening in the hallway.

"You're free," Hank said as he tossed the padlocks to the floor and opened the cell doors. "The city's burning, so be careful where you go."

"Thank you," one man said, then another and another, before a tidal wave of humanity was pouring out of the cells as Hank unlocked them. The men swarmed out of the building, the first three men in line taking guns from the dead slavers.

Harmony and Sharona watched the slaves spill out onto the street and they looked at one another, their eyes asking the same question to one another. *Where the hell was Hank?*

Hank moved down the corridor, opening the rest of the cells. On the last one, after he opened it and the men spilled out, Hank looked into the room to see Chester standing there, waiting to leave with the others, really just going with the flow. He was the last in line, and he seemed in no rush, just another man waiting in line for food or water perhaps.

"Chester, it's me, Hank. I've come to get you out of here?"

"Hank?" Chester said, a big smile through his dark beard. "I missed you, Hank. I don't like it here. The men are mean to me. They call me stupid and feeb and other nasty names."

"You should have hurt them if they were mean to you, Chester," Hank said as the last man left the room and Hank and Chester were standing before one another, alone.

Chester shook his head. "I don't like hurting people, Hank, you know that. I only do it when you tell me I have to so you and Harmony don't get hurt." He looked over Hank's head and into the corridor. "Where's Harmony? I miss her, too. She's nice to me, Hank, not like the bad men here. And I'm hungry, Hank. I'm always hungry now. They don't feed me like you do."

"I'm sorry to hear all that, Chester, but right now we need to leave. Harmony's right outside waiting for us. She's with a new friend called Sharona. She's nice, Chester, you'll like her. She's the one who told me where to find you."

Chester nodded as he followed Hank out of the cell. Chester had to duck or risk hitting his head on the upper doorframe. As the giant of a man walked down the corridor, the top of his head scraped the ceiling, and he had to walk hunched over. "Are we really leaving this place, Hank?"

"We sure are, pal. We just need to find a car or something." He stopped walking and turned to face the big lug. "But there are people in the city trying to hurt us. They're shooting at us with guns. So anyone you see like that is the bad guys and you need to kill them if I tell you to. That way they can't hurt Harmony. Do you understand what I'm telling you?"

Hank could see Chester's mind working, trying to process the information, the giant's face creased in concentration. After almost a full minute had passed, Hank was going to ask the big lug if he was okay, but then Chester nodded happily. "I understand Hank; kill the bad men. I won't let anyone hurt Harmony—or you."

"That sounds great, pal," Hank said, and just as he turned to keep walking, to leave the place behind, gunshots sounded out on the street.

"Shit, I knew our luck was running out," Hank hissed and ran for the door. "Chester, hang back here. I don't want you getting shot."

The building was empty now, all the slaves having run for their lives. As Hank ran down the corridor, he glanced into the rooms, and he saw a few prone bodies here and there. Even his brief glimpse told him that the men were dead. Some of the slaves had died for whatever reasons and wouldn't be enjoying a new-found freedom like the rest of the liberated men.

Hank reached the door leading to the street, and he plastered himself against the wall, then peered outside. Four of the baron's men had Sharona and Harmony trapped behind a set of crumbling stairs to the left of where Hank was. But even as he watched, Sharona managed to shoot one of the men in the neck, killing him or mortally wounding him, but either way cutting the number of enemies down to three.

From where Hank stood, he had a decent vantage point to shoot the men, but they were still too well hidden to guarantee kill shots. He needed an edge, some way to get them to back up a little. The only question was what would that edge could be.

Looking back into the building, Hank studied the area he could see. The office was right beside him, and he went in there to see what he could find. He searched through the one cabinet in the room and even dug through the trash can. He needed something he could use to fool the men into thinking it was a weapon of some sort.

Then he found what he wanted in the corner of the room, an object that fate had seemed fit to leave for him. It was on the floor, hidden under some trash. It was a dog's chew toy from a hundred years ago, and though the paint was faded a little, the plastic it was made of would last another hundred years, if not longer. It was a toy hand grenade, something a military guy would let his dog play with as a joke. When the toy grenade was squeezed by the dog's teeth crushing it, the toy elicited a faint *squeak*. The squeaker had worn out over the decades, only working sporadi-cally, but it was amazing to Hank that it still worked at all.

Pleased with his good fortune, he went back to the doorway and peered outside. The three men were still there, pinned down by Harmony and Sharona.

Hank waited for the right time, and when he thought he wouldn't get shot upon appearing, he stepped out onto the front landing and threw the toy grenade, while yelling, "Grenade!"

Harmony and Sharona heard his warning and ducked down, hiding behind the stairs, and waiting for the inevitable blast. The three men did the opposite, though, and as the grenade landed in their midst, they tried to run. Two of them were breaking cover, jumping up and making a dash for it when Hank, who hadn't moved from the landing, shot each man in the back three times with his SIG-Sauer.

The third man was a little slower to run, which caused him to actually see the grenade land by his feet. Thinking it would be better to get the grenade away from him, he tried to kick it away, but his aim was off and he stepped on it instead. He expected to feel something hard under his foot, but when the grenade was squished he heard the faint squeak from within it.

"What the hell?" he said as he looked down at the toy. He stepped on it again and got another squeak for his trouble. "It's a fuckin' toy!" he yelled, and when his mouth was wide open, Hank shot him, the bullet going right between the man's parted lips, where it then plowed out the back, taking out the lower portion of the skull and severing the spine. The man dropped like a mario-nette with cut strings.

"It's all clear," Hank called out to the two women. "You can come out now."

"I thought you threw a grenade at them?" Sharona asked as she rose, Harmony beside her.

"I did," Hank said and went over to the three bodies, making sure they were dead — they were, very much so. He reached down and picked up the toy grenade and tossed it into the air and caught it. Walking over to the women, he held the grenade up so they could see it.

To their amazement, he squeezed it three times, each time the toy making a faint squeak.

"I found this inside. It worked better than I could have hoped."

Both women were speechless, and slightly irritated that they'd been fooled like the men had been. But before either could say something, a voice called out from the building Hank had just vacated.

"Can I come out now, Hank?" Chester inquired from the doorway. When the shooting stopped he figured it was okay to ask Hank to leave; he didn't want to be alone inside the building any longer.

"Sure, Chester, come on out," Hank called.

Chester lumbered out of the building, his shoulders so wide he had to turn sideways or risk getting stuck in the doorway. He walked down the stairs and joined Hank, smiling down at Harmony.

Sharona's eyes were wide as dinner plates as she took in the gentle giant. She'd never seen a man so big. Her eyes went to Chester's crotch and she wondered how big *that* must be.

"Sharona, let me introduce you to Chester," Hank said with a grin. He saw her eyes go wide and knew what she was thinking. *Thank God this guy's on our side.*

The street was still empty, and had been since the gunfight began, all the citizens running in every direction. The bell still rang in the distance and the cloying smoke was even thicker. It tickled the back of the throat, making Hank and the others want to cough. Over the tops of the buildings, Hank could see a dull orange glow as the fire from the gas reserves spread across the city.

"Hello, Sharona, nice to meetcha," Chester said with a wide grin, taking her right hand and pumping it hard.

Sharona had been told earlier about Chester and how he had Down's syndrome, but to actually see the big lug in person was a whole other thing.

"Same here, Chester," Sharona said, and when she managed to pull her hand back, the Amazon leader had to shake it to get the soreness out of it. She was pretty sure the giant could have crushed her hand by squeezing it in his massive palm.

Chester picked up Harmony and gave her a hug, then put her down when she yelled at him that he was crushing her.

"Okay, now that all the pleasantries are done with and we're all back together, let's get the hell out of here," Hank said. "Grab those automatic rifles off those dead guys, we're gonna need them before we get outta here."

No one argued. Hank gave Chester the toy grenade and the big lug began squeezing it, laughing the whole time.

With Hank and Sharona walking side by side, and Chester and Harmony following close behind, the four friends crossed over to the next street in search of an escape vehicle.

Chapter 32

"Come on, move this fucking thing," the guard in the passenger seat said, snapping at the driver. "Baron Steele said we need to get to the main gate, pronto."

"I'm going as fast as I can," the driver replied, wishing he could shoot the passenger in the head. The guy was always riding him, never having a nice thing to say. "This thing is a piece of shit, if you hadn't noticed."

"Bitch, bitch, bitch," the passenger said. "Maybe you're just a shitty driver."

"Fuck you," the driver snapped.

"Fuck you too," the passenger repeated.

Sitting in the back seat, another man leaned forward and said, "I swear, you two fight like a married couple. How 'bout we just do what we're told and then later tonight, once the fire's put out, we can all go to a whore house and get our dicks sucked."

"Why wait till then?" the passenger quipped. "Joe will suck it right now for you."

Joe gripped the steering wheel tighter, insulted, then turned his head so he was glaring at the passenger. "Screw you, Roy. If anyone would want to suck Leon's cock it's you, you fucking faggot."

Leon began laughing, slapping the back seat with his right hand. "Girls, girls, don't fight over me, you can both have a taste."

"Shit," Roy chuckled "I wouldn't suck your dick with his mouth." He pointed at Joe who once more took his eyes off the road to yell at Roy.

"Screw you, Roy," Joe spit, then swiveled his head back around to see the road ahead. But the road wasn't empty like it had been before he looked away to snap at Roy.

Now there were three people standing in the middle of it. A man was in front, and to either side of him, and slightly behind, so that they formed a triangle, were two women, one woman, the taller one, wore the garb of a common whore. All were holding automatic weapons.

Before Joe could react, to try and swerve out of the way—which didn't matter, for the ambush site had been picked perfectly with nothing on either side of the jeep but decrepit buildings—the three people began to fire their weapons directly at Joe and his buddies.

Joe didn't suffer much, for he received a bullet to the forehead that blew out the back of his skull and killed him instantly. Roy took three to the chest, but none were kill shots. He fell out of the jeep as it swerved and crashed into a building, then began trying to crawl away. He got four more rounds in his back for his trouble, the last one killing him. The engine of the jeep stalled now that there was no foot on the clutch.

Leon, in the back seat, upon getting Joe's brains splattered all over his face, had ducked down low behind the seat, covering his head with his hands, while above him, the jeep was riddled with bullets.

But the bullets were all high, so that other than the seats and the top of the steering wheel, the vehicle itself was undamaged. Not that anyone would have been able to tell anyway. With an all-rust paint job and dents everywhere, not to mention the mish-mash of salvaged parts that had been cobbled together to make the vehicle run, it was anyone's guess what was intentional and what damage was from age.

Suddenly, the shooting stopped, and other than the bell ringing in the distance and the faint screams as men and women fought to extinguish the fires, it was quiet. Leon didn't move a muscle, too scared to do anything. He was nineteen and had never been in a gunfight before. Sure he talked tough around the others guys, but that was all bravado. Deep down, he wasn't a fighter, he was a lover, or that was what he told himself.

The sounds of boots crunching on gravel and debris came to him, and he pushed down lower in the back seat, hoping the ambush was over and that the three armed people were leaving.

But the footsteps grew closer and he knew that wasn't going to be the case. Grasping his pistol in his right hand, he psyched himself up, and with a hoarse yell to keep from chickening out, he popped up and waved his gun around, looking for a target.

One bullet was fired from somewhere close by, and a second later the gun was shot from his hand, his wrist stinging from the impact. Yelping in pain, he turned around to see the man holding the SIG-Sauer, the pistol still raised from when he'd shot the gun out of Leon's hand.

Not knowing what to do, Leon raised his hands high and said, "Please don't kill me. Please."

"Get out of the jeep," the man ordered.

"I…I'm not like those guys you killed, I swear," Leon whimpered. "I don't like working for the baron but it's either be one of his guards or be a slave."

Movement to his right caused Leon's head to jerk that way. He saw the two women, their rifles aimed at him, their faces hard and without mercy. "Oh Jesus, please don't kill me, please. I don't want to die." He began crying, large tears rolling down his face. Then another man appeared behind Hank, this one towering over the first one. This guy was huge, with hands as big as Leon's head. Behind the thick black beard the giant had, his lips were pressed tight together, a grimace if there ever was one. The giant didn't have a gun but it wasn't like the brute needed one.

"I said, get out of the jeep," the man ordered, waving the SIG-Sauer to the side to tell Leon where to go. "Last warning."

Leon did as he was told, climbing out of the jeep, stepping over Roy's body, and standing still. His bladder wanted to let go and it was all he could do not to wet his pants right there. The two women moved closer until they were standing only a few feet from him. Leon closed his eyes and said a prayer his father had taught him. A voice in his head whispered that he was going to die in a second, so he better get ready.

"Kill the bastard," the older woman said, her raven hair cut close to her scalp. "He's one of the baron's men, he deserves to die."

"Oh God," Leon whimpered, his knees going weak.

"Go over and face that wall," the man with the SIG-Sauer ordered Leon, pointing to the worn facade of the closest building. "Now!"

Leon jumped when he heard the man yell but he did as he was told, his feet shuffling under him as he moved across the road and to the wall. They were going to shoot him now, he knew it. He began crying again, his head hung low, his shoulders shaking with each sob.

Behind him, Leon heard voices arguing, but what they were saying he couldn't make out, not with his sobs filling his ears. He assumed they were discussing how to kill him.

From the looks of the older woman, she wanted to make it a long and drawn out process. So he hoped the man was telling her that a bullet to the head would suffice. Leon didn't want to die, but if he had to go, he didn't want to suffer.

"Get on your knees," Leon heard the man say and Leon did as he was told. Oh God, they were gonna do it; he knew it. Any second he was going to feel the warm muzzle of the SIG pressed to the back of his head, then there would be a pop, and finally darkness. His head hung even lower as he sobbed like a little girl.

His eyes were squeezed so tight that he was getting a head-ache, his pulse beating in his head with the rapid fire of his heart. Any second now, he knew it, here it comes. *Oh God, I don't want to die!* he thought.

There was the sound of the jeep's starter working to crank the engine over, then the motor was running. Leon heard the jeep's tires crunching over debris and the clutch being engaged, as the old engine coughed and spit as it had a bad habit of doing—the jeep drove away.

Leon didn't move a full five minutes after the jeep had gone, too afraid to open his eyes, figuring if he did, he would turn around to see a firing squad there. That this was all a joke, and the instant he thought he was safe, they would spray him from top to bottom with bullets, killing him and laughing while they did it.

But finally he knew he had to move, and as he slowly turned around, he saw that the jeep was indeed gone, and other than the bodies of Roy and Joe—the latter having been unceremoniously tossed out of the driver's seat—the street was empty.

Standing on watery legs, Leon started running.

He didn't stop for a long time.

"We should have killed him," Sharona said angrily, her arms crossed over her chest in anger.

"He was just a kid," Hank said. "There's been enough killing. By the time that kid figures out what's happened, we'll be long gone from this place. He didn't need to die."

"He's one of the baron's men. Now he can fight another day," she said. "I don't know why I listened to you."

"We did the right thing, Sharona," he rebutted. "You don't always have to kill people, you know. I've killed more men than I can count. It feels good to know I spared a life, even if this might be the only time I was able to."

In the back of the jeep sat Harmony and Chester. The big lug had to sit on the backrest of the seat for his legs were far too long to allow him to sit like a normal-sized person. He liked riding in the jeep, and he had a big smile on his face.

"Go that way," Sharona said, pointing to a side street. "Once we get on that road we go straight for a quarter mile. Then we'll come to the main gate. It's a chainlink gate on wheels with men on duty all the time. There's a tower, too, with a guard in it constantly. He can see for a long ways up there, that way no enemies can sneak up and attack the wall. But coming from inside, we should be able to catch them off-guard. We can drive through the gate in this jeep before they know what's happening." She grinned. "They won't expect that; the guards only have eyes for what's outside."

"I hope you're right, if not, this is gonna be the worst rescue attempt in history," Hank said as he shifted into a higher gear. The jeep's engine sputtered for a few seconds before evening out.

The bell still rang and the fires continued to rage behind them. In this part of the city, the smoke wasn't as thick, but it still tickled the nose and told everyone breathing it in that the fire was a bad one. When people were spotted, they were always seen running from one place to another.

Many carried packs and old suitcases with patches to hold them together. Hank drove at a steady pace, not looking like he was in a rush.

A few times some of Baron Steele's men were seen on the streets, still searching for Hank, but none of the men took much notice of the jeep as it drove by. Hank was under the assumption that if you acted like you belonged, people didn't give you much thought.

Sharona pointed to the spot where Hank should go and he began to round the corner; it would be a straight shot to the gate. Revving the engine, he put the jeep into second gear and surged forward.

By the time he was at the corner, he shifted into third gear and floored the gas pedal. Swerving around the corner, the jeep shot forward like a rocket, building up speed with each foot he covered.

But what Sharona thought would happen, didn't. Maybe on a normal day the guards were lazy, and only had eyes for what was outside the gate. But now they were on high alert, and the baron had given strict orders to remain vigilant. The penalty for not following his orders was a trip to his playroom to be tortured until he deemed the person fit to return to duty.

The jeep was almost to the gate, and Hank was ready to tell everyone to get their heads down for the crash through it, when suddenly the dirt ten feet in front of the jeep exploded—a .50 caliber machine gun set up at the side of the gate had begun firing. If the gunner had decided to simply shoot the occupants of the jeep, then Hank and the others would have become nothing but shredded meat, bone and flesh.

But lucky for them, the gunner felt taking the prisoners alive would earn him a better reward. The baron had said he wanted Hank alive if at all possible, and the gunner knew better than to disobey the lord of the city, so he didn't shoot the jeep itself for risk of setting off an explosion and killing the passengers.

As the ground erupted, spraying dirt into the air, and the sound of the 50-cal roared loudly, Hank swerved the jeep to the right, thinking he could escape. But the gun roared again and his escape was cut off.

Hank swerved back the way he'd been going, and this time the bullets got so close he could feel their impact as they struck the ground only inches from the front tires. Slamming on the brakes, he put the jeep into neutral and raised his hands slowly, the others mimicking him.

Another ten men appeared from where they'd been on guard, each with their guns aimed at the four newly-acquired prisoners.

"So much for our escape plan," Hank said, frowning deeply, as the guards moved closer for the take down.

Chapter 33

Hank didn't see any way out of the present situation. As the guards moved closer, and the .50 caliber machine gun remained trained on him and the others, he knew his luck had finally run out.

The guards were no more than fifteen feet away when Chester suddenly bellowed as loud as his lungs would allow. The sound shook the very molecules in the air, and for a brief moment, Hank thought there was some kind of monster in the jeep behind him.

"No! Bad men won't hurt me again!" Chester screamed as he jumped out of the jeep, the rear suspension bouncing up and down, as if it was sighing now that the tremendous weight had been taken off it. "Bad men won't hurt Hank and Harmony either!" He was in motion the second his feet touched the ground, running directly at the guards, who were dumbfounded as the behemoth of man charged them, heedless of being shot. "You won't hurt my friends anymore!"

For a few brief seconds no one fired, only stared in shock at Chester. Then one of the guards shook himself free of his stupor and fired at Chester, the others quickly joining in.

Like a charging bull, Chester covered his head with his arms to protect himself and ran at the men full force. Most of the bullets missed him completely, such was the state of the gunmen, but more than one round found his body. But Chester was so angry, not to mention large and padded with muscle and fat, that the bullets didn't even slow him down.

The gunman on the .50 cal couldn't fire at Chester for risk of hitting his own men, so he did nothing but watch as Chester plowed into the middle of the ten guards, punching and swiping at them like he was a giant in a fairy tale and the men were hapless villagers. One man was punched in the chest and his ribcage collapsed. He was thrown fifteen feet into the air before he landed in a tangle of limbs, dead. Another man had his head ripped off, the head then used to bludgeon another man to death.

More gunshots sounded and Chester absorbed the bullets, tiny spots of blood appearing in his filthy clothes, but still he fought on. Another man was picked up and spun around so that Chester had him by his legs. Then the man was used as a club, Chester swinging the guy back and forth, up and down. When the bloody thing that had been a man was so malformed as to be useless, Chester threw the mangled corpse at another guard, then grabbed yet another body and started the process again.

In a minute flat, all the guards were down, either dead or about to be dead. But that exposed Chester to the .50 cal. The air suddenly filled with the roar of the machine gun again, and the ground around Chester exploded with rocks and dirt. Chester began running, moving from side to side to make himself a harder target to hit. The gunner swiveled the gun to the left and right, swinging back and forth so that there was nowhere for Chester to hide.

As the big lug charged forward, bullets began striking him, taking out chunks of flesh in inches. The .50 cal was more than a match for the giant. Still, Chester ran on, not willing to stop for anything.

The gunner kept firing, and Chester soaked up all that the gunner dished out. By the time Chester reached the gun emplacement, his stomach was nothing but a mangled mess of shredded intestines, and his chest had more holes than humanly possible.

A few grazes had come close to his head, and he had a scalp wound on the top of his skull, but the gunner had been too flustered to aim for the giant's head, instead going for the chest and torso, assuming that the simple power of the .50-cal would be enough to stop the behemoth. It would have on a normal man, too, but Chester was far from normal. He was a freak of nature, like the large Fox squirrels or the giant beetles. He was a product of his environment, and so though a gentle soul at heart, he was able to tap into the primal rage that had always been there. He would save his friends, even if it killed him.

The gunner had time for one brief scream before Chester reached him. Grabbing the gunner by his head, Chester ripped him out from behind the .50-cal. The man's hand had still been in the trigger guard of the machine gun, and such was the force of Chester pulling the man up that the hand was ripped from the arm at the wrist, leaving behind stringy tendons and threads of muscle.

The gunner was about to scream some more at the loss of his hand as blood gushed from the open wound, when Chester squeezed the man's head between his massive palms, crushing it like a ripe tomato. The head seemed to deflate, squished brains squirting out the top and bottom of Chester's hands. Chester dropped the body to the ground, already forgetting it. He picked up the .50-cal, which was still firing up into the sky, thanks to the severed hand jammed on the trigger in a death grip.

From the tower at the gate, a man with an automatic rifle began firing down at Chester. Bullets struck Chester in the back, bringing the big lug to his knees, but he roared in anger and stood up, bringing the still-firing machine gun with him. More by accident than design, he aimed the gun right at the tower, and the powerful bullets slammed into the sides, killing the gunman and punching into the ammunition stored there in case of a siege to the city.

A massive explosion erupted from the tower, a flame ball the size of a bus soaring off in all directions. The tower itself shook on its foundation and toppled over, landing right on the rolling gate and crushing it.

As flaming debris fell all around the area, Hank and the others, who could only stare in silent amazement at what Chester had done, finally snapped into action, knowing they had a chance to escape and it was a very short window. Already, more armed men were coming from all the streets behind the jeep, wanting to investigate the explosion and gunfire at the main gate.

The .50-cal finally cycled down, running out of ammunition, and it went silent. This happened at the same time Chester finally succumbed to his wounds and dropped to his knees, falling over, dead.

Hank put the jeep into gear and drove towards the flaming gate, while behind him, guards began to fire at the jeep. As Hank reached Chester's body, he slowed down a little, hoping that maybe, by some chance of God, the big lug was still alive. But when Hank reached the big lug, he saw Chester's face, the eyes wide open, but seeing nothing.

"Thanks, pal, I owe you one," Hank said as he rolled past the heroic giant, drove over the wrecked gate, around some flaming debris from the tower, and sped off into the night, leaving the city behind.

Chapter 34

Baron Steele arrived at the gate ten minutes after Hank and the others had escaped.

He'd been on the other side of the city, trying to coordinate his people in a unified front to fight the fire. Whether it would work was another matter altogether, and it was possible he might just have to let the city burn. He could always move to another section, clear it out, and rebuild his forces and make a new perimeter fence. He still had plenty of slaves to get the job done. In a year or so, it would be like Hank had never darkened his door. He knew it was Hank that had blown up his fuel reserves; the timing was too coincidental for it not to be. The man had hoped to create confusion while he tried to escape, and it seemed to have worked, thanks to the dead giant of a man near the gate, who from reports, had single-handedly destroyed a good portion of his forces, and had done most of it unarmed.

As Baron Steele surveyed the carnage of bloody bodies that were once his men, and doing his best not to cough after breathing in smoke from the fires from the wrecked tower, as well as the flames from the rest of the city, which was still spreading despite his best efforts, he ranted and raved, screaming and yelling at the guards that had arrived with him. He pointed at one of the men higher up in the chain of command he'd set up, singling him out, and said, "You, gather as many men as you can spare from fighting the fire, load them up with any bikes and trikes we have left, and meet back here in half an hour. We're going after the prisoners, and we aren't going to stop until we find them."

"Are you going too, Baron?" the man asked.

"Fuck yes, I'm going, too. I want to be there personally when I see those assholes dead. I want their heads put on pikes for the entire city to see. No one fucks with me and my city. *No one!*" He grabbed another man by the shirt and pulled the guy close so that his face was only an inch from the guard's. Baron Steele then pointed at the fires still burning by the gate, while yelling so loud he spit in the man's face, the guard closing his eyes as he got sprayed with spittle. "I want you to get some men and put those fucking fires out!" the baron raged. "I want this place cleaned up and…"

Suddenly and with absolutely no warning, Baron Steele's head just…disappeared in a glorious spray of blood, brains and bone matter. The hapless guard still had his eyes closed from his berating, and didn't understand why the spray of spittle suddenly got thicker and warmer. But as he opened his eyes and found himself looking at the headless body of the baron, and as a geyser of blood shot upwards from the neck stump, the man shoved the headless body from him, screaming like a little girl. An instant later there was pandemonium as the men fanned out, searching for the shooter that had just killed their leader.

The headless corpse toppled to the ground, the neck stump still spitting blood as the heart pumped a few final times before realizing its job was over. The legs twitched spastically for a full half-minute before finally going still.

The guards began running around frantically, searching for the sniper, but there was nothing to find. A few men went to the destroyed gate and peered out into the night, but all they could see was darkness, and the looming shapes of dilapidated buildings that had been left to rot in the distance, highlighted by the night sky. Though the area before the gate and the wall had been cleared of buildings and debris long ago so enemies couldn't use the objects for cover in a siege, a half block away, structures still stood. But until this exact moment in time, neither the baron nor his men had ever been concerned about an attack from so far away.

As Baron Steele's corpse grew cold on the ground, and blood spread out in a widening pool around the dead leader's shoulders, the city of Lincoln continued to burn.

Outside the circumference of light from the flames of the burning tower, on a rooftop about half a block away, Hank lowered his Heckler & Koch rifle. It had been a tricky shot, but Baron Steele had been backlit from the fire. The 4.7mm bullet had done its job well, and as it had entered the skull, the built-up pressure of the impact had caused the cranium to explode. It wasn't something you saw everyday, Hank had to admit.

"Did you get him?" Harmony asked, as she lay by his side on the two-story building Hank had chosen for his 'hide.' Sharona was waiting in the jeep down below.

"Yeah, I got him," he replied.

"I still don't see why you bothered," she said. "We'd gotten away, why take the chance of getting caught again so close to the baron's section of the city."

"It's simple. If you have a choice, never let an enemy live; it'll only bite you in the ass later." He stood up, then offered Harmony a hand. She took it and he pulled her up. Standing by his side, she looked off to where the city still burned. From the naked eye, all she could see of the fallen gate was shadows moving back and forth. It was chaos over there that was for sure. With Baron Steele dead, the vacuum of power would need to be filled and every man who thought he was tough enough would be vying for his chance at power.

But all that was taking into consideration that the section of city the baron had claimed as his didn't burn to the ground by morning.

"I still can't believe Chester did that for us," Harmony said softly. "He sacrificed himself for us."

Hank didn't reply, not seeing a need. In the time Hank had known Chester, he'd become attached to the big lug, and he felt the loss of the man deep in his soul. He owed his life to Chester, no doubt about it.

Standing up and wiping his knees with his hand, he gathered what gear he'd taken to the roof with him, then led Harmony back down to the street.

"I heard a gunshot," Sharona said upon seeing the couple exit the building from a doorless doorway, the door taken long ago to be used for scrap or for kindling. "Is the bastard dead?"

"And then some," Hank said. "Whatever your future holds for you and your warrior women, it'll be without Baron Steele in it."

Sharona seemed to go limp with relief as she stood against the front fender of the jeep. When Hank reached her, Sharona wrapped her arms around him and kissed him passionately. Harmony stood to the side, not pleased with the awkward moment, and gave the two a disapproving glance.

When Hank was able to pull himself free, he asked, "What was that for?"

"For killing the baron and for getting us out of there alive."

"Well thanks," he replied, "but if you think about it, when we first got to the city my little mission got four of your warriors killed, and then it was you that actually saved me from Steele's little playhouse of torture. Then it was Chester that saved our ass a little while ago. If he hadn't done what he did…well, I don't think we would have liked the alternative."

They all got into the jeep, this time Sharona driving, as she knew where they were going on the return trip back to her Amazons. The jeep started on the second crank of the engine and she steered around some debris and rode on. The conversation started back at the building continued however.

"My four warriors died fighting, Hank, and thanks to you they didn't die in vain," Sharona said as the jeep drove through the twisted remains of a city long dead. "Baron Steele is dead, none of that would have happened if not for you." She grinned. "And best of all, you've taught me that simply running and hiding and attacking from the shadows isn't enough. If whoever takes over the city is as evil as Baron Steele was, this time my warriors and I will be there to stop them, we won't let their tyranny rule this land. I also plan on making raids into the city to free the whores and slaves. This land will be free once more, and I won't stop until I'm dead, and even then, I know my warriors will carry on the fight without me."

"That's good to hear, Sharona, I'm glad for you," Hank said.

She glanced at Hank, who was in the passenger seat, Harmony behind them in the back seat. "You could stay with me, Hank. We could rule my warriors as king and queen." Her hand reached out and touched his thigh, then slid up slightly closer to his crotch. "We're good together, you already know that."

"Ah, yeah, well, thanks for the offer, Sharona but like I told you before, I have someone, and I have friends that need me to return to them, so if it's all the same to you, I think I'll pass."

She shrugged. "Your loss.

"Yeah," he agreed. "I think you're right on that one."

Eventually and without incident, they made it to the Amazon camp, and as Sharona pulled up in the jeep, more than half of her warriors were there to greet her, thanks to a scout seeing the jeep and reporting back to the camp.

Sharona hugged most of the women as she shared the good news of Baron Steele's death, and there was laughter and happiness at the news. But there was also sadness and tears for the loss of the four women that had gone with Sharona and Hank never to return, not even their bodies coming back to be properly buried.

That night there was a grand celebration, and leftovers from the cooked wolf were placed on the fire again, this time the meat used in a thick stew that stuck to the sides of the stomach and filled everyone up fast.

Once Hank had eaten, he excused himself from the festivities and went to bed. He'd seen Harmony among the celebration, and from what he saw, she looked happy with the Amazons, like she belonged with them. When it was time to leave, and if she had asked to come, he was pretty sure he would have let her return to the bunker with him.

But seeing how happy she looked, he knew she had found a home here with the warrior women.

With the rising sun just beginning to kiss the morning sky, and the flames of the burning section of the city creating a false dawn that would now be lost in the new day, Hank finally could go no more and he lay down on his bedroll supplied by Sharona in a guest tent. He'd barely closed his eyes before a shadow appeared at the tent opening. His hand went to his SIG on his hip, but he relaxed when Sharona entered the tent.

"Not again, Sharona, please. I'm exhausted from being tortured all day and night, then almost getting killed about a thousand times."

At first Sharona seemed disappointed, but then she nodded and smiled. "Okay, Hank, I think I owe you that much and more. I won't make you be with me if you don't want to."

"No, you don't understand," he explained. "Sharona, you're a beautiful and vibrant woman, but like I keep telling you, I have someone that I love very much. I want to be faithful to her."

"I understand, and I respect you for that." She moved closer, knelt down beside him, and kissed Hank gently on the lips. "Just know that we could have been wonderful together."

"I have no doubt about it," he said with a grin.

"So, will you be leaving after you've rested?" she asked, knowing the answer already.

"Yeah, that's the plan. I can have that jeep, right?"

"Of course. You need transportation, it's yours to take."

"Thank you. Now, if you don't mind, I can't keep my eyes open any longer. That stew is like a giant sleeping pill."

"A what? A pill that makes you sleep? I don't understand; how can this be? Is it like an herb we find in the mountains that can make you drowsy if you take it with hot water?" she asked, the drug from long ago having been forgotten over the ensuing decades.

"Never mind," he said with a wave of his hand. "It's not worth explaining."

Sharona rose and exited the tent, and before she had fully cleared the opening, Hank was already out cold, snoring loudly.

Chapter 35

Hank slept for the entire day and all through the next night. When he finally awoke, he felt well-rested but starving. Best of all his feet were practically back to normal, and only the barest twinge of pain could be felt when he walked.

After a quick meal of bread and leftover stew from the celebration, he gathered his gear, and some food and supplies the Amazons gave him for his trip. He then prepared to head out and return to the redoubt and his hibernating companions.

Between Sharona, Harmony and some of the Amazons that had lived in the area of the bunker—before being captured for use as whores—Hank was able to get a pretty decent map made up so he had a solid route to take back. Of course, he only had the women get him in the vicinity of the redoubt, and then he picked a random area that was nothing but a blank spot on the land. From there he could easily find his way to the bunker and his sleeping friends, all of who would be waking up in two weeks or so if all went well.

Standing by the jeep, Hank, Harmony and Sharona said their final goodbyes.

"I'm not going with you, Hank," Harmony said. "Sharona invited me to stay and I think that would be a good thing for me."

Hank smiled. "I already knew that, Harmony. I figured it out last night."

"I just hope you can manage to stay out of trouble without me," she joked.

Hank laughed. "I'll do my best but no promises."

Before Hank could react, Harmony suddenly threw herself at him, wrapping her arms around his neck and hugging him tight. "I'll miss you," she whispered into his ear, then kissed him on the cheek. "For the rest of my life I'll always know that each breath I take is because you saved me." She let him go, turned, and ran off. Hank wasn't sure, but he thought she was crying, which touched him greatly.

Sharona and Hank stood looking at one another. For a few seconds neither of them spoke, then Sharona walked up until there were mere inches between them, and she kissed him softly on the lips, her hands going around his neck to pull him close.

"That someone you have waiting for you somewhere is a lucky woman," she said with a grin as she leaned back a little so she could look into his eyes, her arms still wrapped around his neck.

"Nah, it's me who's the lucky one," he replied. "Maybe one day you two can meet."

"I'd like that," she said.

"But do me a favor if it ever happens."

"Yes?"

"Don't tell her about us. It'll only complicate things for no reason."

"I think I can do that," Sharona said with a nod of her head. She let him go and took a few steps back, and Hank climbed into the jeep. He started the engine and it surged to life with a belch of black smoke. The jeep had been through hell long before he'd acquired it, and he just hoped it would get him back to the bunker before it gave up the ghost completely.

A few of the Amazons came out to see Hank off, and they stood together, watching the scene of him and Sharona. Hank saw them and he waved, the women doing the same.

"It's been fun. Let's do it again sometime," Hank said to Sharona as he put the jeep into first gear.

"Let's not. It seems from what Harmony's told me and from what I've seen firsthand, whenever you're around people die."

"Yeah, come to think of it, you might have a point there. That does seem to happen a lot." With a wink and a smile, he began to drive away.

Sharona watched the jeep until it turned a corner of the run-down street riddled with holes and cracks, and when it was gone, she turned, joined her warriors, and together they went back up to the rooftop of their camp.

They had a new initiate to accept—Harmony.

It was a time for a celebration.

Once Hank was out of the rubble that was once Lincoln, Nebraska, his spirit felt infinitely better. Hours passed quickly and soon he was driving down familiar roads that he'd taken with Harmony and Chester. Thinking of the big lug filled him with sadness.

There were a few close calls by raiders and the like on the journey back, but Hank managed to outrun or outgun anyone who tried to mess with him. One time he slowed as a group of men walked out into the road. There were four of them, all holding clubs or other bludgeon-type weapons. But not a firearm among them.

The jeep had no windshield, so Hank, with his rifle in one hand and his SIG-Sauer in the other, rested them on the lip above the dashboard so that all four men could see how well armed he was. Suddenly, Hank didn't seem like such an easy prospect to attack, and the men ran like gazelles back into the woods lining the road. They kept running for a good quarter mile before stopping. With a grin, Hank drove on, glad that he hadn't had to kill any of the men to prove a point. He'd had his fill of killing for a while and was in a mood to choose not to if there was a choice.

Once more he found it hard to believe that only days had passed since he'd left the government redoubt. It felt like months, or even a year. So much had happened, and so many people had come and gone in his life in a few short days. Some had died, Like Chester, and others, like Harmony, were alive today because of him. Baron Steele was no more and hopefully with his evil vanquished, the world would be just a little cleaner than it was before. But no doubt some other scum would simply fill the void of the dead baron.

But that wasn't Hank's problem. When the others were awake in the bunker and it was time to go out and explore, the one place they wouldn't be going would be Lincoln. He glanced over his shoulder at the supplies in the back seat. Dried meats and fruits were shoved in a few cloth bags made from old tarps found in the city. It had been Sharona's present to him. So he had food for his friends when they woke up.

He stopped by the apple tree he'd passed when first leaving the bunker, and here he stocked up on as much apples he could fit into the jeep, then after a brief rest stop to relax, urinate, and stretch his legs, he drove on, knowing he was almost to his destination.

It was late afternoon going on evening when he finally arrived at the field that had once been nothing but grass and hillocks, but was now filled with full-grown trees decades old. Slowing to a crawl, he drove through the trees until the bunker was in sight.

But something seemed different as he got closer, and it took him a few minutes to figure it out.

It was the trees.

Some of them were missing.

Most of the trees that had been close to the crater and the bunker door were chopped down so that only one and two foot stumps remained. He slammed on the brakes, letting the engine chug noisily as he pushed in the clutch with his foot. Something was very wrong here.

A shadow from above was the first inclination that he was about to be attacked. Just before the shape dropped down on him, he managed to glance up, almost as if a sixth sense had warned him to do so.

The shape held a club of some sort, and only Hank's reflexes saved him from a cracked skull. As the shape fell, he threw his body down and onto the seat, the figure's club missing him and striking the steering wheel. Then Hank was pushing himself up and sending a fist into the figure's torso.

Hank saw clearly it was a man who was attacking him, but the man was wearing camouflage netting so he could be hidden in the trees if he wanted to.

The man took the blow in the stomach and folded over, Hank then shoving him out of the jeep. Stepping on the gas pedal and letting out the clutch, the jeep surged forward, but as soon as he began to drive, the ground all around him erupted with more camouflaged figures, at least a dozen by his brief count.

One jumped right in the way of the jeep, as if the man expected Hank to stop, but all he did was grip the steering wheel harder and run the man down. Hank had the brief glimpse of a green and black painted face, then the jeep was rolling over the man, leaving behind a mangled corpse in its wake.

More shapes came at him and a few more even dropped down from the trees.

So far none of the attackers had said a word. Hank didn't know what they wanted and frankly, he didn't care. They sure as hell weren't friendly and that was all he *did* need to know.

The crater before the bunker was coming up fast, and Hank needed to make up his mind what to do. He could swerve hard to the left or right and try to make a run for it, but that would leave his friends in the redoubt without any food, and also unaware that the instant they exited the bunker door, they would be under attack.

As the crater came up, only fifty feet away, Hank did some quick mental calculations, his mind racing at top speed to go through his options.

In the end, he felt he needed to get back into the bunker, to be there for his friends when they awoke. Then, when they were awake and recovered from stasis, they could all figure out a plan to leave the bunker strong, and ready to deal with the attackers.

But the crater had to be crossed, and that was a serious problem. But as Hank saw the wide hole coming closer, he immediately came up with an idea of how to bridge the gap, though if even one of his calculations on what to do was off even slightly, he would probably end up dying quite horribly. He wouldn't get a second chance, either; it was all or nothing.

The camouflaged men were everywhere, and Hank saw that many had guns, hunting rifles by the looks of them. Why they weren't shooting at him was unknown, but once more he had all he needed to know about his enemy. If they wanted to capture him, he doubted it would be because they wanted to throw him a party and welcome him to the new century.

Reaching into the back seat, he grabbed one of the packs of food, and wrapped the rope that tied it together around his arm. He hated leaving the rest of the food from the Amazons, apples and supplies, but he had no choice. Even the one bag he was taking might be his downfall. Next, he slid his other arm through the sling of his rifle, and as the crater came up so that it was only a few feet away, Hank stomped on the gas pedal, shifting into a lower gear so he could get as much speed as possible out of the engine.

The motor redlined and Hank could feel it shaking, as if the engine was about to blow, but he ignored it. In a matter of seconds the jeep would be irrelevant.

The jeep jumped from the thirty mph he was going to fifty, and then he was airborne as the jeep hit the edge of the crater and flew out into open air. But with no ramp of any kind, the vehicle began dropping as soon as the ground was pulled out from under it. But Hank was already moving, standing up and placing his right foot on the dashboard, and pushing off, jumping straight out and forward as the jeep's nose began careening straight down. Hank kept going straight, thanks to his jump off point, and his body slammed against the side of the crater, his hands slapping the lip and preventing him from falling. The jeep slammed into the crater wall, then dropped straight down, landing on its side. It didn't explode which was a pleasant surprise.

A bullet ricocheted off the wall of the crater no more than a foot from Hank, and he struggled to pull himself up. Behind him, Hank heard a man's angry voice yell, "Don't shoot him, you idiot! Baron Sharpe wants him alive!"

Great, Hank thought, *yet another baron wants my head. I sure am a popular guy around here.*

His boots were scrabbling at the side of the cliff and he started to slip. Putting pressure on his arms, Hank slowed his descent. He knew if he didn't get out of the crater soon, either he would slip and fall or would be shot in the back by one of the men chasing him, either on purpose or by accident. With all his strength, he used his arms to levy himself up, then used the tips of his boots to push upwards. His right boot slipped but his left found some purchase on a rock or a root or something that gave him some much-needed leverage.

With a yell of exertion he pulled upwards, as if he was doing a chin-up. The bag of food was weighing him down and his rifle was whacking him in the back of the head, but still, he pulled himself up until finally his waist was even with the crater's edge. With one more shove upwards he fell face down onto the landing before the bunker door, then quickly turned his body to the side to get his legs out of hanging over thin air. He rolled a few feet to make damn sure he was clear of the edge.

More voices from across the crater told him there was no time for rest just yet. Getting to his knees, and feeling like an invalid from the exertion, his arms feeling like limp spaghetti noodles and actually shaking, he crawled over to the keypad inside the metal box. He reached up like a child too short to get at the cookie jar before dinner, and quickly punched in the seven numbers to enter the bunker. He was glad he'd memorized the code when he'd a few minutes to spare, which hadn't been much. He'd said the code over and over until it was embedded in his brain like his own name.

The alarm began to sound from within the redoubt as the door began to recede into the ground, and as it did, more gunshots sounded from across the crater. Hank dropped down flat as bullets struck the bunker door and the frame.

"Get him, he's opened the door!" a man yelled. "Kill him; it doesn't matter if we take him alive now!

"Shit," Hank hissed as bullets whined all around him. Until the door was down more, there was nowhere for him to go. He was a sitting duck. Pulling his SIG-Sauer, he began firing back at the camouflaged men. He shot one and the others ducked for cover. He didn't care how many he killed; he just wanted to keep them at bay for a few more seconds.

But the men didn't stay hiding for long, and a second later the barrage of gunfire resumed, and this time when Hank fired back, no one retreated.

These guys mean business, Hank thought, and if he didn't get inside soon, he was a dead man. As if to make his own point, a bullet struck him in the right thigh, causing him to cry out.

He crawled on his elbows across the concrete landing as the door slowly crept down. When it was halfway, Hank took a desperate risk and jumped up, fired at a few visible human shapes, then jumped over the door to land hard on the cement ramp on the other side. Bullets bounced off the thick blast door harmlessly, and Hank quickly crawled to the interior keypad and reversed the door. It suddenly stopped descending and screeched to a halt, then the door began to rise. The code was still scratched on the wall from when he'd left days before.

As the door began to rise, the gunfire became an onslaught, the men angry that their prey was about to get away. Some of the bullets zipped through the shrinking gap of the door as it rose to the ceiling, the bullets then bouncing off the ceiling before flying down the ramp to be lost.

It seemed to take an infinite amount of time for the door to seal, and just before it did, Hank could hear one man's voice, the same one he'd heard before, yelling in absolute anger and frustration. Then the door slid into the ceiling and there was nothing but silence and the heavy breathing of Hank as he lay on the floor. Off to the side was the piece of plywood he'd used as a ramp to jump the crater with the Triumph.

He idly wondered why his luck was always so bad. Why hadn't he landed on the wood instead of the hard stone floor? Even the plywood would have been softer than the cement. But then he spotted the nails he'd put at the end of the wood to help hold the ramp, the nails jutting straight up like spikes, and he reconsidered his luck. After all, landing on those nails would have been some very bad luck.

He passed out, for how long was unknown in the void that was the ramp of the bunker. When he came to, groggy and confused, he looked around, recalling where he was and what had happened. By the small pool of blood on the floor from his leg wound, and how it hadn't congealed much at all, it looked like he hadn't been out for more than a few minutes.

The first thing he did was cut off the rope holding the bag of food to his arm, and check his wound in his thigh by using the panga to cut the pant leg open. It was nothing but a flesh wound, the bullet barely clipping the meaty part of his thigh.

He was damn lucky for that and knew it. He took off his filthy shirt and ripped it into thin ribbons, then used them to bind the wound until he could wash it and dress it better later.

Taking in a few deep breaths to clear his head, he stood up, while hoping he didn't fall on his ass. He waited for a three count with his eyes closed. When he didn't pass out, Hank felt he was as good as he was going to get.

Though his leg throbbed, he could walk on it. Picking up the bag of food for his friends—and himself, too—and tossing it over his shoulder like he was a hobo, Hank began his long walk to the elevators, limping the entire way.

After showering and cleaning his wound, he wanted to check on his sleeping friends.

Epilogue

Laurie Collins slowly opened her eyes, the bright white light of the room blinding her.

At first she didn't know where she was and her mind struggled to focus, her vision doing the same. Figments of dreams long forgotten drifted through her mind like will-o-wisps. Dreams of her and Hank, together, making love.

"Easy, don't move too fast," she heard a voice say, and instantly, even through her fugue state, she recognized it as her lover.

She heard two other voices as well, coming from a few feet away and behind her. These voices took longer to recall, but soon she knew who they were. Carl Rivers and Stewart Matheson; her traveling companions.

Blinking a few times, her vision began to clear, and though she had to squint, the smiling face of Hank Summers came into focus.

"Hey, how you doing?" he asked as he carefully helped her sit up in the hibernation chamber.

"I don't really know. I'm alive, so that's a start. The rest of you are, too, I see," she said.

"Yes, we are, we all made it," Hank said.

"So you mean it worked? We slept for a hundred years?" she asked, her eyes going wide in amazement, but then she closed them, the bright light too much for her.

"We sure as hell did. Welcome to the next century," he said with a chuckle.

As the fog in her head receded, she got a better look at Hank. His face was covered in bruises, and his arms—exposed thanks to the green Army t-shirt he wore—were also scratched up and red, as were his knuckles. He looked like he'd gone through a war, and when she glanced down at his legs, she saw a spot of blood coming through his BDU pants on his thigh. But it wasn't blood like there was an open wound; it looked like it was seeping through from a bandage of some sort.

"Why do you look like that?" she asked. "What the hell happened to you?"

"For some reason I woke up a few weeks earlier than the rest of you. The countdown had run out so I was able to go out and find some food, seems we still had none inside here with us. I did, too. We have enough food to last us two weeks at least. More if we ration it."

Stewart walked up to Laurie and Hank, followed by Carl.

"I'm glad you did too, Hank, I have to admit I'm starving," Stewart said.

"Me too, I could eat a horse," Carl added.

"The foods in the cafeteria kitchen," Hank said to Stewart. "It's right on the center table; you can't miss it."

Stewart nodded and the two men headed off, overdo for a meal by a hundred years.

Laurie slowly climbed out of the chamber. At first her legs were weak, but in matter of minutes she was standing on her own. Hank hugged her, holding her close, then kissed her deeply. She had the worst morning breath in the history of the world, but to him it was the sweetest nectar. He had her in his arms again; all was right with the world…for the moment anyway.

"You still didn't tell me why you look like this," she said while pushing away from him a little and gesturing to his condition.

He merely shrugged. "There's really not much to say. I woke up early and had to go out and get some food. I got it, and along the way I ran into some new people. The rest can wait until after you've eaten. If you're like I was when I woke up, I bet you're hungry."

The second he brought it up she realized how empty her stomach was. It had been that way when she'd gone into the chamber, and a hundred years in stasis hadn't helped her any.

"Come to think of it, yeah, I could eat."

"Good, let's go to the caf before Stewart and Carl eat it all."

They began walking, but she stopped at the doorway and pointed an accusing finger at him. "This isn't over, lover, you're gonna tell me what happened out there. I want to know what it's like. It can't be too good if you look like that."

"Sure I will, but not right now, okay? For now, I'm just glad you're awake and with me. The guys, too."

"Me too," she said and kissed him again. Suddenly, she pulled back and waved her hand before her face. "Wow, I have some bad breath; you should have said something."

"Really," he said with a genuine smile of happiness. "I hadn't noticed."

CLAN OF THE BIGFOOT

BY ANTHONY GIANGREGORIO

LIVING DEAD PRESS.COM

VICTORY OF THE DEAD
ANTHONY GIANGREGORIO

www.ingramcontent.com/pod-product-compliance
Lightning Source LLC
Chambersburg PA
CBHW070442120726
47910CB00003B/888